By Whit Stillman

Barcelona & Metropolitan:
Tales of Two Cities (screenplays)

The Last Days of Disco

With Cocktails at Petrossian Afterwards

The Last Days of Disco

With Cocktails at Petrossian Afterwards

a novel by

Whit Stillman

Drawings by Pierre Le Tan

Farrar, Straus and Giroux
New York

Farrar, Straus and Giroux
19 Union Square West, New York 10003

Distributed in Canada by Douglas & McIntyre Ltd.
Printed in the United States of America
First edition, 2000

Library of Congress Cataloging-in-Publication Data

Stillman, Whit, 1952–
    The last days of disco, with cocktails at Petrossian afterwards / Whit Stillman.—
1st. ed.
        p.   cm.
    ISBN 0-374-18339-2 (alk. paper)
    1. New York (N.Y.)—Fiction. 2. Disco dancing—Fiction. 3. Young adults—
Fiction. I. Title.
PS3569.T48214 L37 2000
813'.54—dc21   00-28436

For John Sterling Stillman
and Margaret Riley Stillman
in gratitude.
—W.S.

For Piroska.
—J.S.

The Last Days of Disco

An Account of the Real Story

Upon Which the Movie Was Based,

by Jimmy Steinway,

the "Dancing Adman"

Certain Generalizations

Are Made

1

Sag Harbor

"Opposites attract," they say—and it's true. Scoundrels are forever being smitten with angels, and vice versa, and if such terms are objectionable, replace them with the secular equivalent, but it's still true. Like so much that verges on the hackneyed, a wealth of human experience looks out from behind it. Opposites attract, unfortunately, and the cost, in terms of subsequent despair, ruinous legal actions, divorce, fatherless—or motherless—families, cracks in the social welfare system and people falling through those cracks, even suicide and violence, is incalculably horrible. For that reason I pledged myself to oppose the whole sexy "opposites attract" dynamic any way I could.

If after all these years Des McGrath should still resent and hold that against me—well, I'm not sorry.

******

That there has already been a movie on the same subject as this book is a fact too large to ignore or pretend objectivity about. Often the subjects of films—and books—nitpick about how they are portrayed, how the author got this or that wrong, etc., etc., ad infinitum. That was not our case. All of us, except Charlotte, *loved* the movie—not entirely surprising, since so did all good film critics the world over (i.e., not David Denby). Our stake in how the film was received was particularly direct in that we *were* the characters whom the Denbys of this world and the moron from the San Diego paper found so *unlikable*. That was not true. Except for Charlotte we were not unlikable in the least, especially back then. Des said later that the Denby piece read as if some sort of sexual jealousy were involved. Another friend who reviews movies, though he's primarily a novelist, commented that those of his film-critic colleagues who are always finding characters *petty* and *unlikable* tend to be that way themselves.

Why then turn a screen story, admittedly well told, into a book? Art. Self-expression. Taking a corner of our life and culture, and enriching it. Interpreting the times we have lived through and, if not making them one's own, at least preserving them in written memory. For me the events of the story are still fraught with emotion despite their having occurred nearly two decades ago. Watching the movie, I discovered much I had not known before, just as many things I considered important had, given running-time necessity, been left out. The abbreviating nature of film and nearly all audiovisual media is something I had come to understand and accept in a career spent almost entirely in the sphere of the fifteen- and thirty-second television advertising spot.

I come from the tail end of that generation in advertising when there was usually an unfinished novel in the lower desk drawer. It was still the glory days of the baby boomers. While we might have sought to fit into society in economically useful or at least minimally remunerative ways, we still refused, at least initially, to let go of our aspirations to accomplish something beyond that, be it artistic or otherwise. Unlike some other people, I do not think our generation was entirely selfish or bad.

As a fiction writer *manqué* who had never gotten beyond Chapter 3 of a novel, and then only once, I found the offer from Jess Wittenberg of Castle Rock Entertainment's business and legal affairs department to turn *The Last Days of Disco* into a novel an opportunity too compelling and rare to let pass, whatever problems and pitfalls might seem to go with it. That I was one of the participants in the original story would, I hoped, take it beyond what is normally thought of as a film "novelization," and to further underline the distinction, publication was not intended until long after the film had already passed through the traditional film distribution "chain." That this would coincide with the film's free television premiere on the well-regarded VH1 music channel— one of only three feature films to be so selected—was a fortuitous coincidence.

Once, at a dinner during a return trip to New York I heard the novelist Tom Wolfe talk fascinatingly about what film could and could not do well in terms of narrative storytelling. I forget what he said film could do well, but as to what it could *not* do well, he cited as an example "shoes." In a novel, he said, if you wanted to discuss a character's shoes, you could describe not just the shoes' external appearance— the film or TV ad spot equivalent might be a tight close-up—

but everything about them. Perhaps the shoes had been handmade at enormous expense at Lobb in London; maybe the character under study would not have known (or cared) about Lobb when he first came to New York from the South in the late 1950s, but over time and with increasing prosperity in a certain social milieu, perhaps he'd come to care about just that kind of thing. Was it to show off and keep up with his peers, or simply an enthusiasm for beautiful objects of craftsmanship, along with the resources to buy them?

Later when I read Wolfe's *The Bonfire of the Vanities*, I admired how he used such sociological detail to weave a portrait of Manhattan in the 1980s that memorialized a world we all lived in, the way Thackeray and Trollope had theirs.

I remembered this "shoes" story at the screening of the first rough cut of *The Last Days of Disco* when, after the opening title cards set the scene as "Manhattan—The very early 1980s," the first striking pictorial image flashed on the screen and was, again *footwear*: in this case, a tight shot of a woman's shoe-clad feet (Alice's) striding along the sidewalk, keeping pace with another woman wearing a pair of modish low black boots (of course, Charlotte's). Then the camera tilts up and we see the cool actresses attached to these shoes and boots. In the movie it's the music (Carol Douglas's early disco hit "Doctor's Orders"), the sound of the actresses' voices, and their stylish body language that strike one so strongly—the shoes hardly register at all. It was another example of the enormous difference between a story told on film and one told in writing.

For the majority of us, the real story began not outside the Club that night but weeks earlier at Kate Preston's famous party in Sag Harbor Labor Day weekend.

Kate's father was the publisher and de facto editor of the

magazine *Futura* and, as such, a big figure in our Harvard firmament. Maybe later those in our group moved on to careers in advertising, the law, or nightclub management, but that didn't mean we had given up our intellectual interests and aspirations—quite the contrary. There is a too-common assumption among professional intellectuals that the world of thought and ideas is in some way owned by them. In truth, some of the best minds have fled the mediocrity, jealousies, and low pay of the literary-intellectual ghetto.

Sag Harbor is one of the resort towns on the southeastern fork of Long Island, two or more hours from New York City, that are collectively referred to as "the Hamptons." It is the Hamptons town with the "literary" reputation—a reputation that is, frankly, deserved. Many writers, editors, and people active in the theater and the allied arts do tend to vacation or live there—and those who don't, often visit. Like the other Hamptons, Sag Harbor has a particularly intense summertime social whirl which it has long been fashionable to decry. This is one of those poses, fairly tiresome, that everyone seems compelled to adopt. But to be honest, I've always found the social life there pretty terrific—from that first party at Kate Preston's on.

Kate's Labor Day bash was a curious affair that started at about one in the afternoon and ended long after dark. We were all supposed to bring food and drink and help out. Tom Platt and I had been given responsibility for the condiments and hamburger buns (we found that moist and good-tasting brand of potato rolls—Martin's, I think—they sell on the Island). My turn on the grill came first, and it was in that context that Alice and I met. She claimed the burgers I was cooking were much too rare.

"That's disgusting," she said each time I took one off.

I accused her of being anti-meat, an unconfessed vege-
tarian.

"Not at all. I like hamburgers—properly cooked."

Before I moved to Europe, all the women I fell for liked
their meat extremely well cooked, practically burnt, and their
favorite color was always blue. I don't know if there was any
connection between these preferences. (Oddly, the French
word for meat that's so rare it's essentially uncooked is, in
fact, *bleu*.) Alice was the last and by far the greatest of these
infatuations.

What kind of first impression did she make? A very strong
one. In my opinion she did not greatly resemble the attractive
blond actress Chloë Sevigny (*Kids*), who played her in the
movie. She was more petite, her hair darker, her figure less
sensational, though still perfectly fine. She was only twenty-
one then and in some ways even younger-seeming than that.
I should mention that not everyone found her attractive. To
them, she was merely "normal-looking." Thank God for
divergences in taste and aesthetic judgment—and other people's lack thereof!

For those sensible to such things, Alice had an extraordinarily sad and romantic look around her eyes—lovely light
brown eyebrows, diagonals sloping downward, above warm,
sincere, kind, dark eyes that promised the most interesting of
companions to anyone lucky enough to become her friend.
Through absolutely no fault of her own, she had an expression
that could break one's heart—at least anyone sentient to such
things. While normally such a look might portend a sad, poetic,
romantic—and, often, unhumorous and quasi-depressive—
personality. Alice was instead (and thank God) funny, charming, and cheerful—at least to the extent that she had any rea-

son to be. (She was not "inanely cheerful," the way some very tiresome people are; in fact, I've been accused of that.) Of course, like anyone in her twenties, she got into funks and "depressions"—but hers tended to be for actual reasons, not trumped-up ones, and then she found ways out of them without making everyone else in Creation miserable, too.

An observation which might not be wholly true but which I'll risk proposing anyway: Most women who seem fascinatingly silent, romantic, and mysterious turn out to be just . . . not so bright or communicative. Getting deeply involved with them can mean, at least in my experience, a one-way trip down the well of loneliness. Perhaps that sounds cruel, and they could probably say the same; granted that. All I mean is, what a loss, what a shame: if people were only as fascinating as they looked, how life might be. On the other hand, to be balanced about it, many people who *don't* look at all fascinating, mysterious, or interesting turn out to be. You tend to encounter this most often in working environments where there are so many opportunities to meet people who seem completely unattractive and uninteresting—but then turn out not to be. I think that's one reason I've always liked the working world so much.

Next it was Tom's turn to take over the grill. I sort of expected or just assumed that Alice would join me, drifting away to explore the rest of the party together. We had really hit it off. I thought a real connection had been made. Instead, she remained glued to the spot, leaning against the table where hamburger and hot-dog preparation was taking place, chatting with Tom and monitoring his grill technique. So I decided to hang around, too.

Evidently Tom was also one of those entirely susceptible

to that heartbreakingly romantic-sad look in a young woman's eyes. It was pretty surprising to see. For years he had been romantically linked to a very attractive, extremely-sexy-for-the-cardigan-set Wheaton girl, Jennifer Robbins by name (not to be confused with all the other Jennifer Robbinses). In college they had been among the most visible couples, Saturday-evening drinks at the Hasty Pudding bar and all that. I think she was the first young woman I noticed drinking whiskey sours. They were one of those couples envied by both sexes, including me.

With Alice, Tom was completely different—much lighter and funnier than had been his mode in college. Maybe it was the Labor Day atmosphere and release of tension. Similarly, with him, Alice dropped the teasing tone she had taken with me, not harassing him about the "rareness" of his hamburgers at all.

When Tom stepped away to get another platter of hamburger patties, I asked her about the apparent inequity of this.

"It's just that his hamburgers are properly cooked," Alice said. "We're free to talk about other things."

"I thought you were just teasing me about my burgers being rare."

"No. Your hamburgers *were* too rare. It was a health hazard."

"Haven't you ever heard of steak tartare? People eat raw meat all the time. I love it."

"Yes," she said. "I noticed."

"I thought you were just saying that for effect."

"I don't say things for effect."

"Oh, you don't," I replied in that fairly obnoxious, skeptical tone it's all too easy to slip into, regretting it even while saying it. In situations of any kind of social tension at all, I tend to act in one of two ways: like a bit of a jerk, or like a total jerk.

"No, I don't," she said.

Alice was not, as it turned out, one of those people who make themselves interesting, or flirt, by teasing or criticizing someone of the opposite sex. She really did think the hamburgers I was cooking were much too rare, and our conversation, though it had seemed great from my point of view, in fact never got much off the barbecue level.

On the other hand, the way she and Tom communicated was like bursts of microwave transmission, with vast quantities of information, opinions, and insights almost instantly interchanged. Tom acted as if injected with sodium pentathol or some other alleged truth serum, spilling his guts out to Alice in a way I had never imagined before (though later it turned out that he was filtering out *some things*).

I did not hold it against Tom personally, but it was intolerable being around him in the presence of girls. They collapsed in puddles before him, sometimes in the most abject way, and Alice, terrific as she was, seemed not entirely an exception in this case.

Despite firm resolutions to the contrary, I did let myself get bent out of shape by it and finally slipped away in a skulk, fortunately not attracting Alice's adverse attention. She had been pretty charitable in not noticing my querulousness while she devoted her concentration pretty much exclusively to Tom. As with any humiliating experience (and competing with Tom Platt was always going to be a humiliating experience), I immediately tried to put it out of my mind, and the girl with it. There are all kinds of things we do, against our own ultimate best interests, in order to immediately protect our egos and *amour-propre*. That the remarkable rapport between Alice and Tom did not have any immediate consequence or sequel is something I did not stick around to notice. An unobserved or unacted-upon romantic opportunity is the same as no romantic opportunity at all, at least in my experience.

None of this was directly portrayed in the movie. The filmmakers, seduced perhaps by the title they had come up with and the potent reference to "Disco" embedded within it, began their account instead on the south Manhattan streets outside the club where we coincided that night and often subsequently gathered.

The downtown section of Manhattan—specifically that nowhere land between Greenwich Village on the north and Wall Street or Chinatown on the south—had for most of a century been desolation personified at night. Until recently the area's only late-night patrons had been financial printers on the lobster shift and young corporate finance types pulling all-nighters proofreading their work, documents on which hundreds of millions of dollars of stock market financing could depend. Serving them were two taverns with greasy barbecue, several takeout places, and a couple of Italian restaurants which time and all but a few nostalgic mobsters—and their closest business associates—had forgotten. Then sometime in the 1970s, what would later be endlessly referred to as the "downtown club scene" was born. By the time of the story—the very early 1980s—Hudson and Varick Streets had begun their new roles as dual parallels of late-night beauty and romance.

Which brings us back to Charlotte and Alice and their search that night for love. They were walking up Hudson Street from the subway station in the direction of the legendary disco those of us who became regulars there made a point of referring to only as "the Club." It would be hard to explain today the promise of social and romantic magic the

Club seemed to hold out (and often delivered) in those days.
But first there was always the nightmare of getting in.

Alice had been worrying about it as they approached the
corner with Van Dam Street.

"I heard you have a better chance of getting in if you
come by cab," she decided to mention.

"You're really worried about getting in?" Charlotte asked.

"Yeah—I am."

"I thought you'd been here several times before."

"Not the front way. They were private parties. We came
in the back."

Charlotte glanced at her. "We look really good tonight.
I'm sure we're going to get in."

Rounding the corner, Alice and then Charlotte slowed to
a stop. As they looked up the street, their expressions turned
somber. The sidewalk outside the Club, about a half block
away, was already a tragic mob scene of rejection, a horde of
people forced to wait ignominiously while a pallid chosen
few were whisked inside. Members of the crowd who sought
to slip in with them were cruelly rebuffed. One young
woman sobbed as four bouncers hustled her boyfriend out to
the curb, shouting and squirming.

"Let's get a cab," Alice said, stepping off the curb and raising her arm to flag one.

Charlotte followed her. "Maybe you're right."

A cab that had just discharged its passengers at the Club
swerved to pick them up. The street was crowded with
vehicular traffic—taxis and "limos" dropping their clients off
into the mob, everyone seeking to make as impressive an
entrance as they could within the realm of plausibility, and
occasionally beyond it.

I was similarly at that moment a block farther up the street, riding nervously in a black "stretch" limousine the agency had hired, with three out-of-town clients whom the agency's new "powers that be" had decreed I *must* get into the Club. Though we had not yet crossed the intersection nearest the Club, I already had that terrible doomed feeling.

Once again I was supposed to use whatever fading entrée I had with the all-powerful front doormen to get three highly unlikely prospects into the hottest club in the world—that at least is how we saw it then. It was described in the film's shooting script this way:

Looking through the limo windshield, JIMMY STEINWAY, a thin, worried type in a sharp suit, about 25, watches the same mob scene outside the Club. He then turns to address three CLIENTS in business suits in the back seat.

JIMMY

When we get out, don't stop where the crowd is. Follow me right in.

One of the three clients, the eldest and seeming nice-guy boss type, MARSHALL MURIE, wears noticeably ugly clothes—a brown and red check polyester-look suit and a less garish but very wide tie.

CLIENT #3

When we get out, just follow you in.

JIMMY
(*turning to them*)

Yeah.

He swivels back to look out the window but seems worried.

They were right—I *was* worried. A strange aspect of human nature was that precisely because I had never been turned away from the Club, the possibility of it finally happening had grown into a prospect of inconceivable horror and humiliation. Looking at Marshall's outfit, I dreaded what was about to happen. He was a nice guy but a terrible dresser—it was famous.

Anticipating a colder night, I had brought with me the navy blue cashmere coat I'd acquired the previous winter, the crazy sort of extravagance the city's ferocious wind-chill factor could inspire. Contrary to what many people think, junior-level ad jobs don't pay well at all.

As the limousine approached the Club, I panicked. To be honest, between lack of sleep and all the agency pressures, I was pretty thoroughly frazzled by this point. Drinking gives you the illusion of control, but unfortunately little of the reality.

Turning to Marshall, I grabbed the coat and held it out to him.

"Why don't you put this on. . . ."

"What?" he asked.

"Just until we get inside . . ." I tried to sound cool about it.

"I don't get it. . . ." Flustered, Marshall took the coat anyway. His younger colleagues, Hap and Steve, better dressed in early-eighties business style, looked pretty uncomfortable about the whole situation, too.

2

Running the Gantlet

Des McGrath had been my original "meal ticket" at the Club. We had met sophomore year in college in Professor Walter Jackson Bate's legendary Age of Johnson course. Des was a passionate admirer of the poet Alexander Pope and took some of Johnson's not entirely admiring comments about Pope pretty hard. He felt that Bate identified too closely with Johnson's viewpoint, which led to some fireworks in class, unprecedented for that course, which was a large lecture-hall affair not really designed for classroom discussion. Des felt that much of what Bate said, though it sounded great, was undermined by his adherence to the dubious theories of the philosopher Alfred North Whitehead. He also felt that Bate misrepresented Johnson's Toryism.

As one of the Club's managers, Des had gotten me in in its early days, but over time I felt I had come to be accepted on my own as a Club "regular"—those who got in without problem and with the unstated permission to bring others in, too, provided that this privilege not be abused. In recent weeks, though, it *had* been abused. The agency's new "powers that be" had put me under huge and indiscriminate pressure to get clients into the Club. The guardians of the red velvet rope had noticed this and started giving me a lot of static about it, especially the number-two guy, Rick, who had recently started throwing his weight around a lot, much to Des's irritation.

The common parlance for nightclub gatekeepers in those days was "door-Nazi." Not terribly complimentary, but that was the general feeling then. Both Rick and especially Van, his boss, really looked the part—tall, angular features, dark blond hair, early-Wehrmacht good looks. Van wore his hair longer than the Black Shirt norm and affected a black-blue cashmere overcoat (much like mine) draped over his shoulder rather than the standard black leather. Of course, describing them this way implies feelings of hostility and resentment I did not yet have. I was still then at least nominally part of the in crowd who admired Van's taste and good judgment in always raising high the velvet rope on our behalf.

Back in the limo, I waited until Dom, our habitual driver, pulled as close to the Club as he could get. Signing the hours for him, including a healthy gratuity, I was somewhat betrayed by a crack in my voice—I hoped barely audible—on the "thanks" of the clipped "Thanks, Don" I managed to squeeze out.

I jumped out and—trying to disguise whatever nervousness I felt—moved with alacrity to a spot on the edge of the crowd where, stretched to full height and standing on the balls of my feet, I could catch Van's eye.

Van, who stood on a low podium about ten feet behind the rope to see over the crowd, spotted us and nodded me in. I led my clients through the crowd, which opened almost magically before us with looks and murmurings (I imagined) of envy and respect. The heightened-reality exhilaration and adrenaline rush of getting into the Club swooshed back, filling me with all sorts of positive emotion, shaded with worry. I glanced back at the clients. Hap, identified as CLIENT NO. 3 in the screenplay excerpt, wore an expression of cautious joy, while Marshall and Steve still looked pretty intimidated.

As I approached the red-velvet rope, Rick coolly snapped it open—had it been up to him alone, I doubted I'd have gotten in at all. I remember thinking, *Evidently my front-door credit has not yet entirely run out.* Higher forces still seemed to be working on my behalf.

Then the boom dropped. Just as Marshall approached, Rick fastened the rope again. For a moment I simply stood where I was, not reacting at all. I remember thinking it was colder out than I had expected—a coatless reflex of some kind.

Walking back to the rope, I insisted, "We're together." Rick just stared back impassively as if he could've cared less.

I turned to Van, who pretended to ignore us, looking out over the crowd for other arrivals.

"Van . . . ?! Hey, Van?!" I called, trying to get his attention.

When he finally looked our way, I nodded to indicate the others.

He looked them over, then turned to Rick. "Only him."

"But *we're together,*" I said, trying not to sound too pathetic but probably not entirely succeeding.

Van faced the crowd, nodding to an arriving couple who looked like models. The rope was lifted and they strode in with their affected model walk.

This is admittedly a digression, but: are contemporary models really so "beautiful"? Exactly who decided that? This couple had the raw and faintly animalistic, fat-pouty-lips-and-tiny-noses look then and now in vogue; "pretty" mostly in the sense of "pretty vacuous-looking." It was not always thus. Harry Potter's mother, who was a model in the late fifties/early sixties, really was beautiful. I have the feeling this changed when everything got "cool"—sometime in the sixties, like everything else.

"Come on, Van," I asked confidentially. To reaffirm his authority and control, Van would sometimes jerk the guests of even a "regular" around a little—but finally let them in.

Van ignored me to nod in an incongruous-looking couple who were just approaching the crowd's periphery: a petit white-haired gent wearing a black Asian-style jacket and an odd pointy beard, accompanied by a lovely, tall, fine-featured woman who for some reason struck me as probably Belgian. Van liked to say he mixed a salad selecting those who entered at the door. Which elements of the salad were this couple? The olive, radish, or avocado? Or, if she really was Belgian, perhaps the endive?

"This is important, Van," I persisted. "These are my friends."

Van looked down at my "friends." They seemed awkward and out of place: nice guys who never should have been put through this. But the thinking then was that such abasement was "worth it" if that's what it took to get in.

Van said, "You can go in, but they'll have to wait." Glancing at Marshall, he added, "Hey, nice coat." Marshall sort of grimaced.

At this point I'm afraid I kind of freaked out. Impulsively, without a further word, I turned and pushed back out through the crowd in the grip of raging feelings of fury and humiliation. When I got out to the curb, though, I had no real idea where I was heading, I just kept moving. The limo we had arrived in was gone. Marshall had wanted it released. He despised the sort of wasteful extravagance that had limousines waiting all night outside nightclubs. I frankly agreed with him: the waste as agencies sought to "butter up" out-of-town clients was shocking, but you didn't normally get that kind of frugal thinking from a client: the car would, after all, have been on the agency's dime. Now we could have really used it; there was no place to go or hide, no immediate refuge.

I wasn't thinking anyway. Anger and shame clogged my brain. I just stalked down the street away from the Club, heading reflexively east, getting back on the sidewalk when I could. Marshall, Hap, and Steve chased after me.

"Don't worry, Jimmy," Marshall said when they caught up with me. "We don't care."

"I can't believe it . . ." I started saying, but couldn't continue.

"Yeah, what an asshole," Steve added sympathetically. We were now walking three abreast, with Hap slightly behind.

"You know, that had nothing to do with you guys," I said. "Van just wanted to put me in my place. Apparently, it happens all the time."

"What a jerk," Steve said loyally.

"It's happened to you before?" Marshall asked, sensing my fib the way smart bosses often uncannily do.

"No," I admitted, backtracking, "but it was overdue."

"You know, none of us really wanted to go," Marshall said. I couldn't believe it. He was so great about it. Even after what had happened, his concern was still to make me feel less bad. This was very unusual behavior for a client.

"No, I really wanted to go," Hap piped up from behind.

One of the greatest spurs to romance is knowing, or thinking, that someone likes you. Conversely, thinking that they *don't* like you can be an enormous inhibiting factor.

Unbeknownst to us as we marched along the sidewalk, the cab carrying Alice and Charlotte around the block so they could make their "more impressive" entrance was at that very moment passing us on the street.

Had I been privy to what Alice said that night, it could have changed the whole course of my life. The knowledge might have decided the toughest question we face in our romantic lives: whom to be in love with. This snatch of dialogue within the cab, a bit of a "throwaway" in the film, was for me the key to everything that happened later.

(For those scenes I was neither a participant in nor a witness to, I have essentially relied on the script's earliest drafts, which closely followed extensive interviews with nearly everyone involved except Charlotte and Berrie, the Club's owner, or directly on the transcripts of those interviews. The final film diverged somewhat from these scripts. Several parts of the story I checked further by calling those involved. They generally did check out. When they didn't, I will say so. Although there was some "studio interference" in the final version of the film, those sequences will stand corrected in this account.)

Alice had spotted me and swiveled around to follow us as the cab went by and our forms receded down the street.

"There's Jimmy Steinway!" Alice exclaimed. A note of real disappointment entered her voice. "I can't believe it—he's leaving already?"

Charlotte turned to look out the window in the same direction.

"You like him?" she asked, as if surprised. "I could never be interested in anyone who worked in advertising."

Then Charlotte leaned forward dramatically to look out the front window at the intimidating mob scene swirling before the Club.

"God. You were right. This place has gotten really hard to get into."

Alice had resolved that if they had any trouble getting in she would just leave and go on with Charlotte to some completely accessible bar or club, where "getting in" was not a problem, rather than just slink back to St. Catherine's, the somewhat dreary residence where they were staying.

"Who was the other guy you were interested in?" Charlotte asked as they got out of the cab. Alice, with all the hullabaloo outside the Club, either missed the question or just dodged it, stepping forward and standing on tiptoes to see over the mob. Van immediately spotted her and signaled them in. With some difficulty they threaded their way through the crowd, Alice still visibly nervous, to within a few feet of the red velvet rope. Just as they were about to reach it, Bobby, one of Rick's sidekicks, lowered the rope as if to refasten it—Alice was on the verge of turning around and rushing away—when he pulled it up again as if he had just misjudged their speed.

They continued through the milling throng and two sets

of doors, after which Alice bent over and practically hyper-ventilated with relief at having gotten through.

"*Phew. Oh God. We made it!*" she gasped, trying to catch her breath. "This is the last time I'm coming here. I want to be able to say, 'I always got into the Club.' "

"Of course we got in," Charlotte said. "Who was the second guy you were interested in?"

"Uh . . . Tom Platt."

"Well, *that's* better . . ."

"How do you mean?"

"Tom Platt's smart and somewhat cool, a lawyer involved in environmental causes—not to mention *tall, blond, and incredibly good-looking.*"

As Alice and Charlotte glided toward the crowded dance floor, which resembled a circa-1980 multi-ethnic United Nations of Cool, a beautiful young woman, Nina Moritz, hurried past them in the opposite direction, very upset, her eyes moist, on the edge of full-scale crying. Des, described in the film script as "a young Helmut Berger, his hair slicked back Racquet Club–style," followed closely behind. Many women and even some men did consider Des devilishly handsome, particularly when he dressed the part.

Traditionally the women Des pursued were themselves beautiful heartbreakers, used to making men suffer with little compunction, often taking pleasure in it either as an exhibition of their power or as an expression of the age-old Miss Havishamite game of squashing bugs of the male gender. (Let's face it, under the cloak of feminism there's been a lot of such behavior.) Nina was not like that at all. She was in fact far too sensitive and perhaps unstable to cope with the sort of problem Des posed.

Now she hurried through the Club lobby, out the doors,

and up the ramp past Van's station and through the mob outside, moving quickly in the reverse direction of everyone else.

"Nina . . . Please—stop . . . !" Des called, trying to catch
up.

Bursting through Van's station, going the wrong way, Des
tried to dodge the rope but, as the bouncers stepped aside,
brushed against one on the other side. In his wake a metal
stanchion hit the ground with a bang and started rolling.

"Hey, McGrath!" Van shouted after him. "Come back
here!"

Des glanced back but hurried after Nina as she wandered
unsteadily down the street, occasionally looking over her
shoulder for a cab.

"Nina . . ."

By this time she had stopped, turned around, and raised
her arm as she looked for a cab, her breathing still near weep-
ing. Des reached her and stopped, also trying to catch his
breath.

"It's not what you think. I'm . . . uh . . ." He hesitated. "I
think I'm gay."

"What?!"

For a moment they just looked at each other.

"That's not possible," Nina said.

Des scrunched up his face and shook his head in the
affirmative.

"How . . . ?"

"It's always been there, I guess. I've only begun to
acknowledge it now."

Nina's breathing returned to a more normal pattern. She
looked at Des as if she were going to X-ray him with brain-
waves, but also seemed strangely relieved.

"You really think you're gay?" she asked matter-of-factly.

In Manhattan real estate circles convenient location was considered everything, and this was certainly the case with the venerable Acropolis Coffee Shop, a half block from the Club and popular for pit stops to refuel on burgers, eggs, or various platter specials of Greek or New York cuisine before or after a grueling night at the Club. As was well known, virtually all New York coffee shops were owned and run by Greek-American families, hence all the classical references in the names and decor. The overall color scheme of the New York coffee shops in those days was darker, warmer, and more inviting than it is now: all dark burgundy vinyl and walnut Formica, while now it's pastel colors and lighter shades of imitation wood.

Des would often stop by the Acropolis (it was open all night) after the Club closed or for a second breakfast before work in the evening. Des was one of those New Yorkers on a three-breakfast-a-day schedule. In college we had gotten accustomed to such nocturnal hangouts as the old Hayes-Bickford cafeteria in Harvard Square, where students, night-shift workers, nurses from the university infirmary, and strays and oddballs of all kinds would linger. Characteristic of the overall difference between Boston and New York, the population at the Acropolis was far less forlorn. Its customers were just those who, for whatever reason, wanted to eat coffee-shop food at very strange hours.

Josh Neff and Tom Platt occupied one of the Acropolis's larger booths, having a bite to eat after getting off late from their law jobs. Among starting lawyers in New York there was a perverse competitiveness about working the longest hours possible—perverse except that at firms like Tom's the extra hours were billable at high rates by bosses who would be deciding, within the next seven or so years, whether they would "make partner," too. It was a morbidly fascinating subculture, with its own unforgiving rules, like the geisha districts of old Kyoto. Josh, as a public employee, had less of an excuse for working such hours, but it was in the air: as well as being so many other things, the early eighties was a time of hard work and maximum productivity.

Tom and Josh were then, like me, twenty-seven. In retrospect, it was a significant year for all of us. It's the age when a college graduate working in the city might meet, fall in love with, and marry the person he was destined to spend the rest of his life with. Or meet, fall in love with, and *not* marry that person. Or be part of a couple that, after five years of living together, decides the time has finally come to either marry or else go their separate ways.

Tom was an "Associate" at the prestigious firm of Cravath, Swain & Moore, known familiarly as just "Cravath," who also contributed his time *pro bono*—"for the public good," i.e., without charge—to several organizations concerned with protecting the environment. Even under the coffee-shop lighting he had the sort of looks which women considered divinely attractive, though blond. Tom wore a come-from-work gray pinstripe and had propped up next to him one of those cool beat-up soft leather briefcases lawyers often carried. Josh had changed earlier in the grubby office he shared (deserted at that hour) in the Hogan Building near Foley Square downtown. He had chosen to wear the somewhat ugly greenish jacket that had kept him company in his sparse leisure hours since college. It was rather overlarge, like all his clothes, and gave him an appearance that was not exactly prepossessing. But he was an engaging presence whom Tom always enjoyed being around.

Others found the intensity that Josh brought to the subjects he was enthusiastic about a little worrisome.

"I was just starting law school at Penn when the first 'up-tempo' Philadelphia International hits broke," he said. "Some people don't consider that disco—because it's good—but I remember feeling *absolutely electrified* and thinking, Finally, dance music's back! Dance places can't be far behind—"

"Well, you feel electrified often—"

"But this was different. I loved the idea that there'd be places for people to go dancing after the terrible social wasteland of our college years. Uhff."

"You've been to a lot of discos?" Tom asked.

"No. In fact, practically none. For me, Penn wasn't easy, and I haven't had much social life since coming to the city, either. But I still consider myself a loyal adherent of the Disco Movement—"

"It's a Movement?" Tom asked.

While talking, they reached for their wallets to pay the check, which at the Acropolis tended to be pleasingly small.

"It sort of is," Josh affirmed. "What I found terribly encouraging was the idea that when the time in life came to have a social life, there'd be all these great places to go to. Because, as you'll remember, for many years there were none."

Tom nodded in agreement.

Josh continued: "What I didn't realize is that they'd get so *impossible* to get into."

Meanwhile, I was huddled with the clients on the sidewalk about a half block east of the Club's main entrance, near the alley leading to the back, pondering what to do next.

"I'm exhausted," Marshall said. "Let's just call it a night."

Marshall started taking off the long dark cashmere overcoat I had lent him.

A long limo, though not exactly a stretch, turned into the alley near us.

"No, wait," I said. "I think I have an idea."

I took off at a half-run down the alley the limo had just gone down. There were a few calls of "Jimmy!" urging me back, but I heard their steps and assumed they were behind me.

An interesting aspect of the downtown area where the Club was located—and crucial to the events of this story—was the web of strange alleys and tunnels giving access to the often large open areas or courts behind the buildings that lined its streets and avenues. The Club had taken over the structure of the former Van Dam Opera House, built in 1888 amidst the optimism that the area, then so active during the day, would become a popular nightlife center, too—which did finally happen, though not for another nine or so decades.

Rounding the corner, I could see the limousine pull to a stop not far from the old opera house's backstage door, which served as the Club's semi-secret back entrance. A limo door opened, and as the driver walked to the back, a group of five models started getting out, some of them not just model-looking but austerely beautiful. As I approached, one apparently recognized me from the Club and spoke to me in a very normal, friendly-girl voice belying the severe aesthetic of her looks.

"Oh, hi," she said.

"Hi."

"You're Des's friend."

"Yeah."

By this time Hap, the most junior of the three clients, had caught up with me. As the models approached the Club's back door, it swung open and Hap and I merged with them to unobtrusively slip into the passageway. *The gambit had worked!* I couldn't believe it: *we were in the Club!* Hap was thrilled, too, but suddenly it occurred to me that the others were nowhere to be seen. The models were already heading down the corridor. I went back to the door and looked out.

"Where are Marshall and Steve?" I asked.

"They've gone back to the hotel."

I leaned out the door and looked around. Deserted. No one.

"Come on," Hap said, pulling me away, still anxious about getting in. "Let's go."

"I can't believe it."

At Hap's urging I slowly turned away and followed him down the back corridor, cluttered with scenery and miscellaneous objects used in the Club's parties and spectacles, as well as boxes of extra glasses, mixers, and bar supplies. Antique signage and other colorful relics of the old "opera house" days—it had really been a vaudeville theater—remained, too. Maybe it was all very interesting, but I felt numb, in an utter funk, once again having snatched defeat from what, if they had given me only another three minutes, could have been a magnificent triumph.

"They wanted me to apologize for them," Hap explained. "They were really bushed."

"What a . . . disaster," I managed.

"No."

Hap handed me back the infamous overcoat I had loaned Marshall. I took it almost without registering the fact, at several points later panicking that I had lost it. Full of naïve—I had to think rather innocent—enthusiasm, Hap led the way through the backstage opening to the cavernous disco now reaching the apex of writhing hyperactivity. The models we had slipped in with, going on ahead, had by now disappeared into the crowd where the inevitable boyfriends—or just friends who were boys—waited. In any case, it was no big deal. Even if I had been thinking of romance at that moment (which I wasn't), I had no expectations of or aspirations to date models, nor had ever done so—I couldn't even imagine how anyone would go about it. An outsider might consider this just a defensive, self-protective pose—and it was probably that also—but even at a young age one sometimes recognizes that there are behavior patterns that would simply be a waste of time for everyone concerned, which leads you to put them out of your mind or avoid them until you reach a certain stage of inebriation, whereupon everything is reconsidered again.

One of the more immediately notable things about the Club on a night like this in the early eighties was that there was almost nothing about it that would be identified today as "Disco Era"—none of the corny clothes, fabrics, hairdos, and behavior—almost no specifically "disco" dancing that I could discern. Which, frankly, was fine with me.

Hap seemed completely oblivious to the disaster of the evening, the discouragement that Steve and Marshall must be feeling—with their sad, face-saving "turning in early" on what by rights should have been a fantastic night on the town—completely forgotten.

"Wow!" he said, overwhelmed by the energy and romance of the Club going at full blast. I'd like to paint a gaudy picture of how extravagant it was, but looking around there were in fact no beautiful naked women on horseback, no baby elephants or fabulous semi-naked people painted gold or silver or wearing ostrich feathers, no voluptuous Cleopatras or ebony Nubian Guards, not even a run-of-the-mill music or film star immediately visible. Though over the past year and a half I had seen most of those things—and there's nothing quite so great as a baby elephant in a disco—what you basically found in the prime hours and nights of the Club was a huge crowd of fairly normal-looking, often stylish people who felt they were celebrities because *they were in the Club*—and because they were often fairly smashed.

3

In Complete Control

I think another secret of the Club's popularity—part of which involved attracting a mixed crowd of older and cooler people as well as the usual army of the young—was that the selection of dance tunes played was great but not *painfully loud.* The Club's sound engineers had taken advantage of the auditory fact that low-register tones can be amplified at a high volume without hurting the ears or entirely obliterating conversation. The acoustical design was brilliant in that volume was focused where it was needed most, at the center of the dance floor—not on the booths along the walls, the mezzanine, or the balconies farther above. These functioned almost as conversation pits, much like what was achieved at the nightclub Nell's later in the decade. That's what struck me as so off about the "Oh, you couldn't talk in discos" criticism the movie sometimes later faced—obviously they hadn't been to the Club.

Another good place for talk was the so-called "Ladies

Lounge," which was actually operated more on a unisex basis, with guys filling the superfluous chairs and sofas of its outer room, talking, smoking, rolling joints, hanging out. The disco sound reached the plush lounge in two ways: as a thumping bass coming through the building's walls and infrastructure, and as a seemingly more distant melodic line carried through the smoky air.

Charlotte and Alice were waiting in the lounge's inner room (where the plumbing was) for some of the scarce washstand space. A young blond woman stood in front of the mirror trying to adjust the tubular part of her tube-top dress for comfort, without much success. Finally, annoyed, she yanked it down, momentarily freeing her petite breasts before adjusting the dress over them again, with a last scrutinizing glance before heading back to the dance floor action. This was the mood of those times—freer, more spontaneous, less inhibited, with no prudishness or priggishness, or at least very little.

"I like the dark side of things," Charlotte was saying as they took the young woman's place at the mirror, through which she could address Alice. "To stay open to that side of experience. I want to *undergo* life in all its colors, even those which seem terribly dark, sordid, and disturbing . . . For instance, I've tried heroin."

"You're kidding!" Alice said, incredulous.

Charlotte shook her head no.

"Do you like nightmares?" she continued.

"No."

"Well, I do . . . It's not obviously related but . . . I think that's what made me a little more tolerant of the guys at Hampshire."

"What do you mean?" Alice asked.

"You were a bit critical. The guys there preferred women more . . . laid-back."

"*I'm* laid-back," she said.

A compassionate look crossed Charlotte's face. "Well, for whatever reason," she went on gently, "you didn't have much of a social life there."

"I had a social life," Alice answered, "just not one of those terrible pretend-marriages. The Hampshire guys were jerks, hippy-dippy suburbanites with all this hair"—she opened her hands by the side of her head to indicate lots of hair—"and extremely dim intellectual interests. I'm sorry, I don't consider the guy who did the Spider-Man comics a serious writer."

Defensively she tilted her vodka-tonic, took a long sip, and sat on one of the little lounge sofas.

Charlotte turned to her. "Alice, one thing I've noticed is that people *hate* being criticized. Everyone *hates* that. It's one of the great truths of human nature—I think it's why my parents got divorced."

Alice looked implicated. Her eyes began to water slightly.

"I'm sorry," Charlotte added, apparently sincerely. "It's just that you're so terrific—it makes me sick to think that you might get in that terrible situation again where everyone hated you—"

"*Hated* me?"

"You're wonderful," Charlotte said, sitting next to her. "Maybe, in physical terms, I'm a little cuter than you, but you should be *much* more popular than I am . . . It'd be such a shame if what happened in college repeated itself."

"Why would it repeat itself?" Alice asked, her voice sounding pretty upset.

"You're right," Charlotte said reassuringly. "I just think it's so important to be in control of your own destiny—not to fall into that fifties cliché of waiting by the phone for guys to call. The right ones never do. The ones who do, you've got to make the most ridiculous excuses to; the nice ones get hurt feelings and hate you; the jerks inevitably corner you into going out anyway. Late at night you find yourself with some awful guy with disgusting breath thrusting his belly against you, sticking his slobbering tongue in your mouth . . . Ugh, yecch. Thank *God* this is a whole new era in music and social models!"

As they passed through the portals of the ladies' lounge area, a wave of music washed over them. The beat of the brilliant Chic-produced Sister Sledge classic "He's the Greatest Dancer" took over their steps while Charlotte led the way to the mezzanine balustrade.

"Look down," Charlotte said, indicating the dance floor below: "*We're in complete control.*"

Trying to enter into Charlotte's supremely confident and exalted spirit, Alice examined those dancing below, too.

"*There are a lot of choices out there,*" Charlotte concluded triumphantly.

Meanwhile, I was slumped, very depressed, in a booth along the wall on the main floor. I don't know whether Alice and Charlotte had seen me or not at that point, but I was certainly oblivious to them and nearly everything else as well. According to the film script, I was "in an almost comically tragic state." Ha, ha, ha.

Hap stood watching the dancing, weaving slightly to the music. We had both gotten drinks, but they seemed to be affecting us in opposite directions.

"*Fan-tastic!*" Hap said, not for the first time. "This place is far better than I could have possibly imagined. Too bad

Steve and Marshall didn't come—they would have really loved it here."

Taking a gulp of his drink, he noticed my continuing depressed state.

"Don't worry about it," he said. "So what."

Charlotte and Alice, coming down the stairs, now definitely spotted us.

"No, it's him," Charlotte said. "I saw him coming in the back with some lummox."

"I think it's much better to wait until things happen naturally," Alice replied, looking over to where we were. "Forcing things never works."

"No," Charlotte countered. "Forcing things usually works beautifully . . . You know, even if he's in advertising, someone will want him. I just think it's really important that we be in control of our own destinies."

Meanwhile, Hap was still trying to buck me up. "It doesn't matter," he said. "Marshall's a good guy. He doesn't care about this kind of stuff."

"Uh, excuse me," Charlotte said, addressing Hap. "Has anyone ever told you you look just like Kate Preston's brother, *Rod*?"

"Who?" Hap asked.

"Rod Preston. Do you know him?"

"No."

Charlotte turned first to Alice and then to Hap. "Have you ever noticed how people who look 'just alike' *never* seem to know each other?"

"Huhn," Hap said, intrigued.

Alice was watching me when I finally looked up and managed a (fairly depressed) smile.

"Hi," she said.

"Hey . . ." I managed. "How've you been?"

"Fine. How are you?"

Hap interjected, "He's really depressed."

As the deejay started his mix, snatches from Evelyn "Champagne" King's "Shame" started to become audible, until it finally took over entirely.

"God," Charlotte said, looking around, "isn't this place great?"

"It's fan-tastic!" Hap replied. "I love it." This was about his fourteenth "fan-tastic!"

"I really like this song," Charlotte said.

"Huhn," Hap observed, but with the intonation clearly positive.

"Do you like to dance?" Charlotte asked him.

"Would you, uh . . . ?" Hap indicated the dance floor.

"Sure," Charlotte replied. "Great."

She looked to Alice and then back to Hap.

"Should we *all* go?" she asked, indicating me.

"I think he's too depressed to dance," Hap said. Then he addressed me directly: "Hey, Jimmy, we're going to dance— come on."

"I'm too depressed to dance," I said. "You go ahead."

Charlotte gave Alice a significant look and threw her jeans jacket on the banquette before taking off for the dance floor with Hap in tow. Alice wandered closer to the banquette.

"What's wrong?" she asked, sliding gracefully onto it while tucking her legs under herself, totally relaxed and natural. Sometimes it's like that; when we're with someone who's totally distressed, we're conversely put at our ease.

"An absolute disaster," I managed to reply.

"What?" she asked.

"I had to get some clients into the Club, and gave the boss my coat to wear—'Here, wear this.' I can't believe what an idiot I am."

"Why?" she asked. "Your coat's nice."

"That's just it: it is nice. But this guy's—Marshall's—clothes are hideous. It's famous. But giving him a coat to put over them—it's so stupid. Just incredibly stupid."

"It's not stupid. The Club is really hard to get into."

I looked at her, a little surprised and annoyed—not at all in the mood for contradiction.

"It was unbelievably, incredibly *dumb*. He's a really nice guy and I insulted him. And this nice guy I *stupidly* insulted is basically my boss. It was really *stupid*."

"Maybe you're right," Alice finally conceded, reluctantly. "I guess it *was* a bit stupid."

There was something about hearing the word "stupid" from someone else's lips, describing my conduct, that at that moment completely enraged me. Despite what I'd said, I guess I was not looking for agreement about my stupidity at that moment but, rather, continuing, consoling assurances. I bolted up with my coat and drink glass and started to walk away, in a huff and a little disoriented. All my life I have ignored the explosive combined effect of unhappiness and booze, with some disastrous results. Then, catching myself and aware of overreacting, I stepped back, trying to recoup and act minimally polite.

"Can I, uh, get you a drink?" I asked her.

Alice took a moment to reply. "Yeah, thanks."

Then I took off, leaving her alone in the big banquette booth, though with every intention of coming back with some drink for her.

Alice looked around, first, to notice if anyone had witnessed what had happened and, second, to try to appear a "people-watcher" or nightclub observer, rather than just another stranded single girl.

Outside the Club on Van Dam Street, in the quiet beyond the front door mob scene, Des stood with Nina, who had by now recovered from her earlier crying. It was that poignant and bittersweet moment after the storm—they were breaking up, but both had now accepted it, their mood soft and very mellow, silences punctuating their phrases.

"Des," Nina said tenderly, "you're a wonderful man."

She glanced down the street, and Des signaled the approaching cab, which pulled to a stop near them. Nina turned to Des, giving him a last kiss of the gentlest kind.

"Take care of yourself, Des," she said, then stepped into the waiting cab. Des closed the door carefully and watched the cab drive off before striding up the crowded Club entrance to where Van was.

"What's up, Van?" he asked.

Van had stepped off his platform to confer with Rick—something very serious seemed to be afoot. Bobby and the other bouncers had been left to control the swollen crowd.

"Keep that ad guy friend of yours out of here," Van replied, as he spoke moving the short whiskey glass in his hand around in a vaguely threatening manner. Perhaps it should be mentioned that Van could have been pretty well sloshed at this point. Alcohol is something that can lead even the best of us to aggressive, quarrelsome, erratic behavior. On the other hand, it can also induce a wonderful feeling of pervasive well-being.

"What do you mean?" Des asked him.

"When I turned him away with a group of his 'clients,' he snuck around back, where you let them in—"

"I didn't."

"They're inside. Rick just saw them."

Rick, Van's good-looking protégé, nodded his head in confirmation. Des looked to him a moment, then paused to regroup and try another tack.

"Is this really important?"

"I'm not out here on *jerk patrol* just so you can let them in the back way . . . I've talked to Berrie and he promised me he'd fire you if that guy's in the Club."

"I can't believe that!" Des said. "You made Berrie *promise* to *fire me*?!"

Van nodded emphatically. Des shook his head and walked to the Club doors, throwing back one comment— *"You really think Berrie keeps his promises?"*—before continuing into the Club.

4

Like Something out of the Nazis

Des took the main stairs to the mezzanine level two steps at a time, more or less to the rhythm of "Le Freak" by Chic playing at the Club's maximum volume level, though still well short of the threshold for pain inflicted at lesser clubs. Music was part of Des's domain and he and the then very young Michael O'Brien—the deejay whose career Des started, later famous as a record producer and for his entanglements with Madonna—had the idea of "anthem" moments throughout the evening, when an irresistible disco standard would be played at higher than normal volume to get everyone back onto the floor. Throughout the night there would be crescendos and lulls but always what those of us who cared considered great music.

At some point in the darkest years of anti-disco opprobrium, the Chic Organization emerged as the disco group it was okay to say you liked. Though among Chic songs "Le Freak" was not one of my personal favorites, like a lot of disco standards which might not seem so great heard on the radio, it sounded incomparably better when played in the environment for which it was intended—the floor of a dance venue.

The circumstances of "Le Freak's" composition were emblematic of the earlier period when Studio 54 was *the* place of all places. By the early eighties, when the Club held sway, "Studio," as it was colloquially known (*not* "54," as the title of a competing disco movie had it), had been closed and padlocked for quite a while, its owners heading to prison on tax fraud raps. "Le Freak," which became the top-selling single of all time up to then, was created in response to its writers being excluded from Studio on the night of a party supposedly partially in their honor. Bernard Edwards and Nile Rodgers, the musical geniuses behind Chic (not to discount the contributions of others, such as the lovely vocals of Norma Jean Wright), had rented tuxedos and frilly shirts for the party for Grace Jones, with whom they were then collaborating, but nothing they said or did could get them beyond the Studio ropes. Perhaps it really was "full"—the usual excuse given—that night. Or maybe Mark—the Van of Studio 54, who rarely slipped up about such things—was not around, or the frilly multicolored After Six–style evening wear they'd hired fell afoul of Studio's snobbish dress code (dark colors, natural fabrics, etc.; *footwear* was particularly important, one of the owners was quoted as saying). Furious, the songwriters finally left, screaming "F★★★Studio 54" as a sort of chant, went home, and, still wearing their party finery, opened some champagne set aside for celebration and let their angry mood metamorphose into songwriting joy, somehow from the "F★★★Studio" refrain getting the totemic "Le Freak—c'est Chic."

The Club echoed with the Chic instrumentals as an agitated Des climbed the last flight of stairs to Berrie's third-floor offices. He passed a bouncer type lounging near the door and a young woman carrying a cash tray back to a register downstairs before coming to the club-like inner room where Adam and Victor, the two sleek turtleneck types who served as Berrie's assistants, were doing a preliminary count of that night's cash. An open balcony onto the Club rotunda allowed the spinning, refracted light of the disco ball to scrape the ceiling and walls to incongruously beautiful effect.

"I need to see Berrie," Des announced.

Adam looked up from his count. "Berrie's not around."

"He's pretty mad, Des," Victor added. "Van told him you were letting people in the back again."

"When you let people in the back, is a cover being charged?" Adam asked. "Because that money should be coming here."

"Of course we're not charging a cover in the back," Des replied, an exasperated "*Gahd!*" escaping as he turned to go.

Des clomped back down the stairs two or even three at a time. The long stairway below Berrie's office was a private zone roped off and watched by Travis Sanchez, a tall flunky incongruously named after the colonel who commanded the Alamo when it was overrun by General Santa Ana's troops. Des flew by Travis but had to pick his way through the mezzanine and lower stairs, which were mobbed with standing, sitting, drinking, smoking, talking, laughing, kissing, toking, show-offing Club flotsam and jetsam (though more of the former).

Reaching the main floor, Des edged through the main bar area to intercept Berrie Rafferty, the Club's scumbag owner, near the main register just as he was collecting two fat wads of bills from Alex, the bar manager.

Unlike the actor who played him in the movie, Berrie was older, less of a hipster, a smooth businessman of once-athletic good looks in a dark cashmere turtleneck shirt and tailored jacket, probably in his mid-fifties but tough, energetic, and—to put not too fine a point on it—*very* scary. How he had come up with the name "Berrie" none of us knew. There was a rumor it was an affection he had picked up during a sojourn in France in the early seventies—"Berrie" a version of how the French pronounce "Barry." Or perhaps he just greatly admired the founder of Motown Records, Berry Gordy, but preferring his own eccentric spelling, which is actually characteristic of jerks.

"Uh, Berrie . . ." Des started diffidently. Berrie turned to him while stashing the bar cash in his jacket's inside breast pockets. "This thing that Van's saying about your promising to fire me if Jimmy Steinway's in the Club—that isn't true, is it?"

"No, it's true," Berrie said. "I can confirm that. This Jimmy Steinway I don't want in the Club."

"Why?" Des asked.

"Come here," Berrie said, and led Des to the backstage hallway, where it was quieter and they'd not be observed. The moment they were through the doors he started in on Des. "You promised you'd stop letting friends in the back."

"No," Des said. "You said we could still let people in from the list."

"Don't contradict me, Des. I don't want a lot of ad people in the Club, particularly not this guy—"

"I didn't let him in. If Van didn't either, then he's not in the Club—"

"Did I ever tell you that my first job was in advertising—at Y & R?" Berrie asked, not out of the blue. Berrie had told Des of his stint at Y & R many times.

"In those days the big thing was to be *nice* to everyone," Berrie said, a kind of anger or disgust in his tone, "to the secretaries, the media department, the *art directors*, the Client—"

"Well, I don't think it's that way now . . ."

"I don't care," Berrie said, leaning on one of the doors leading to the main room. "I don't want *that element* in the Club."

"Jimmy's, like, my best friend—"

"And you've been a good friend to him, Des; but this Jimmy's not a good friend to you. He's out of control—an *egomaniac*."

Berrie pushed through the door back to the main part of the Club. This whole exchange was amazing to me, though I don't doubt its veracity. You wear a suit and have a job in advertising, no matter how essentially humiliating, and suddenly you're a big "egomaniac," and pond scum like Berrie feel authorized to hold you in self-righteous contempt.

Des caught up with me almost immediately after leaving Berrie—apparently he found my usual movements in the Club fairly predictable. I was just carrying my Scotch and Alice's vodka-tonic back toward the booth when he intercepted me.

"Uh, Jimmy—" Des said, panting as if he had run.

"Where *were* you?! What a nightmare!—"

"Listen," he said, "I don't know how you got in, but you'd better go—"

"What?!"

"This way."

Des had started leading me toward the back.

"You're asking me to leave?" I was incredulous. Absolutely stupefied.

"Van's gone crazy. He made Berrie promise he'd fire me if he found you here. And Berrie hates ad agency people. It's nuts."

"I can't believe it! It's *like something out of the Nazis!!*"

I'll admit that I had completely lost it at that point. Maybe getting thrown out of a nightclub seems trivial when so described. But it didn't seem so that night.

"Come on," Des said. "I'll get you back on the list, but tonight it's best you go . . ."

While Des was leading me hurriedly toward the back door, he caught sight of Van talking with one of the young Club flunkies not far away. Des edged behind me to block, I suppose, any glimpse of me Van might have gotten, while still trying to hustle me out.

"Could I at least tell my client that I've got to go—"

"No."

"Please," I insisted. "Tell him what happened. His name is Hap."

"Okay," Des said.

I tried to chugalug my Dewar's before Des hustled me out but insisted he take Alice's vodka-tonic to her.

"That's for this irritating girl who's occupying my booth—Alice," I said.

Des took the drink and looked in the direction of Alice, still sitting stranded in "my" booth. I was already embarrassed at how I had behaved and would have loved to have started making up for it by at least giving her the cocktail. In retrospect this whole evening, what transpired and the way things were left, turned out to be one of the tragedies of my life. But to say so reflects a huge quantity of hindsight being brought to bear on events that seemed at the time to be nothing more than "events."

"She's irritating?" Des asked. "I thought she seemed nice."

"You know her?"

He took a sip of her drink, wincing slightly at its sweetness, while still trying to hustle me out of the Club the back way.

"Well, she's been here two times before. How's she irritating?"

By now we had pushed through the doors to the back corridor, Des trying to guide me out, holding a bunch of fabric from my suit jacket. I broke away from his grasp.

"God, I can't believe this?!" I said, coming to a complete stop. "You're really going to throw me out?!"

Des nodded.

"Thanks, Des," I said, my voice dripping with sarcasm of the about-to-sob hurt-feelings variety. "You've really been a good friend to me!"

Turning on my heels, I started to head down the corridor, for a millisecond checking that my cashmere overcoat was still on my arm and, verifying that it was, stalking off. Noticing an enormous gold metallic sphere on top of a pile of other theatrical props and seeking some way to express or dramatize the anger and frustration I was feeling, I reached out and knocked it off its perch. Instead of dropping with the great metallic clang I expected, the balloon-like prop slid to the ground with a pathetically anticlimatic plop.

"Oh, that's mature," Des said behind me.

I turned around. "Oh, McGrath," I called down the hall, using his surname coldly as if I barely knew him. "One last thing: *Cram it!*"

This, however, did not seem enough. After a few steps, I turned around again. "I'm never speaking to you again. Find someone else to bore with your pathetic ramblings! *Good! Bye!*"

With that I departed the Club without another word.

Des was left standing alone in the hallway, the vodka-tonic in hand. He took another sip and winced again. Once you've outgrown the stickily sweet bittersweetness of tonic drinks, there's no going back again.

Alice, abandoned in the booth, had no idea where I was or what was going on. She felt devastated but did a very good job of not showing it. She looked around, tried to appear the equanimous people- and club-watcher, examined all the different costumes and dancing styles, and finally— seeing no indication of my return imminent or otherwise— got up and crossed to where Charlotte and Hap were dancing, matching her movements to theirs with her usual effortless grace.

"Are you okay?" Charlotte asked her solicitously.

Alice nodded and continued dancing. Hap, now with two partners, was in a great mood, and renewed his energetic if klutzy dancing with even greater enthusiasm.

As soon as Alice left her booth, members of the Club's fun European crowd moved to occupy it—there was a huge premium on good booths at the Club, particularly at the height of the evening.

"You really think we'll be able to get in?" Josh asked Tom as they crossed Van Dam Street diagonally toward the Club. With their long raincoats and floppy legal briefcases they were hardly the typical idea of cool nightclubbers of the period, but in a sense they really were.

It would not have occurred to me at the time, but Tom and Josh approaching the Club could be seen as two powerful agents of attraction—in Tom's case, clear and overwhelming; in Josh's, subtle, goofy, but from my point of view perhaps more insidious—about to be added to a lab experiment. This version of the Club, as some sort of test tube for romance, was not far from the truth. But it turned out not to be a controlled experiment that could later be endlessly repeated. These results were often long-lasting. There would be Club marriages, and the offspring of those marriages, and soon the grandchildren will arrive, the destinies affected by any given night at the Club increasing geometrically with each subsequent stage.

Tom didn't immediately answer Josh's question about getting in. He seemed to be thinking or strategizing. They passed through the outlying reaches of the crowd as if wading through a field of rye.

"This usually works," he said finally, with a certain amount of bravado. "Try to avoid eye contact with the guys at the door and just follow me in."

Although this was pretty much the opposite of the usual system for getting in, it worked for Tom, who found a hole in the crowd leading to the velvet rope, which snapped open just as they got to it. Striding down the tunnel to the

Club's main set of doors, Josh gave a long exhaling sigh of relief, shivering with *Schadenfreude* at the thought of those not so lucky.

"*Phew*—thanks for getting me in."

"Not at all," Tom replied.

Des, carrying the cocktail, approached the banquette area deserted by Alice, now occupied by the European crowd.

"*Ciao*, Sandro!" one of the European girls called to a passing guy, who just nodded back and kept on walking as if he were looking for someone else, perhaps someone more fascinating or attractive, or maybe of a different gender entirely—or, perhaps, all of those things.

Des looked around at the adjacent booths to make sure he had not missed Alice elsewhere. She was definitely *not there*. While he wandered toward the dance floor to check there, still holding her cocktail, a lovely-looking but quite tense young woman approached him from out of the crowd.

"Des," she said dramatically, with the hint of an English-German accent in her voice, "I think we need to talk."

In fact, I knew all about this girl: her name was Diana. She was from Düsseldorf, but with her pretty English accent had gotten small parts in several television movies and miniseries—the rape victim in the shower scene, etc., etc. I knew that Des considered her a little too "heavy"; now she was very tightly wound up, as if about to explode. It was an emotional state Des knew well, since at some point virtually every woman he ever dated had gotten into it.

"Yes," he said. "There's something I want to talk to you about."

Taking her hand gently but decisively, he led her—frankly a little surprised at his resolve—to a nearby booth where there was just enough space to sit and talk in reasonable privacy—a privacy that seemed heightened once they were seated and the booth's other occupants left for the dance floor.

Alice's former high spirits had recovered considerably while dancing with Charlotte and Hap. Hap was silly but a lot of fun and Charlotte really sweet, leading Alice in all sorts of new moves, some cool, some just entertaining. For those nearby it was entrancing to see these two young women, graceful and high-spirited, dancing in unison to a great disco song—Chic's "Everybody Dance!" again featuring Norma Jean Wright's lovely liquid vocals—with Hap bounding around cheerfully near them.

A few moments later Tom, his coat and briefcase checked, appeared on the raised area overlooking the dance floor. Charlotte spotted him and immediately leaned in toward Alice to alert her—though on the dance floor whispers had to be shouted.

"I think Tom's here!"

"Who?!"

"Tom Platt!"

Alice stole a brief and ultra-casual glance in Tom's direction. As if on this cue, he started down the steps to the dance floor toward her. Alice smiled and spun around a few times with Hap until Tom arrived. Immediately and miraculously, everything fell into place. They danced beautifully together, or so it seemed, Alice occasionally looking up and smiling. Disco mercifully overthrew one of the big, tiresome concerns

of the rock era: avoiding too frequent smiles or looks at your
partner so as not to seem too uncool. The dance floor was
made safe for unshaded happiness again. Disco versions of
some of the most optimistic songs of the gregarious twenties
and thirties—"Puttin' on the Ritz," "We're in the Money,"
"Mountain Greenery"—seemed to express this. Finally the
deejay's switch to a not-so-good song, always a downer, gave
them—sweaty, exhilarated, and exhausted—the excuse to flee
the dance floor, joined by Hap and Charlotte. As they crossed,
a sexy "older" woman in a clinging cheetah-pattern cat suit
who had been dancing in a highly voluptuous way with a
much younger man bumped into Tom, quite hard. By way
of apology she made a big cat growl. Tom laughed and nodded to her, also sharing a complicit smile with Alice.

"Who's she?" Alice asked.

"They, uh, call her 'Tiger Lady,' " Tom said, as if it were a
scientific term.

"It's actually a cheetah pattern she's wearing."

"At some point she wore a tiger pattern," Tom said. "It's
always something very slinky and sexy."

"You consider her sexy?"

"*Yeah.*"

"Here's a booth," Charlotte said, and moved to claim it
from some departing older types. Hap looked toward the
booth where he had left Jimmy, which was now full of
strangers.

"Where's Jimmy?" he asked.

"I don't know," Alice answered. "He went to get drinks . . ."

"What would you like?" Tom asked.

"Uh—a vodka-tonic," she said.

"Me too," Charlotte added.

"I'll go with you," Hap offered. As he and Tom left for

the bar, the girls slid into the banquette. Behind her Alice noticed a young woman, apparently crying.

In the booth immediately behind Alice, Des and Diana were at a difficult part of a very hard conversation. Diana's face was already wet from tears.

"Ever since I was six years old or so, I sensed that I was somehow 'different,' " Des said.

"Then every time you made love to me," Diana, her voice very strained, asked, "you must have wanted to . . . *vomit . . . ?!*"

"No, no, not at all!" Des said. "You're beautiful! You don't have to be some sweaty, horny, hetero he-ape to admire and appreciate . . . female beauty. Only very, very recently did the final realization come."

"When? Exactly when did the final realization come?"

"Two days ago," Des said, trying to collect himself. "I . . . get up late and usually turn on the TV, sort of a reflex action. Wednesday afternoon there was a rerun of *Wild Kingdom*, Mutual of Omaha's old nature show with Marlin Perkins, and that . . . attractive . . . younger guy. It . . . triggered something. Suddenly everything fell into place: 'I'm gay—and always have been.' "

"You only found out you were gay on Wednesday?"

"Only then, definitively," Des said. "Wednesday was Gay Day for me."

Alice watched, completely drawn into the unfolding story, unobserved by either of them though only inches behind Diana.

"Finished eavesdropping?" Charlotte asked.

Alice, startled, turned around. "I wasn't eavesdropping," she protested.

"Oh come on." Charlotte smiled conspiratorially. "Anything interesting?"

"Shhh. Gahd," Alice, embarrassed, whispered.

"Listen, it's much better you're with Tom than Jimmy," Charlotte said. "You two really look great together."

"You think so?"

She nodded. "It's too bad we weren't closer friends in college; I think I might have really . . . helped you there." Charlotte leaned closer, whispering: "For most guys, sexual repressiveness is a turnoff."

"You're saying this for *my* benefit?" Alice asked.

In her sweetest and most sympathetic tone, Charlotte explained: "You're a good conversationalist but . . . there's something of the kindergarten teacher about you—it's really nice, but . . . the guys you like also tend to be on the 'ethereal' side—it can get pretty far away from any kind of physicality."

Confidentially, she added, "This'll sound dumb, but it really works: Whenever you can, throw the word 'sexy' into your conversation. It's kind of a signal. Like, uh . . . '*There's something really sexy about . . .*'"

The strobe lights just then began to flash, creating eerily beautiful stop-motion effects on the dancers.

" '. . . *strobe lights.*' Or—"

Charlotte closed her eyes and sank more deeply into the banquette. "Ahh . . ." she gasped, tenderly kneading and caressing its fabric. "This fabric is *so . . . sexy!*"

Tom and Hap were just returning with the drinks. Hap

sank into the banquette next to Charlotte, leaned back, closed his eyes, and, stroking the fabric, sighed sensuously.

"Yeah—*it is!*" he said.

Alice turned to Tom and smiled, too. Charlotte's plan was working—Alice felt less ethereal already.

5

Exchanges of Ideas & Points of View

Near the dance floor Des thought he recognized someone he knew from the not especially pleasant past. The man, who might have been considered handsome by those who did not know him, wore a too-big jacket and trousers, and his hair was escaping at all angles from an attempted wet-down. He stood along the raised edge of the dance floor gazing with enthusiasm and identification at the spectacle unfolding there. Des approached him a little cautiously.

"Josh?"

Josh turned to him. "Uh, hi," Josh replied, oddly reserved and laconic.

"God, what are *you* doing here?"

"In New York, or in the Club?"

"In the city . . ." Des said.

"I'm an A.D.A. in Morgenthau's office."

This was actually quite a common post for young law school graduates to try to get, one of the classic paths for success—or failure—in "the Law." But Des acted as if he were unaware of any of that—his face remained a big blank.

"An Assistant District Attorney for Manhattan," Josh elaborated. "They call us A.D.A.s."

"You're a *prosecutor*?" Des asked, as if very surprised.

Josh nodded.

"How did you get that?"

"It's not such a big deal."

"But . . ."

"I'm perfectly competent to do the job, Des," Josh said, a bit tensely.

"Great. Good," Des said. "I wasn't implying anything. I was just surprised . . . to, uh, see you here."

Josh returned to watching the dance-floor action, depressed at the thought that the college baggage he thought he'd left behind might in fact never be, if Des's questioning was any indicator. Des, recoiling again from the sweet-bittersweet taste of Alice's drink, continued to watch him with some trepidation.

The truth is that there were two theories concerning Josh based on the same set of facts. All concerned, including Josh, would have stipulated that some of his behavior in college had been pretty crazy. But from this same set of facts, a very positive overall picture of Josh could be drawn and was by his closest friends. Tom subscribed to that view. On the other hand, another picture could be extrapolated that was very negative. That was the one Des held.

Henry was Charlotte and Alice's "gay friend." He was funny, smart, fastidiously dressed, and slightly tormented—

seemingly one of the last editions of a dandy type on its way to extinction since the ending of the good ol' repressed days. Dave, who accompanied him, was more boyish and athletic. Wearing tight jeans and shirt, he seemed the classic chorus-guy-friend-of-a-lawyer type but was actually the director of a small museum just north of the city dedicated to historical preservation—the sort of place that might lovingly preserve the snuff boxes, desk sets, and a manuscript or two of Washington Irving's or Edgar Allan Poe's. Dave was as smiling and relaxed as Henry was intense and hypercritical. It was not just heterosexual couples who paired up that way.

While the two of them spoke with Charlotte and Hap at one end of the booth, Alice and Tom were having a tête-à-tête at the other.

"Going to Harvard must have been great," Alice was saying.

"Well . . ." Tom replied doubtfully. He actually hadn't liked it much—though he knew he was lucky to have had the experience, etc., etc.

"The people at Hampshire were nice," Alice explained, "and pretty smart, in a non-traditional way. But I was out of place there. I'm sorry, I don't consider the guy who did the Spider-Man comics a serious writer."

"Yeah," Tom said, "I thought it was the Green Hornet people took more seriously."

Alice smiled. Her going to Hampshire, notorious for its hippy-dippy, touchy-feely atmosphere—objective character-istics acknowledged even by those who went there then—was a bit of a puzzle to everyone, including her later self. The story was a familiar one: a relatively brief enthusiasm at age sixteen ends up being one's entire lamentable higher education. The summer before her senior year in school, Alice found herself with time on her hands in a baby-sitting job on the less populated side of Martha's Vineyard island when a battered copy of Theodore Roszak's influential *The Making of the Counter Culture* fell into her hands, resulting in a brief period of countercultural thinking (though no drugs or Hermann Hesse), which coincided with the collapse of her first-semester grades and bad interviews for Swarthmore and Harvard.

"Hey, Tom," Des said, showing up out of nowhere and leaning over the back of the banquette, still holding Alice's by now wilted drink.

"Excuse me . . . are you 'Alice'?"

Alice, surprised, nodded yes.

"Jimmy Steinway gave me this vodka-tonic to give to you, but I'm afraid I've sampled it. I'll get you another."

"Jimmy's gone?" Hap asked, disconcerted.

"You're 'Hap'?" Des asked. Hap nodded. "Yeah, well, he wanted me to tell you that he's sorry but he was ejected from the Club."

"He was *ejected*?"

"Apparently he snuck one of his clients in the back of the Club," Des said. Hap looked thoughtful for a few moments and finally nodded.

"That's odd he knew I drank vodka-tonics," Alice said. "I never told him."

"It's uncanny."

Alice looked at Des, trying to decipher this. "You mean it's a complete cliché? 'All women recent college graduates drink vodka-tonics,' or something like that."

"Well," Des said. "Maybe."

At this point Adam, one of the turtlenecked guys from Berrie's office upstairs, slunk up next to Des and whispered in his ear.

Turning to Charlotte, Alice said, "So, Jimmy thinks I'm a total cliché."

"I ordered a vodka-tonic, too—so what," Charlotte said. "You're plenty original without having to order some weirdo drink."

"Yeah, I wouldn't worry about it," Des said. "Can I get you another?"

"Thanks," Alice said. "Actually, if you don't mind, I think I'd prefer a . . . uh . . . whiskey sour."

Des nodded and went off with Adam. Alice turned back to the group. Henry watched Des leave and then leaned in toward her and the others.

"Be careful with that guy. He's a monster—the worst."

"What do you mean?" Alice asked.

"He uses his position in the Club to get girls involved with him—then brutally dumps them," Henry said. "He's a notorious liar and womanizer."

"How can they let someone like that work here?"

Henry liked Alice, but he had to smile at her naïveté. "You think only highly moral people work at clubs like these?"

A great aspect of the very early eighties was all the connections being made. None of us were in any sense "New Wave," but we liked the effect it had on mainstream fashion with narrow ties, narrow lapels, sharper cuts, and the cool neo-1962 look which was then the rage. I liked 1962 the first time, so it was good to have it back again. People from different groups and subsets more readily appreciated each other in the early eighties, even if it was by error or misinterpretation. I remember one such experience when at a party a rather hip girl was incredibly friendly to me. My hair had just been hacked short by an incompetent barber, I was especially pale and thin and wearing a sharply cut old suit with narrow lapels and a similar tie—not from some cool vintage store but from the wardrobe of a family where nothing got thrown out until it fell off, and sometimes not even then. She evidently mistook me for a cool New Wave heroin user rather than just a junior-level ad wonk with an unhealthy pallor, bad haircut, and secondhand clothes. This was a strategy a lot of us tried to play in the period: if you took "uncool" to its farthest limits, you stood a good chance of being mistaken for cool by someone.

When the colossal hit of the season—Blondie's "The Tide Is High"—came on, everyone except Des was on the dance floor. This melodic masterpiece brought into play a multiplicity of influences, including the lovely original 1968 Jamaican version by The Paragons, the operative dance culture of the early eighties, and Blondie, a music group and vocalist associated with the New Wave. The result was dance-floor nirvana, the culminating anthem of the night. When the Club's heavens opened and all the balloons and confetti came streaming down, everything was wonderful once again. Part of the Club's magic was the nightly renewal of its population. On any particular night a large portion of the revelers were entirely new to the scene there—as it was that night for Hap, Charlotte, and Josh—with everything fresh and unexpected.

Alice and Tom were on the dance floor, having lots of fun, when the loud bangs of the bursting metallic-colored balloons gave Alice a momentary fright and Tom wrapped his arms around her and they slow-danced through the rest of "The Tide Is High" and Harold Melvin & the Blue Notes' beautifully poignant "Bad Luck" from the pre-disco period. It was these sorts of juxtapositions that made Michael O'Brien's music mixes so popular with the Club crowd.

For Alice, who was not completely new to the Club, having come to two private parties before, the night seemed particularly extraordinary. To state at the beginning of an evening that you like someone, and then to run into that same person by chance at a great place, where everything was arranged for getting more closely involved in the easiest and most graceful way possible with dancing, drinks, music, and the companionship of the rest of your generation, and other ages, seeking the same thing. Such an evening of consummate but spontaneous romance was almost unheard of in American nightlife, though far more prone to happen in the disco era than before or since. The events of that evening were not just a chimera or phantasm, as both Alice and Tom were terrific people who between them had all the elements for creating a great or at least a very good relationship.

Tom already had his raincoat on and was talking with Des on the side of the main bar toward the coat check and Club entrance when Josh, leaving the dance floor with his hair and clothes matted with perspiration, encountered them there.

"You're going already?" he asked Tom.

"Yeah. It's really late."

Josh looked as if that hadn't occurred to him.

"I didn't peg you as such a nightclubber," Des said.

Josh looked at Des, but did not immediately reply.

"I mean, you really seem to like it," Des went on.

"I do," Josh said, not holding back any longer. "This is a great place. It's what I always dreamed of . . . Cocktails, dancing, conversation—exchanges of ideas and points of view . . ."

He looked around the Club.

"Everyone's here," Josh continued, his enthusiasm mounting a little strangely. "Everyone you know and everyone you don't know . . . You should be proud, Des. This is quite an accomplishment."

"Yeah," Des said, looking around the Club, too. "I am."

Josh turned to Tom. "Who's the girl you were dancing with?"

"Alice Kinnon."

They looked toward Alice, who was just putting on her coat twenty or so feet away. She looked lovely, her hair now a little loose and frizzy around the temples but pulled back along the top.

Josh nodded and looked wistfully in Alice's direction.

"Thanks again for getting me in," he told Tom before heading off.

Des looked after him. "I'm a little worried about that guy," he said. "I think he could be having a 'manic episode' of some kind."

"Come on, Des. Don't start in on that again."

"No, I was just making an observation."

Hap, now with his coat on, rejoined them.

"So," he asked Des, "you're one of the Club's managers?"

"Yeah."

Meanwhile, near Alice, a girl in a revealing metallic gold halter top burst into tears as her boyfriend was explaining something to her. She broke away and ran with a sob toward the downstairs ladies' lounge. Charlotte stood alongside Alice, looking in the same direction as the crying woman had gone.

"You knew Tom'd be here tonight, didn't you?" she said. "God, you're much craftier than I thought."

"No, I didn't."

"We're going to check out this after-hours club Jimmy told Hap about," Charlotte said. "Why don't you come? Jimmy might be there."

"I don't know."

Tom and Hap came up, and they all turned to walk out together. From some distance away, Des watched them go before turning back to work himself. It was at this point, toward the end of the night with the registers starting to close, that Des's responsibilities in the Club grew heaviest. There was a lot of tension involved in the control and counting of the vast quantity of cash and credit-card receipts that flooded into the Club every night, and Berrie's strange attitude made it no better, at least as far as Des was concerned.

Walking in the fresh night air, warmer than it had been earlier, Tom and Alice skirted the edge of Washington Square Park, a leafy September green and seemingly deserted at this hour. A yellow steam pipe by the curb issued voluminous white steam, on which a lovely, undulating image was projected—the shadow of a nearby leafy tree.

No matter what people say to the contrary and no matter how superficial it might seem, no matter how intellectual and judgmental we pretend to be, never discount the importance in life of looks. Tom, though tired and grimy after a long day's work and night's dancing, with a "4 a.m. shadow" of beard beginning to show, was more handsome than ever, and had that magnanimous confidence which went with it. Alice was not only entirely smitten, she felt smitten and consciously liked the sensation, especially after the disaster of her Hampshire years.

"How did you get involved with environmental causes?" she asked, adding quickly, "I think that's great."

"You're interested in the environment?"

"Very much so," Alice said.

"Actually, there's one theory that the environmental movement of our day was sparked by the rerelease of *Bambi* in the late 1950s," Tom said. "For many members of the baby-boom generation, it was traumatic . . . The hunters killing Bambi's mother?"

"Yeah," Alice said, "that was *terrible*."

"For six-year-olds, it's devastating. To this day, no one wants to identify with those hunters."

"I think you're right," Alice said thoughtfully. "Hunh."

"You're living at some women's residence, aren't you?"

"Yeah. It's terrible . . ." Alice said. "No guests."

"Where would you like to go, then?" Tom asked. "Some after-hours club?"

For someone just two years out of law school, Tom Platt had a surprisingly well-arranged apartment. Dark colors predominated, mostly brown. There was some nice worn old furniture. Tom made some noise with the keys opening the door and then held it open for Alice. Then entering he took his raincoat off and threw it over the back of a chair, as young people often will. For a moment he watched while Alice leafed idly through some mail, mostly of the "junk" variety, that had accumulated in a pile on the sideboard.

"Anything interesting?"

"Not so far," she said first, then added, "Actually, I find it all interesting."

"Would you like something to drink?"

Alice nodded.

"What?" Tom indicated the liquor bottles and bar stuff on a sideboard near him. Alice looked them over, her eyes first stopping on the squarish brown bottle of Jim Beam whiskey before spotting a more exotic green one.

"Uh, could I have a . . . Pernod?" she asked.

"Sure," Tom said, and started preparing it.

"You know," he said, indicating the Pernod, "this's supposed to be very good for cigarette mouth . . . Do you smoke?"

Alice nodded affirmatively. "When I drink or go out at night, I usually smoke. I live dangerously—on the edge. I'm no kindergarten teacher."

Tom laughed. Ever since their first marathon conversation that day in Sag Harbor, he had thought Alice terrific. But since arriving at his apartment, a New Alice had emerged—a recent-college-graduate version of the Tiger Lady: slinky, seductive, and a little mannered in a "sexy" direction.

Alice sat perched lightly on the furniture and, when she moved, trod catlike on the balls of her feet. A well-lit lucite display case in one corner attracted her attention while Tom prepared the drinks.

"What's this?" she asked.

Tom came over, bringing her a little glass of Pernod.

"I collect original-edition Scrooge McDuck comics," he explained. "I know it sounds a little odd—"

"No. Not at all," Alice said.

"This is original artwork by Carl Barks, who created the Uncle Scrooge comics," he said, indicating some framed artwork on the wall. "He's considered a bit of a genius."

Tom went back over to the stereo to adjust the tuner. Alice examined the drawings with considerable attention before turning back.

"There's something very . . . sexy . . . about Scrooge Mc-Duck," she said.

"You really think so?"

On his stereo Tom found WKTU, the preeminent disco radio station of the period. The Andrea True Connection's sexy, evocative "More, More, More" came up in volume gradually, the way the older hi-fis used to. Alice liked the song and started moving to it, downing the rest of her Pernod in one long sip.

"I *love* Uncle Scrooge," she said.

Tom smiled, too. He did not know if Alice was entirely aware of the seductive effect she was creating. He put his drink aside and crossed the room to join her on the improvised dance floor—a space between the furniture and the wall, actually. Alice danced really well—and, now, very sexily also. They moved in almost perfect synchrony. Alice laughingly dodged one kiss, but not a second one. They danced down the hallway to where Tom had his bedroom—all this was very much of that period, though such evenings are not entirely unknown even today.

6

Dawn Reverie

The first rays of dawn's early light are not always so excellent. On overcast days the early light can have a dirty, messy quality and seem hardly worth it. And from night's point of view, that first daylight, no matter how great or mediocre, is Death—the End. Kaputski. As for those of us who lived by night, there you might be, very probably were, reveling in the magic of night, the romance of darkness, with seemingly no time being marked at all, or at least no sun (and very few people) around to mark it (seven in the evening and four in the morning looking pretty much the same most places most of the year), when out of the blue, daylight has arrived and it's over, the spell broken. Busted. Though you might try to keep that old nighttime spirit going, it was almost impossible to. There might be a dawn revival, a dawn high, but it's deceptive and soon that pain-in-the-neck "It's a new day" feeling takes over, all the same daytime obligations to go through yet another time. Again it's the world of "Button up your coat, dear" and "Thanks, Mom," even if you've ostensibly gotten an apartment on your own or shared with some people you don't want to spend the rest of your life cohabiting with anyway. Fatigue and crankiness set in. Better hit the sack, because between nine and ten comes the waking dreamland, and you are about to start feeling and acting very, very weird.

But that was not the kind of dawn Alice walked into leaving Tom's apartment. The sky was crystalline, with rays of sunlight illuminating the still opulent green of the treetops along the rise in Central Park at Ninety-third Street across Fifth Avenue, and in the different gradations of shadow along street level the coloration subtly beautiful. Tom's building was one of those "sunken" brownstones (the entrance slightly below street level) of five stories on a beautiful tree-lined street in the low Nineties between Madison and Fifth Avenues. In the building's anachronistic vestibule, a light still burned, the brightness popping out of the light gray-green of the side street's shadows. Any excess of detail here is consonant with the highly responsive and aesthetic mood Alice felt in as she stepped from Tom's building into the dawn.

(If more specifics are available for characterizing this scene than could typically be derived from script drafts or interview transcripts, it's because in her late twenties Alice published two essentially autobiographical short stories set in the period. She had become a protégé of the fiction theorist-teacher-guru Gordon Lish, who later published several of her stories in his highly regarded literary magazine, *The Quarterly.* Most of what was published there was a little over-stylized, in my opinion. Even Alice's stories, good as they were, suffered somewhat from this highly introspective, slightly weird, stylization.)

Alice ascended the few steps from the brownstone's sunken entrance, running a hand through her hair and wrapping her light-colored raincoat more tightly around herself against the chill of the early-morning air. There seemed to be absolutely no side-street traffic at this time on a weekend morning and, rather than remain on the sidewalk, she crossed into the street, slightly teetering for a moment in her shoes, to walk diagonally down it toward Fifth Avenue beyond.

How a young woman might feel leaving a man's house early in the morning after the first night of her first adult love affair seems to me totally mysterious and worth further study and understanding. Would she feel completely happy, joyous at having finally found someone and having that passion so quickly reciprocated, physically and emotionally fulfilled, perhaps even with the triumph of conquest and of having her femininity, skill, and allure confirmed? Or on the other hand, would she feel vulnerable and exposed, in a strategically weakened position with the man involved, and perhaps open to criticism for having moved "too quickly" and acted in a way that, from the outside in the eyes of the critical or moralistic, might have even seemed a little bit "slutty"?

None of the above would have been possible to read in her facial expression as she reached Fifth Avenue, deserted at this hour except for the most pathetically dedicated joggers heading for Central Park's famous "Reservoir" track, and hailed a cab.

Alice sank back deeply into the passenger seat and allowed the waking city to roll by her.

When the cab deposited her outside St. Catherine's, she again teetered slightly on her heels as she made her way to its doors, her balance not improving any with increased grogginess. Trying the door, she found it locked—at St. Catherine's residents were *not* given the exterior door key. She rang for the night porter, but after almost six minutes there was no response and no sign of life within. Now she was cold and a little upset, but in characteristic Alice style, rather than get hysterical and lose it or make a scene, she spotted a deli across the street that had opened early and proceeded calmly to it.

Inside were a few tables, so she ordered a hot chocolate and to pass the time started leafing through a slightly smudged copy of the previous day's *Daily News*—not, incidentally, her favorite paper but one that did have a few occasionally promising features such as the Jumble (a game involving scrambled words), a well-written daily horoscope which could be read for its commonsense insight into human nature and upbeat tone, and the legendary Ann Landers advice column, which Alice now found and read. What she did not notice or dwell on was the depressing array of small health-related ads for abortion and VD clinics on the facing page: "PREGNANT?" "ABORTION?" "STDS?" "HERPES?" they asked unembarrassedly.

Night and Day

7

The Night of San Gennaro

It was late afternoon, though the sun was hidden behind the haze when Alice and Charlotte got out of the subway at Spring Street in Manhattan's "SoHo" district, a recently coined designation derived from its location *So*uth of *Hous*-ton Street, and probably also inspired by London's Soho section—though this was rarely mentioned. Until shortly before then I had, frankly, not heard of either—Gramercy Park or Greenwich Village were about as far downtown as anyone would go residentially. Soho in those years was still what would be called "urban frontier," along with TriBeCa and more problematical areas such as "alphabet city" (Avenues A, B, C, & D; fortunately, it stopped there) and various parts of Brooklyn.

Even then Soho was considered prime weekend brunch country—that was part of its early vogue. From late morning Saturday and Sunday, the area filled with not just the usual uptowners but also brunch-hunters in from the suburbs, hence all the expensive cars (including the good-looking, curvy Jaguars of the period) with New Jersey and other out-of-town license plates parked along its low-density streets. Soho had largely been built in the 1880s, just as the new "cast-iron" building methods had come in vogue, allowing spacious floor-through construction and enormous windows—masonry walls no longer had to support the buildings' weight.

Charlotte and Alice hurried out the subway steps west of Lafayette Street in the direction of West Broadway.

"What time did you finally get back?" Charlotte asked.

"I don't know."

"You don't know?" Charlotte asked, a little incredulous.

"I didn't check."

"Was it light or dark?"

"Why do you care what time I got in?" Alice asked, increasingly irritated and a little defensive.

"Sorry. No reason," Charlotte said. "I guess I was just making conversation. When I can't think of anything brilliant to say, I tend to fall into that '20 Questions' thing. I know it's obnoxious—sorry."

The restaurant they were headed for was called, simply, 'Spring Street'—it was a stylish glassed-in triangle at the corner of Spring and West Broadway that was then very modish. (The space was actually quadrangular, but designed to feel triangular.) Seeing them approach, I held open the door. Hap and I had been waiting for them at the restaurant, or on the sidewalk just outside, for upwards of two hours. In fact, Hap was just then leaving, carrying his garment bag–style traveling case with him.

"You're going?" Charlotte asked.

"Yeah, it's four-thirty."

"You can't go—we just got here."

"Yeah, I know. You're two hours late."

"That's impossible. Can't you stay just a little longer?"

"No. The Sunday trains are a mess. If I don't get there early, I might have to stand the whole way."

"Would that be so terrible? When's the train?"

"It's the five-fifteen," he said and looked at his watch. "I've got forty-three minutes."

"That's plenty of time. It only takes ten or fifteen minutes to get to Penn Station, which still gives you half an hour to have a drink with us."

"I *think* you might have a punctuality problem," Hap said. "Sorry, I'd have loved to but . . . it's really late. I've got to go."

Charlotte watched Hap cross West Broadway with his bag.

"*Gahd*, that's so lousy," she said disconsolately. "He didn't say anything about a train."

Alice looked concerned. "I had no idea it had gotten so late. Has Tom Platt come yet? Have you seen him?"

"Tom's coming?"

"I left him a message but said four o'clock, not four-thirty," Alice said. She looked through the bar's big glass windows onto the street as if he might be out there. "He could have come, not seen us, and already left."

"No," I said. "Hap and I saw *absolutely everyone* who came in or left through that door. I can assure you Tom wasn't one of them."

"I can't believe it," Charlotte said, still preoccupied and fretting about the misunderstanding with Hap, the way people do when they are obviously completely in the wrong.

"How could he think we'd be going to the San Gennaro Festival at *three o'clock* in the afternoon?" she asked. "My God. Obviously we meant to meet later than that."

At this point I am going to make no comment about what I really think about Manhattan's famous San Gennaro Festival. Suffice it to say that it was then very popular.

The geometry of downtown seemed simple. West Broadway, Soho's main street, actually ran up and down its western side. Four blocks east was Broadway, the only avenue to extend the entire length of Manhattan from Battery Park near the Atlantic waters of New York Harbor and up through the Bronx. In fact, as Route 9, it extended all the way north to the border with Quebec, or so they said—I never checked. Two blocks east of Broadway was Lafayette Street, the dividing line with Little Italy proper, and one block farther east, at Mulberry, the neighborhood's true start. From here on the San Gennaro Festival was already in full swing.

As it got dark and the lights came on, the neighborhood did have a festive aspect, all sorts of lights, sounds, and smells, with a spinning, illuminated Ferris wheel presiding over it all. At street level Alice, Charlotte, and I made our way past the booths where Italian sausage was being grilled and Beck's beer sold.

"I don't think he even got your messages," I told Alice. "They were still on his machine, apparently unplayed."

"You listened to his messages?"

"Yeah—most use a simple code. It's quite easy to crack."

With my right hand I made the gesture of punching in phone numbers—if you tried enough, it usually worked.

"You're somewhat technically inclined?" Charlotte asked.

I nodded.

"Can you use that at all in advertising?"

"Actually, I often get into the editing room when we do TV spots."

Alice asked, "What did you say in the message to Tom?"

"That he should just meet us at Luigi's."

She seemed somewhat reassured by this.

I added, "Since we don't really know whether he'll get here or not, I also called Des. He *can* come."

"Des McGrath?" Charlotte asked, incredulous.

"Yeah."

"But he's *terrible* . . . Henry was telling us about him . . . Didn't he eject you from the Club last night?"

"Well, he sort of had to do that."

"What was the code on Tom's machine?"

"Two. It was actually the second number I tried."

As we approached Luigi's, it was obviously a mob scene, with an enormous line outside. Luigi's was famous for the mob-style killing of a Mafia boss there some years earlier, still within journalistic memory. Its speciality was shellfish, which in our price range usually meant pasta with "white" clam sauce (actually more clear-colored).

From out of the chaos, Des appeared. It was actually kind of strange to see him that early in the evening and outside the usual Club environment.

"God, what a *nightmare!*" he exclaimed. "Let's go—I've been able to get reservations at Raoul's."

"What?" Charlotte said.

"Let's get out of here," Des went on. "*Arrivederci*, baby!" he called, waving goodbye to the San Gennaro Festival.

"We came downtown to go to the San Gennaro Festival," Charlotte said, "not to some restaurant in Soho."

" '*Some restaurant?*' Raoul's?" Des asked rhetorically.

Alice had gotten in line for Luigi's. "We've got to get in line," she reminded us.

"Do you know how hard it is to get a reservation at Raoul's on a night like this? It's, like, impossible . . . a miracle."

"But, Des," I said, "you can always get reservations."

With his clout at the Club it was well known that Des could get reservations anywhere.

"Okay," he conceded after a pause, "that's true . . . But you can't assume that you'll be with me every night."

"This is the last weekend of the San Gennaro Festival!" Charlotte said.

"Good!" Des said. "Thank God!"

"You don't like the San Gennaro Festival?" Charlotte exclaimed.

"No."

"We *can't* go anywhere else," Alice said. "We told Tom we'd be at Luigi's."

"Tom Platt's coming?" Des asked.

"Maybe," I said. In view of Alice's rather obsessive concern, I felt a little guilty not to have tried harder to reach Tom. I should have called him at Cravath, where, it being Sunday, he almost certainly was. In those days associates at Cravath rarely took Sunday evenings off—particularly if they had gone out on Saturday night.

Charlotte, Alice, and I held our place in the line outside Luigi's—the street and restaurant continued to be mobbed—while Des ducked into a nearby grocery store, coming out with both a large brown bag and one of the very little ones used for single cups of coffee or tea.

Charlotte and I had gotten into a fairly controversial conversation.

"I can always tell if a guy is gay," Charlotte insisted.

"How?" I asked, rather skeptically.

"There's something in the eyes," she said. "Maybe it's related to how they look at you."

"I got some beers," Des announced as he approached.

"Great. Thanks," I said. From the brown grocery bag he extracted beers for the three of us, then put the bag down on the sidewalk between his legs and opened the lid of the cup of coffee he had gotten for himself. As a reflex, he blew into the cup to cool it off.

"Schmidt's?" I asked him, regarding his beer selection.

"Well, it's 'popularly priced,' " he said. "How is it?"

"Cold." I actually liked Schmidt's, especially when it was fresh and frosty, though the pose was you bought it for price. In our group it was modish to be very, very cheap—which was fortunate, because none of us were earning very much. Alice, though, affected none of the beer-snob pretensions many guys had—up to that moment she had rarely drunk beer and never liked it.

"This is the best beer I've ever had," she said, marveling at the subtle Schmidt's taste. "It's delicious."

Des and I exchanged a look. We had recently had a long conversation about just this subject—how young women, often quite abruptly, acquire a taste for beer. Des thought it was related to sexual experience—that women, when they become sexually active, find something in the taste and texture of beer that they never appreciated before.

Des took a large sip of his coffee and winced. "Yuck," he said and, stepping over to the storm sewer drain near the curb, poured his coffee carefully down it.

Coming back, he asked Charlotte, "What were you saying about being able to tell if a guy is gay or not?"

"Yeah. I think you can tell."

"How?" Des asked, a little incredulous.

"Well, it's hard to define. Basically, looking into their eyes. It's either there or not. I think for most women it's the same."

"No," Alice said.

"Are Jimmy or I gay? Do you see it in our eyes?"

Before Charlotte could look, Alice interrupted. "Excuse me," she whispered, "I've got to go to the washroom; could you come, too?"

"Why?"

"Well, I've got to go—come on, come with me."

Charlotte looked at her a moment. "Okay. Fine," she finally agreed, albeit slightly weirded out.

As they entered the restaurant looking for its rest room, it occurred to me that the beers seemed to have hit the girls pretty hard.

Inside Alice and Charlotte joined a short line of women waiting for the ladies' room.

"You've got to be more careful," Alice said.

"What do you mean?" Charlotte had no idea what she was talking about.

"Des *is* gay," Alice whispered.

"That's impossible."

"No, it's true."

"How can you know that?"

"Well, I do, and some of what you're saying could sound really offensive—though I know you don't mean it that way."

"No, I do mean it to be offensive. Did you hear what he said about the San Gennaro Festival?"

"So."

"He's terribly arrogant. Henry told us all about him, 'Des McGrath.' Don't you remember? He's a monster—in fact, a terrible womanizer—"

"No. He's gay, and you should be careful what you say, because it sounds really bad."

"Well, I don't like him. I think he's a total fraud, and I'm going to take that fraud apart. Think what you want—but don't get in the way."

When we finally got a table and attracted the attention of one of the overwhelmed waiters, we all ordered quickly, except Des, who examined the menu with extreme skepticism, perhaps justified.

"Uh, the, uh, white . . . clam sauce . . . ?"

"It's the house specialty."

"Does, uh, this month have an 'r' in it?" This was a reference to the old rule about eating shellfish only in months with the letter "r" in them. No one really answered, and Des continued fatalistically, "Okay, the capellini with the . . . white clam sauce."

He made a face of trepidation. The waiter took back all our menus.

"*Gahd*," Charlotte said, "you're such a complainer."

"Excuse me?"

"You *whine* about everything—Luigi's, the San Gennaro Festival, whether the sauce has garlic in it—"

"I'm sorry, I happen to be allergic to garlic."

"Oh, that's so pathetic. Nowadays it's not enough for people to simply *not like* something; they have to say they're *allergic* to it."

"No. I like garlic. I'm just allergic to it."

"You're *allergic* to garlic and you come to an Italian restaurant?"

"This wasn't my idea. I made reservations at Raoul's. We could still go, you know."

"No," Alice reminded him, "we mentioned Luigi's to Tom."

"I knew you'd get back to your *reservations* at *Raoul's,*" Charlotte said. "You're *so* cool, *so* important—you can get reservations at restaurants."

"You're right, it's a small talent compared to being able to tell people's sex preference by looking in their eyes, but it's all I've got. I can't stand that—you probably believe in astrology and the prophecies of Notradamus, too."

Charlotte looked momentarily stunned.

"Omigod. You've got something against Nostradamus and astrology?" she asked.

"I've got nothing *against* them."

"You know, Voltaire believed in astrology."

"Oh, give me a break," Des said. "Maybe you could get away with stuff like that at Hampshire, but don't try to feed it to me."

"What?" Charlotte sputtered. "Oh, I see. You went to Harvard. You're above all that."

"God, I hope so."

Charlotte turned to me and Alice for support. "Have you ever noticed that you can't talk to anyone from Harvard for fifteen minutes without them bringing it up somehow. Every ten seconds something about how *they* went to *Harvard*." To take the sting out of that, she added in an aside to me, "I know you're not that way, but it's pretty exceptional."

"Actually, I didn't bring it up," Des said.

"Do you think Tom could be working tonight?" Alice asked. "Maybe we should call him at his office."

For a few moments no one said anything. While Des and Charlotte were still stewing, I was undergoing another guilty twinge about not having tried harder to track down Tom.

"You're probably right—I should have called him there earlier," I semi-confessed. "But it's pretty late now. Maybe it'd be better to leave it for another day."

"I don't know," Alice said. She thought a moment. "What about giving him just one last call?"

After dinner we walked back through San Gennaro, the smoke from the grilling Italian sausages hanging heavy in the humid air. It was far warmer than normal for September and the sounds and smells were stacked on top of each other like planes over LaGuardia Airport on a Friday evening in summer. Alice and Charlotte walked ahead, also talking but out of earshot, while Des and I trailed behind.

"She's really stuck on Tom Platt, isn't she?" Des asked.

I nodded. It was a problem.

"I thought Tom was still going out with that terrific Wheaton girl. What was her name?"

"Jennifer. Jennifer something—Robbins, I think."

"What happened to her? She was terrific."

"They must have broken up. Tom's not the type who'd two-time someone."

Des gave me a dirty look. "What's *that* supposed to mean?" he asked, pretty aggressively. "That *I am* the type who'd two-time someone? Is that what that's supposed to imply?"

"Well . . ."

"I've never intentionally two-timed anyone *in my life.*
There was just some inadvertent overlapping."

Ahead of us, Charlotte and Alice paused to watch a carnival
attraction in which a row of paying contestants, most rather
well lubricated I would say, used a sort of high-powered
water-pistol contraption to shoot streams of water into the
open mouths of a row of large plastic clowns; the water
"swallowed" by each clown then propelled a symbolic horse
figure rapidly across a racetrack backdrop. The fastest horse
won, of course. Des and I watched from farther away.

"I hate this whole idea that I'm such a *bad guy,*" Des said.
"I'm not a Bad Guy. I'm a perfectly good guy who occasionally does somewhat Bad Things."

"Well, you'd have to admit, there's a bit of a difference
between someone like Tom, who's been with the same
woman for five years—"

"Yeah, I know. That's kind of dull—"

"—and someone who, frankly, goes through about, uh,
twenty girlfriends a year."

"No," Des said. "Actually, I'd say it's more in the thirty to
forty range."

"Okay. My point is, those numbers are quite large. It's a
lot."

"I don't really like to judge things in numerical terms,"
Des said. "To me that's not romantic. It depends on what
you're used to. Five days can actually be quite a long time to
be with one person. You can get to know them awfully well.
Maybe, for Tom, five years seems normal. I'm not criticizing
him for that."

He looked to me as if for confirmation that he was not
criticizing Tom. I just nodded. While we talked, the man

running the carnival stand gave Charlotte an enormous bright yellow stuffed animal in the shape of Tweety Pie, the big-headed yellow character from the Looney Tunes cartoons. So, in addition to beautiful and smart, it turned out that Charlotte was also a crack shot. This was the very fair way God had chosen to distribute talents.

The girls started moving on again, so we did also, maintaining a pretty even distance, safely out of earshot.

"My problem is . . . I fall in love *a lot*," Des said. "It's not that I like ending relationships so much—not at all. In fact, I dread that. My problem is, I like *beginning* relationships far too much."

I nodded again. This was a plausible interpretation of Des's behavior, casting it in a more sympathetic light, though without modifying its essentially reprehensible nature.

"That's what interests me about this girl so much."

"Alice?"

"Yeah. She's complex, 'hidden depths' and all that, but apparently without the neurotic or 'difficult' dimension that often goes with it. No, not at all. Maybe it's crazy to say this without knowing her better, but she seems like the kind of person who would well reward spending five years with—or even fifteen. Those eyes—there must be something behind them. I see her as deeply compassionate . . . and yet sweet. I'd like to be with someone who's really . . . kind. And she's smart—you don't hear her talking about Nostradamus or the signs of the Zodiac—nor will you: she's way, way beyond that kind of thing."

"*Come on*, Des."

"What?"

"Leave her alone."

"Oh, I know what you're thinking. That I'll 'act badly' and she'll get hurt, or something. I don't think so. Not this time."

"Why not?" I asked.

"Okay," he said. His voice was quieter; his mood turned strangely reflective, somber, and philosophical. "I didn't want to make a big deal about this, because I know how cynical and—skeptical—you are, but . . . I've been thinking about changing my life. I can't keep on going as I have been." We passed a caravan filled with rows of big-eyed stuffed animals staring out blankly. "People have no idea how hard it's been emotionally."

While Des and I walked through the *festa*, picking our way through the crowds, Beck's and calzone stands, and caravans chockablock with not very nice prizes and gift items, Charlotte and Alice walked ahead of us, talking also. At the time I had no idea what their conversation was—that was part of the point of staying out of earshot—and in any case, the psychodrama of Des's self-analysis and confessional had been pretty absorbing. It wasn't until much later, when Castle Rock Entertainment, as part of the agreement for the novelization, turned over their whole stash of interview transcripts and very early script drafts that I found out what Alice and Charlotte had really been talking about that night.

"Of course, I don't *really believe* in Nostradamus or astrology," Charlotte said, according to the notes. "No one of any intellectual seriousness could. But that doesn't mean they are not interesting to talk about. I don't *believe* in all of Nostradamus's prophecies—obviously—but have you ever read them? It's uncanny. There're so many things he gives the *impression* of having foretold. Is there any truth in that? I don't know, but it's certainly interesting and worth serious discussion."

Alice nodded, though more in the "I hear and register what you are saying" mode than specifically agreeing or disagreeing.

"God, that guy's such a bigot!" Charlotte continued. "I don't see how you can stand him."

"I didn't say I could stand him."

"You know, he's not the first Harvard guy I've known. They're all that way. The moment certain subjects come up, or certain areas are gotten into, the arrogance is unbelievable. I'm sorry, I'm not going to go up with that guy in the Ferris wheel. I couldn't bear being trapped in one of those little seats next to him."

"Des McGrath?"

"Yeah. Would you mind terribly if I went up with the other one?"

The only parts of the San Gennaro Festival Des would admit he liked were "the Ferris wheel ride" and "the inebriated women"—then he retracted the latter comment and said it was really just the Ferris wheel he liked. In the amusement park world, Ferris wheels are now usually considered tame and uninteresting—little more than a carousel for children arranged vertically rather than horizontally. What made the Ferris wheel at San Gennaro so interesting was its being jammed into a break in the line of tenement buildings on the west side of Mulberry Street—a couple of empty lots provided just enough space for it. With most of the buildings no higher than four or five quite low stories, the Ferris wheel raised its riders just over the roof line for a tantalizing glimpse of the neighborhood from above before pulling them down again. The upswing lifted you quickly above the thick atmosphere of frying food and mobbed humanity to the cooler night air higher up. Shared with the right sympathetic person, or even with the nearly right such person, it also had a romantic dimension.

As we were buying tickets at the little pink-and-green ticket booth, which looked like something out of *Dumbo*, Charlotte made things easier by pairing off with me. Alice and Des went ahead, getting the chair just before ours. The loading up of a Ferris wheel can be a somewhat protracted business. We were slowly ascending to the top of the wheel when all movement stopped. By then we were too high up to have a clear view of what the matter was below. Charlotte and I were already in a pretty animated conversation, and could only glimpse Des and Alice in the chair ahead and above, though their conversation was reconstructed in detail in the script's early drafts.

"I suppose this happens a lot," Des said, and then looked down toward the base of the wheel. "They don't seem too worried." His view of what was going on was better than ours.

"Do you know Tom well?" Alice asked.

Des's mood had not changed greatly from his near-emotional meltdown before. He was somewhat sad, reflective, gentle with Alice—a little bit sweet, actually, not at all cynical or even ironic. He was at the edge of that sort of irrational crying fit people can go into when they crash from "speed" or similar drugs, though that had not been what he was taking.

"I don't know," Des began. "We go through life accompanied by people. . . . They come from the same city we do, or go to the same school. We like them. Our paths often cross. Or, if they don't, other friends keep us informed about what they're doing. One day, we see from an obituary that their father has died. We mean to write them, and keep the article around for the longest time . . . You feel a bond, but that bond is not acted upon. Meanwhile, we wonder if we're ever going to get off this Ferris wheel."

Des looked down from the other side.

"I wonder where Tom could be?" Alice asked.

"They work really hard at firms like his. And Tom does all that *pro bono* work for environmental organizations on top of his regular workload, which must be mind-numbing. I find it tiring just thinking about it. Sometimes I'm glad I'm a failure."

"But you work really hard, too. I heard you hadn't taken a night off since the Club started."

"You heard that?"

"Yeah, Jimmy said so."

"Well, it's a little different: you'll find at the top law firms there's very little disco beat to keep things lively, or else the volume's very low. And, uh, being a nightclub flunky is not exactly challenging work."

He looked down again. "My most serious task is getting there on time."

Des kept looking to see if any rescue attempt might be under way below. "This is getting serious," he said.

From their static position on the Ferris wheel they could

see into the windows of the adjacent Little Italy apartment building. In one partly lit, uncurtained window a man with a handsome, muscular torso was kissing what turned out to be another naked man. Then he dropped down.

"I wonder if sexual identity is as important for women as it is for men," Des said.

Alice was then looking elsewhere, down back to where Charlotte and I were stuck in another Ferris wheel chair, talking animatedly, teasing each other, and smiling a lot. If only I could have looked up and seen her looking at me, that might have been enough encouragement to maintain hope alive, but as it was, all I saw was really how very pretty and charming Charlotte was and that Alice was hopelessly stuck on Tom.

Des, noticing that her attention had wandered in our direction, finally answered his own question: "Somehow I suspect it isn't."

Alice turned back, looking again toward the building window.

"I think you're right," she said.

8

A Theory of Bestsellers

In the glass towers along Park and the nearby avenues, within a radius of approximately ten blocks from Grand Central, all the companies aspiring to make a serious business of publishing had over the years relocated—and redecorated. In spaces designed to impress capitalists into relinquishing their fortunes to investment advisors and corporations into turning their marketplace destinies over to geniuses at ad agencies like mine, commas were now to be moved, story lines summarized, and unpublished authors rejected yet again. The commercially unambitious houses could be left to their prestige and Union Square, or other such dowdy confines; before long, all such profit-disoriented concerns would surely be consigned to the ash heap of publishing history and the real estate long march uptown. Never had the commerce of literature existed in such spectacular quarters.

In one such modernist, international-style environment of glass, steel, chrome, and limitless gray carpeting, Alice's adult

working life was just beginning to unfold. In June she had
started in the publishing training program at Edward Riley
Publishers—apart from Doubleday's, the only one of its
kind—and had recently landed with Charlotte as an editorial
"secretary" in Riley's Trade editorial department. Unlike
Random House and elsewhere, there had been no "title
inflation," nor, in fact, inflation of any kind, at Riley Publishers. The controversial wage freeze instituted by the Nixon
administration in the early seventies had pretty much rubber-
stamped what was already a long-standing company policy.
Nor had the company's anti-inflationary stance weakened
through the intervening Ford and Carter years. So, after finishing the training program, Alice and Charlotte had become
"secretaries"—not "assistants" or "editorial assistants," which
were higher job categories—and as such could look forward
to gross annual wages of $6,500. Riley Publishers might have
opened up its budget lines for office rent and decoration, but
there would be no precedent-setting hikes in editorial pay.

The "bay"—a broad open-plan corridor where Alice and
Charlotte worked—had five desks for the secretaries or assistants working for the more senior editors. The editors' window offices ran along the exterior side of the bay, while filing
cabinets and the interior offices of the editorial assistants ran
along the other. Dominating life in the bay was the commanding presence of Josephine Baker—no relation to the singer—
an elegantly dressed British West Indian woman who was
executive secretary to Carol, the Editorial Director, though the
authority she exerted seemed more personal than hierarchical.

Charlotte sat at her desk finishing typing a reader's report
on her beige IBM Selectric II typewriter, while in the
glassed-in office nearby "her" editor spoke into a Dicta-
phone—the recording of which Charlotte would later turn

into a messily typed letter. Her typing somehow fared better when the thoughts she was expressing were her own, and now the "letterball" on her IBM Selectric bounced comparatively steadily—without too many corrective back-and-forths—over the narrow sheet of inexpensive pad paper that was used for reader's reports at Riley:

> . . . Tibet's predicament as a small, old-
> fashioned country caught between the enor-
> mous land masses of what is today India
> and China.
>
> Summary: A somewhat incoherent account of
> an apparently fascinating story — one fam-
> ily's struggle to escape political oppres-
> sion in Tibet in the 1950s. The author's
> brother is, according to Tibetan Buddhism,
> God.
>
> Recommend: Very kind decline.
>
> Charlotte Pingree

Carefully Charlotte rolled the pad paper out with the carbon set behind it, then separated them, took the report, and, getting up, slipped it on top of a pile of three manuscript boxes with reports already attached. Alice stood at her own desk preparing a similar stack of four manuscript boxes.

"Anything interesting?" she asked.

"Not really."

Carrying their boxes, Charlotte and Alice set off for the manuscript room, entirely oblivious of the watchful glances of Dan Powers, the bay's lone editorial assistant—at Riley a far more responsible post than at more title-inflationary houses. At Riley "editorial assistants" actually "edited books," as well as helped departmental higher-ups with theirs (Carol was Dan's "editor").

That day, as pretty much every day, Dan wore a blue shirt, gray chinos, heavy black industrial tie shoes, and a choppy haircut. Since Alice and Charlotte had landed in his department, Dan had kept up with his filing at the built-in cabinets near their desks much, much more regularly. Dan was another Harvard guy (though Leverett House), but his strongest personal identification was with the militant wing of the American labor movement. At the publishing house the project he was most involved with was a massive encyclopedia-like undertaking called the *Solidarity Almanac,* essentially a *Whole Earth Catalog*-style history-of-the-world project as reinterpreted from an American labor perspective. For those who care about such distinctions, Dan was more C.I.O. than A.F.L., but still "a guy" not at all immune to the attractions of bourgeois girls, particularly those as attractive and dynamic as Alice and Charlotte appeared in the pallid environment of Riley Publishers.

As Charlotte and Alice walked down the main corridor, Charlotte continued to muse about the manuscripts she had just consigned to the rejects bin. "It's terrifying to think that some author's going to spend years sweating and agonizing over his book and then have its ultimate fate depend upon people like us."

Alice agreed. The excessive power to destroy had bothered her also. They were both already well aware of how things worked at Riley—which was far from the worst publisher of its kind, by the way.

"I think that the problem is," Alice said, "that the editors have to spend so much time and energy reassuring authors that they're doing everything they can to make their books successful that they really don't have time to do much."

"I also get the feeling no one's getting enough sleep," Charlotte said. "If we were well rested, how different would our judgments be? I don't mean just us—have you noticed how terrible most of the editors look?"

Alice nodded.

"We've *got* to get our own apartment," Charlotte concluded. "Do you know how long it takes to become an editor?"

"You mean, 'Associate Editor.' "

"Yeah, Associate Editor."

They turned in to the manuscript room, which was full of card files and shelves loaded with manuscript boxes and presided over by Zenia, an Eastern European woman in a brown dress and a not very becoming wig. Zenia looked as if she could have been a character in an Isaac Bashevis Singer story, and in fact, there were rumors within the company that they had had some sort of affair in the late 1940s. The woman in the story said to be based on their romance was portrayed as a dark-eyed seductress whose insistent erotic demands exhaust and finally alienate the story's narrator. Now she was just another religiously Orthodox grandmother in an old-fashioned brown-print dress. Of course, the entire Zenia-Singer connection was almost certainly just "house legend" (the term "house," derived from "publishing house," was publishing slang for "the company"; for instance, at some houses the acronym "H.E." was used, perhaps ironically, as a designation for company loyalty and staff enthusiasm for the books being published, or "House Enthusiasm") manufactured for its incongruity by some "House Comedian." Singer himself *had* visited Riley several times during this period, as he was contributing the text to a picture book its Religious Books division would be publishing.

As Alice and Charlotte entered, Zenia was just removing a teabag from a glass of steaming water as she chatted with Helen, an "assistant to" (this is how they were called) with several years' seniority to them. Helen sat leaning against a table with some manuscript piles on it, sipping coffee from a blue paper cup decorated with Athenian monuments and the printed motto *It Is Our Pleasure to Serve You.* She had stopped by while waiting "for her carbons to dry." In those days, which were the latter end of the carbon paper and the start of the Liquid Paper (or Wite-Out) era, typing mistakes could be corrected with the application of liquid paper but had to be left to dry before corrections could be typed over them. This left time for a coffee break and perhaps socializing.

As Alice started the rigmarole of putting her manuscripts on the "read" stack and filing her reader's reports in the gray metal cabinets, Helen slid over to give her more room.

"What's the minimum amount of time to become an Associate Editor?" Charlotte asked. "How many years?" Her tone was intense.

"It's hard to say," Helen said.

"Approximately . . . ?"

"Maybe . . . four years," Helen guessed.

Charlotte looked sunk.

"But," Zenia added, "more than years, before you can become Associate Editor, you haf to haf a bestseller."

"How can you be sure you'll get a bestseller?" Charlotte asked.

"You cannot."

"But what if you don't find one?"

"You haf to . . ."

A look of worry crossed Charlotte's face.

Helen leaned toward Zenia. "Show them the outline," she suggested.

"Oh, *yess*," Zenia said, "you might want to see thees." She pulled a slender manila file folder from the metal rack atop her desk and extracted a single page from it. Meanwhile, Dan Powers entered with a stack of "read" manuscripts and started going about filing his reports.

"Eet's the Scott Meredith bestseller outline," Zenia explained, starting to read snatches from it in summary style: " 'Create sympathetic characters with whom readers identify . . . Give them problems . . . Make thees proplems big . . .' et cetera, et cetera."

Charlotte approached Zenia's desk and, handed the page by her, looked at it closely. Alice tried to read it over her shoulder.

"Could I photocopy this?" Charlotte asked.

"Yess, but I need eet back," Zenia replied.

"I'd like to get a copy, too," Alice mentioned to Charlotte while they both continued examining it.

"That stuff is such crap," Dan interjected.

Alice looked up from the sheet. "This does describe a lot of bestsellers. It's true."

"It's completely formulaic," he said.

"Of course it's formulaic," Charlotte pointed out, "it's a formula."

"That's why I prefer nonfiction," Dan said.

Charlotte looked annoyed, but then seemed to shake it off.

"It's goot you vant to be an editor so much," Zenia said.

"In this era of television, you are devoted to the printed vord."

"Actually, ultimately I'd like to work in television, but right now what I need's a raise." She looked to Alice. "Alice and I've been looking at apartments but we can't afford one on what we get as assistants."

At this, Dan snorted aloud. "That's so comical."

"What?" Charlotte asked.

"That girls like you really worry about paying the rent."

They looked at him, confused but annoyed.

"Aren't your fathers heavily subsidizing your living expenses with big allowances?"

"They're not big at all," Charlotte replied.

"Then in a few years you'll marry some incredibly rich corporate lawyers. It's not as if you're really worrying about paying the rent like the rest of us."

"You worry about paying the rent?" Alice asked.

"Yeah," Dan said, a little too woozy with self-pity at that moment to spot what was coming.

"Then," Alice pointed out, "you're *way ahead of us*, because we don't even have an apartment."

Dan just looked at her for a moment.

"What if, in a few years, we don't marry some corporate lawyer?" Charlotte asked. "What if we marry some meatball like you?"

At this point, and before everyone feels too sorry for him, it should be mentioned that until Charlotte's arrival in the department, *Dan* had always been the harasser in intraoffice class warfare, never the harassed; always the needler, never the needled. For him the shift was not a particularly welcome one.

"Not you, *personally*," Charlotte specified, "but someone with similarly low socioeconomic prospects."

On that note she departed. Alice, leaving with her, tried to give Dan a sympathetic look, but he seemed too surprised to take anything in. The moment they were out the door, he turned to Zenia and Helen for support.

"Can you believe that? They really think that way," he said, his voice strained.

Dan went to the doorway and called down the corridor after them, "Disco *sucks!*"

As they walked back toward the bay, Charlotte rolled her eyes. "What a *dope*."

Alice nodded, but she felt a little sad for Dan. Underneath all the ideology and "class" bullying, there was something sweet about him, or at least the promise of a human core of some kind, though it was pretty well buried.

"Would you ever go out with anyone who worked in the company?" Alice asked as they walked back toward the department.

Charlotte looked incredulous and shook her head—"No.

"Fortunately," she added, "there's absolutely no temptation."

From the other end of the hallway, Josephine waited for them, a phone receiver in her hand.

"Charlotte!" she called. "Telephone!"

Charlotte nodded.

"It's a . . . *man*," Josephine said.

Charlotte now hurried a bit, taking the phone call from the passageway side of her desk as she slipped smoothly into her chair, a swivel deal on roller wheels.

"Hello . . . Oh, hi—thanks . . . We were thinking of having some people over for dinner Saturday and wanted to know if you could come?"

Back at her own desk, Alice moved some of her paperwork around while unavoidably listening in on Charlotte's side of the call, an apprehensive expression on her face.

"Good . . . About seven-thirty . . . Actually, I'll have to call you back with that. We don't have one yet . . . (Laughs.) Yeah . . . Thanks . . . Okay . . . 'Bye."

She hung up.

Alice looked at her inquiringly.

"That was Jimmy Steinway; he's coming for dinner Saturday night."

"You called him?" Alice asked.

Charlotte nodded.

"I thought you said that you 'could never be interested in anyone who worked in advertising'?"

"No one could say something like that seriously," Charlotte said. "It was obviously a joke . . . Anyway, it's not like a date or anything. He's invited as part of a group. It's really important there be more group social life—not just all this ferocious pairing off."

Alice looked pale and stony-faced, giving Charlotte the faintest twinge of a guilty conscience.

"Anyway, you like *Tom*," Charlotte said. "Invite him."

"We don't have an apartment," Alice replied. "How can we have a dinner party?"

"Well, it's another incentive to get one," Charlotte said, turning back to the *Times* real estate section spread open on her desk, already full of her red circles and markings. She picked up the phone to call the real estate agent.

9

In the Matter of Railroad Apartments

In those days Riley's Manhattan corporate and editorial offices were at a strategic spot at the intersection of Park Avenue and East Fortieth Street, just where the ramp around Grand Central starts its ascent and the divided avenue below slopes down toward the legendary station's main entrance and the nexus of subway and commuter rail lines within.

The precise street address was 99 Park Avenue; across Fortieth Street, at 101, the old Architects' Building still stood, soon to be replaced by an enormous black glass tower. Alice and Charlotte left the building and joined the stream of commuters heading toward the station.

"Does the Lexington Avenue Express stop at Eighty-sixth Street?"

"I think so," Alice said.

"We'd better hurry."

They walked at a hurried pace toward the station's stately Forty-second Street front, a statue of Commodore Vanderbilt gazing down on the raised roadway wrapping around it, with imagery of Mercury supported by moral and mental energy—Hercules and Minerva—crowning the façade above.

Alice looked preoccupied. "Do you think we really know each other well enough to room together?"

"Maybe that's good," Charlotte replied.

"It's not just that we don't know each other well," Alice explained. "It's that . . . I'm not sure we really . . . even . . . like each other."

Charlotte looked thoughtful. "That's okay," she said slowly.

They walked together in silence for a while.

"You know, Alice," Charlotte added, "I'm not as much of a bitch as I might seem."

On the subway ride uptown, Charlotte thought she should tell Alice something about Holly, their prospective roommate, before getting there.

"You'll find she's a little sensitive about her intelligence," Charlotte warned her.

"She's dumb?" Alice asked.

The girls stood hanging on to the subway car's chrome horizontal and vertical bars, already "straphangers," though the original leather straps had long been replaced with clean-looking, greasy-feeling chrome poles.

"Well, it's more that she's *so* good-looking. Holly went to Pine Manor, near Boston, within striking distance of all the Harvard preppies. Harvard guys—even the ones who seem good-looking and reasonably cool on the outside—are all essentially wimps and bookworms on the inside. They loved being seen out with this beautiful, lovely girl. But after a date or two, rather than risk rejection, they'd pretend to drop her, going around complaining about how 'dull' she was."

"Is she dull?"

"A little; but that's not the point. Once you start worrying about something like that, you're lost," Charlotte said. "You really *do* get boring. Holly was devastated. She stopped dating entirely and weekends either went home or just hung around the library at Pine Manor."

"Gahd," Alice added sympathetically.

At this point something happened the details of which have never been fully clarified. Apparently a guy pushed up behind Charlotte much more intrusively than required by the usual rush-hour crowding. Charlotte later said it was actually worse than just that.

"What do you think you're doing?!" she exclaimed, spinning to confront him.

The man looked completely taken aback.

"Shove off, *Mac*!"

As the train slowed for the Fifty-ninth Street stop, the man, evidently caught red-handed at whatever he was up to, slunk toward the other end of the car.

"Deviant! Creep! Off!" Charlotte insisted, pointing to the subway car's doors. The man waited near them and clearly wanted nothing more than to comply. He was not the repulsive-looking degenerate one might expect but a reasonably presentable guy about our age; she later said he looked like a better-groomed version of Josh.

Alice had come to admire Charlotte's way of dominating any situation, even the most difficult, with not only aplomb but something far, far beyond aplomb, though the extremes she could go to had lately begun to worry her, too. She'd have hated to be on the wrong side of any dispute with Charlotte, who since they graduated had only been incredibly nice to her—except for a couple of things very, very recently.

At the Fifty-ninth Street stop, the masher did leave the train. Charlotte gave his departing form a last look before turning back to Alice.

"So," she concluded, "I wouldn't develop any illusions about Harvard guys. They can be amazing creeps, too."

The Lexington Avenue Express did, it turn out, stop at East Eighty-sixth Street. Leaving the train in a hurry—Alice and Charlotte were late for their rendezvous with Holly and the real estate agent in front of the building they were supposed to take a look at—they then walked east on Eighty-sixth Street to First Avenue, the heart of the old Yorkville neighborhood. Once this stretch of Manhattan had seemed like the last outpost of the old Austro-Hungarian Empire—the *Mittel Europa* atmosphere and charm were thick on the streets—but by the early eighties not so many vestiges of its former identity remained: a few cafés with names like the Heidelberg or the Edelweiss, some bakeries, beer halls, and specialty sausage shops. It was still pretty interesting.

The girls walked north on First Avenue and then turned east on Eighty-ninth Street. Some of the buildings were fairly run-down. Old-style metal garbage cans, grimy and beat-up, were bunched up next to the stoops, giving them a decrepit air. Drab-looking older white people—some had what Alice thought of as "drinker's eyes"—hung around the stoops dispiritedly as if the external "drabness" extended inside, too. Their forlorn aspect reminded her of the angular characters in a George Price cartoon, but without the funny punch line—not the image normally conjured up by terms like "Manhattanite" or "Upper East Sider." Most throttled and depressed-seeming of all were the junior-high-schoolers on the block, as if the violent corridors of Julia Richmond High School looming in their future had already gotten them down. Only the girls in the plaid-skirt uniform of the local Catholic school—chattering and making plans—seemed to escape the grim atmosphere.

Alice felt a little guilty noticing all these things, that the tenor of her observations could be considered "elitist," but it just seemed the way things were.

The real estate lady, in a golden beige suit-dress, heavily made-up and coiffed, was waiting for them in front of the building, a five-story walk-up on Eighty-ninth Street, east of First Avenue. Some of the building's apartment windows were decorated with trim flower boxes. Others looked quite derelict.

"Holly hasn't arrived yet?" Charlotte asked. The real estate lady shook her head—her name was Mrs. Madgette and she seemed a little mature and "grand" to be showing bottom-of-the-market rentals to twenty-year-olds at this stage of her life, but she was still trying to get her bearings after a recent and typically unhappy divorce. All three looked up and down the street, but there was no sign of Holly.

By the time Holly did arrive, Mrs. Madgette seemed a little wilted. She led the way up the building's stairs while Holly, still out of breath, followed at her heels.

"I'm really sorry," Holly said. "I forgot which way the numbers went on the East Side."

Alice and Charlotte, bringing up the rear, exchanged a glance.

Looking around, Alice noticed the cracked linoleum on the stairs and landing, the dirty dark gray stucco of the walls, and the fluorescent lighting dim and flickering. From one apartment spilled the sounds of a TV game show, while from across the hall came the cheerful jingle for an Italian wine: *"Riunite on ice / Riunite so nice / Ree-yew-nee-tee! / Ree-yew-nee-tee!"* The smell was none too pleasant, either.

They entered the apartment from the living-room side and ritually looked out the front windows at the street they had in fact just left.

Mrs. Madgette revived as she led them through the long, narrow apartment, turning lights on as she went. As they walked their feet kicked wire coat hangers, fallen plaster bits, and other detritus.

"It's what's called a 'railroad apartment,' " she said. "Long and rather narrow, like a railroad car. Each room opens directly onto the other."

"It's very nice," Holly said.

It wasn't really very nice. The original configuration had probably been ratty enough before a former tenant with a do-it-yourself streak used some secondhand plywood and two-by-fours to make a clumsy half-partition between the living room and the first "bedroom." The apartment was dark, dirty, and had a peculiar smell which Alice did not relish the prospect of getting used to. It was not "terrible"—there were many, many far worse; maybe it could even be made relatively okay, but after sporadically apartment-hunting all summer she was discouraged at the idea she might now be pressured into settling for this, especially considering the almost total lack of privacy the layout afforded.

After passing through the two very narrow bedrooms, they entered the kitchen and the real estate lady opened the door to a cramped bathroom, which was very convenient to the kitchen sink. Each poked her head in to have a look.

"So," Alice asked, not exactly hiding a certain skepticism, "to get to the bathroom from the living room, you have to clomp through both bedrooms?"

"Well, actually there're two outside doors," Mrs. Madgette said, crossing to the kitchen entrance door and opening it. "In theory you could use the exterior hall to go between the kitchen and the living room."

"Huhn," Charlotte said, taking a look out the door.

"Even for two roommates, the layout's a bit awkward," the real estate lady said. "You can't afford anything bigger?"

"We all work in book publishing," Charlotte explained.

"Couldn't your parents help?" the older woman asked.

"They already are," Charlotte confessed, and looked to her friends. "So what do you think?"

"I think it's nice," Holly said.

"The layout's pretty awkward," Alice said.

"Well," Charlotte said impatiently, "I think we should take it."

A Saturday afternoon, several days later. A VistaCruiser-style station wagon—or maybe it was more of a country-wagon type—was pulled up before the building and Alice, Holly, and Charlotte—all dressed in fairly grubby clothes—were unloading its contents with the help of Alice's mother and younger sister, who were now inside sweeping.

Some of the boxes and oversized suitcases they really had to struggle with. Other objects, such as Alice's inexpensive stereo, were surprisingly light. "Plastic," almost universally derided in our culture and with none of the prestige of steel or iron, has the distinct advantage of being easy to carry.

Dan Powers first made his presence felt by a rather chiding remark from across the street, though he had actually intended it to sound ingratiating.

"Ahhh," he said, "it's good to see bourgeois girls building up a sweat."

"Why's that 'good to see'?" Charlotte immediately responded. "And what's your interest in 'girls' sweat'? I don't think I like the sound of that."

"You live around here?" Alice asked.

"No. There was a guild meeting at Asphalt Green," he said, crossing the street toward them.

"A guild meeting?" Alice asked.

"The Newspaper Guild is organizing clerical and editorial staff in book publishing," Dan said. "I'm supposed to organize our department."

"Oh-my-God, we're all going to lose our jobs!" Charlotte yelped, pushing open the building's door with her back and disappearing with her load inside.

"You should support this," Dan called after her. "You were just complaining how lousy the pay is!"

Alice carried her load inside, too, leaving Dan alone on the street with Holly.

"You're rooming with them?" he asked.

Holly nodded.

"That's going to be *really tough*," he said. They both looked toward the door, Holly a little apprehensively.

Shrimp were being sautéed in a beat-up old Teflon pan with lots of butter, changing color from pink to orange as Charlotte moved them around with a smallish metal spoon.

"Aren't we behind schedule?" Alice asked from the bathroom washstand, which was actually only a few feet away. Moving-day decor was still all over the apartment.

"No," Charlotte said, "this recipe's extremely fast."

She grabbed an opened can of Campbell's Cream of Mushroom soup and upended it over the pan. A solid light-brown cylinder oozed out slowly, then dropped with a *thwush*-plop into the pan. The brown tower tottered atop the shrimp until Charlotte mashed it down with the little spoon and started adding cream and lots of curry powder. Rice simmered in a separate pot.

The intercom buzzer sounded. Alice, dressed for the evening in a daring reflective metallic tube top and tight pants, stepped out of the bathroom to get it.

Pressing the Talk button, she leaned in toward it: "Hello?"

A weird staticky voice responded: "Dan."

Alice gave Charlotte a perplexed look. "Dan?" she asked.

Holly, still in a bathrobe, bolted into the room and across to the intercom, displacing Alice. "Hi—come up," she said.

She pressed the intercom buzzer and then turned to them. "Dan, from your department—I invited him."

Alice and Charlotte exchanged looks.

"Departmental Dan?" Charlotte repeated.

Alice looked a little worried.

"You know," she said to Holly, "he went to Harvard."

"So?" Holly asked.

Alice's mother and the others must have done a lot of work on the apartment, because by the time Dan and I got there that evening it seemed pretty nice. Maybe there were still boxes around, but the windows had been left open for an all-day airing, and now the warmth and scents of good cooking—Charlotte had prepared a delicious shrimp curry based on a family recipe—filled the rooms.

Alice and Charlotte were still arranging the improvised dining table and place settings. Dan leaned against the doorjamb nursing a beer, in observer mode. Holly looked decorous. I had brought the wine and was opening it with a corkscrew—always a good sign. My wine-buying system in those days was, first, always a cork. Second, I looked for bottles with the soft metal around the top you could peel off and later toy with—preferably in red or black, though that was hardly vital. The label—and this did seem important—should have an old-fashioned look, not too colorful. Pretty basic, but: the word "vin" somewhere on the label was always a good sign. If a gift for others, never less than five dollars; for home consumption, never more than three. If it were a "Selection Monsieur Henri" or "Jacques Reynaud," so much the better—one had to assume they knew their stuff.

"Yeah," I was saying in response to a question of Charlotte's, "I've got to meet some clients at ten and get them into the Club."

Alice was counting the place settings and suddenly removed one.

"Tom isn't coming?" Charlotte asked.

"If he does, he'll be very late."

Alice went to the icebox, took out a Rolling Rock, popped the cap with an opener, and upended it. She was pretty cool. I started to pour the wine after officially "tast-ing" it myself. Frankly, I couldn't tell if it was good or not. I guessed it was okay. To be honest, wine that is considered "good" always tastes on the bitter side to me.

Looking around, I asked, "Isn't this what they call a 'rail-road apartment'?"

"Uhn-huhn," Charlotte said.

"People always say how terrible they are," I said, "but it seems pretty nice."

Charlotte smiled.

"Well, the layout's not so good," Alice countered. "It's amazing the little things in life one doesn't appreciate until they're missing—such as hallways."

"These apartments," Dan said, pointing with his beer bot-tle, "were actually planned in the last century as tenement housing for working-class families. Now," he added, with an undeniable sting in his voice, "all the yuppie roommate com-bos are crowding them out."

The girls all looked in Dan's direction. There was a com-plete lull in the conversation, finally broken by Charlotte.

"Well," she said. "*That's . . . just . . . tough.*"

The phone had started ringing. Charlotte immediately turned to Alice. "Maybe it's Tom," she said, and stepped back to let Alice get it.

10

A Suggestion of . . . Possible Illegality

That night one of those weird incidents took place which had immediate consequences, consequences later that night within the Club, and then—months later, after we had all nearly forgotten about it—consequences that came back to haunt us, me in particular.

A confrontation between Van's bouncers (Bobby and his friends) and some frustrated waiting guys from the outer boroughs descended into 'fraidy-cat semiviolent taunting. There were calls of "Bruno!" and "Rocky!"—then a couple of them ran up and took a swat at the bouncers, who responded more aggressively.

Van got involved, too, though not directly in the scuffling. Des, who had been with the cashier near the front doors, watched the fracas from there, calling encouragement as if parodying someone egging on a gang fight: "Fight! . . . Rumble!"

To Des the whole situation seemed like some incongruous Van-version *West Side Story*. "Officer Krupke!" he called.

Van, in the midst of the fracas, turned and shot him a dirty look, furious. The sound of approaching police sirens had just begun to be heard in the distance when a more serious scuffle broke out between three of the guys and Bobby's bouncers. Finally, the broadly built black-clad Chinese guy in Van's retinue rushed up from the interior doors and punched the ringleader, "Bruno," hard in the stomach, doubling him up and dropping him. As this was all getting a little more serious than Des had anticipated, he shut up (wisely) and disappeared inside the Club, yet another jocular misfire behind him.

Two police cars pulled up in front of the Club on Van Dam Street and the cops jumped out, but it was almost all over except for the mercurochrome, with those involved scattered or melted into the crowd, except for two who, lingering behind and getting into a shoving match with Van's guys, were finally detained.

The bubble lights on the police cars were still spinning as the Checker cab carrying Charlotte, Holly, and Dan—with Alice on the small jump seat facing them—approached the Club.

The whole trip downtown Dan had been strangely subdued. There had been no comments at all of a socio-economic dimension. The Gentrification of Downtown and how rising rents had forced the closing or relocation of the small manufacturing concerns based there, throwing their often elderly work force onto the street or into premature retirement, went unmentioned.

Dan now had a real worry—not that the others were not

real worries, but this was one that actually *affected him personally* and which *he had something to do with*—and this real, personal worry was whether he was going to get into the Club. And if he did get in, whether he was going to seem horribly out of place there. And what Holly and Alice might think, because Dan found them both utterly alluring, and in recent years he had encountered surprisingly few objects for romantic obsession. Since college his romantic life had been a null set; when it existed, confined entirely to his head, and not so much there, either. He did have the *Solidarity Almanac*, but was beginning to suspect that man does not live by solidarity alone—something that he had actually long known but, as we tend to do, periodically forgot. That night Holly and Alice were Dan's real worry—mixed in with that horrible nose-on-the-glass left-out feeling and the defensive maneuverings that went with it.

"Actually, I was thinking I'd go home," Dan said, looking out the cab window.

"What?" Holly said, surprised and upset.

"You should come," Alice insisted.

"I don't know," he said. "I'm not really a 'disco' type."

"Well, *who is?*" Charlotte asked.

"I probably wouldn't get in anyway."

Charlotte was a little impatient with all this pessimism. To her it was just self-indulgence.

"*Of course* you'll get in," she said. "*Holly's gorgeous!*"

Holly gave Dan a big smile. He smiled tentatively in return, then looked out the side window apprehensively toward the approaching Club mob scene.

*＊＊＊＊＊

A police car was pulling away with a gratuitous *whoop* of its siren as the Charlotte group, trailed by Dan, cut quickly through the large and now law-abiding crowd.

"Who are *they*? *Charlie's Angels*?" a woman in the crowd complained. There *was*, in fact, a resemblance between the three roommates and the stars of the television show *Charlie's Angels*, which featured three beautiful female detectives getting into a lot of exciting adventures. Charlotte looked particularly like the actress Jaclyn Smith, though in a more East Coast–Publishers Row version—less fit, complexion pastier, hair flatter, more tense—but still great-looking.

Dan trailed closely behind, watching everything with an expression that was increasingly hopeful, even exhilarated. Each step he took—the vibration passing from each footfall up his leg and spine into the cerebral cortex—had acquired a significant, dramatically heightened quality. The domestic beer he had had before dinner, the French-wine-with-a-cork I had brought during dinner, topped off by icy Champagne which Alice's mother had left as a housewarming present, conspired to give him a perspective on experience that was entirely altered. Sociopolitical formulations were, frankly, not at the forefront of his consciousness at this precise moment.

As they walked through the Club's famous tunnel to its inner doors, the syncopated beat of Diana Ross's 1980 classic "I'm Coming Out" caught them in its rhythmic grasp, picking up their steps to its pace and their hearts to its exhilarating message of hope and virtually limitless possibilities.

A silly, giddy smile appeared on Dan's face once he was safely inside; then he tried to muffle his ecstatic look a little, perhaps in consideration of the jobless and larger economic realities.

Whatever tensions and even violence there had been on the outside—and however frazzled, strung out, and furious those who ran the Club were with each other—Van had again "mixed" a great party that night. As Josh might have said, everyone was there: everybody you knew and everybody you didn't know. In Dan's case, it was everyone he didn't know, but that was great, too; in some ways, better.

The girls plunged onto the mobbed dance floor. Dan paused for a moment on its rim and looked around, thrilled, his expression one of almost naïve enchantment. Holly, already dancing, looked back and flashed him a dazzling smile. She had a crazy weakness for socially backward intellectual types. Dan joined her on the dance floor, trying out some steps, a little awkwardly at first, in modified rock 'n' roll style, the way one might imagine Bruce Springsteen dancing in a disco—though not quite that studly, not so bad either. It turned out that, to the surprise of many, on the dance floor Dan was cool.

Coming into the Club from Des's domain in the back, wearing a flamboyant harlequin costume with an ill-fitting mask headdress, was a disorienting experience for me. I could not see anything very well, or in context. Vision through the headdress was unidirectional, requiring pointing your head in the precise direction you wanted to look. But it was a huge relief to get in without having to run the gantlet before Van with clients in tow.

"Thanks a lot, Des. I really appreciate it."

"Fine. Cool," he said.

Maybe it was also the drinks, but I felt very, very grateful to Des. Behind me, like refugees from Mardi Gras, came a woman and two men dressed in *Wizard of Oz* costumes—Dorothy, the Tin Man, and the Cowardly Lion—who looked around, excited to be there, too.

"Have fun—Harry, Jack," I said as they passed us headed for the dance floor. It was a little sycophantic. But each of them turned and nodded gratefully as they went by.

"Thanks, Jimmy!" the Cowardly Lion called, his voice somewhat muffled by the rubberized costume.

Des flagged down a waitress, who let him take two drinks—they looked like Scotches—off her crowded drinks tray, one of which he handed to me.

"Thanks, Des."

With no peripheral vision it was actually quite hard maneuvering the glass in the crowded club. Similarly I had to be somewhat careful sipping the drink through my headgear.

"Phew," I said. It was actually the second night I had entered the Club this way. "I'm starting to realize how important eye contact is. I can't really talk to people in this thing. They get nervous. They don't know who I am."

"That's the point," Des said.

"Do you think this might be a good time to talk to Van—you know, try to patch things up?" I asked. "Get a reprieve of some sort?"

"Uh, no," he said.

"My job's sort of on the line, Des," I said, trying to keep the pathetic whine out of my voice, not too successfully. "Not all clients'll be such good sports as Harry and Jack."

I nodded toward the dance floor, where the Cowardly Lion and Dorothy were essaying a basic, though still to me impressive, disco step. The Tin Man danced by himself—not far from the cool gay crowd.

"If it's a question of *groveling*, I can do that. Just . . . point me in the right direction."

"Sshh. Gahd," Des said, whispering—one of Van's flunkies was in the vicinity. "Listen, can I . . . show you something?"

"Sure. What?"

Des just nodded and led me in the direction of a nondescript unmarked door not far from the main bar area. Before opening it, he paused and looked around, probably to make sure that none of Berrie's spies were in the area. The door opened onto a basement staircase in the gray-paint industrial style, with the lighting quite dim.

As we went down it, Des asked, "You know something about banking, don't you?"

"Yeah, Manny Hanny was a client—Manufacturers Hanover."

"I know what Manny Hanny is!"

Des was increasingly impatient and irascible with me in this period.

From the stairs we went down corridors and passageways to a large room with old-fashioned air-ventilation equipment that could have dated from the building's construction and had been, evidently, long in disuse. It was like an antique machinery exhibit at a dusty Smithsonian. Finally, more corridors and a metal door, which Des opened.

"Note," he pointed out, "no lock." He shook his head in mild amazement.

Des entered the room and pulled on a light. There was another metal stair-ladder which we had to step down, but as the area was deserted, I could at least take off the harlequin hood. In the dark sub-basement we passed a weird concatenation of enormous metal cylinders stretching horizontally across the space—another relic of the antique air-cool system. Des walked around the pipes and crouched by a cache of old-fashioned canvas air-shipment bags and next to them super heavy-duty black plastic trash bags. All seemed full. The only other paraphernalia in the area related to packing and air shipping. Des undid the plastic tie fastening one of the plastic bags. Inside were smaller bags with writing on them. He opened one. At first it was a little difficult making anything out in the dimness. Des pulled the bag's mouth open further and I could see it was full of packets of used U.S. currency, almost all tens.

"Ten is the cover charge," Des said.

"God, paying a cover charge to get into a club?! How humiliating."

"That's your reaction?" he asked.

Des moved over to a padlocked canvas sack. "Look at this."

He indicated a shipping label with a Zurich, Switzerland, airport address. For a while we just gawked, looking around at the cash sacks, astounded by the brazenness of it all. What had they been smoking? Or what mislinks, in whichever hemisphere of the brain governed tax evasion, when combined with whatever they had been smoking, could have led to this?

"Kind of worrisome, don't you think?" Des asked.

I nodded. "Yeah."

Being in the room with so much untracked cash made us both feel implicated. We went back up the metal stair-ladder and returned the way we had come.

"If it were just a question of banking the cash," Des said, "there's a Chemical Bank branch around the corner where I am sure they can count perfectly well.

"To me," he said, "shipping cash to Switzerland, in plastic bags, doesn't *sound* honest."

Whispering, he added, "To me, it suggests . . . *possible illegality.*"

"What are you going to do?" I asked.

"Well, I'm not going to go in that room anymore."

11

Knock on Wood

At the bar area Dan was positioned to order drinks—just waiting for Charlotte and Alice to decide what to have.

"A gimlet," Charlotte requested. Gimlets are essentially vodka–lime juice cocktails: great, if you like that kind of thing, but lethal.

Alice took a little longer. "A . . . whiskey . . . sour, please," she said.

For himself Dan ordered "a, uh, domestic beer—a Bud."

He waved off their proffered five-dollar bills and himself paid with a twenty, surprising them greatly.

That night, as it turned out, Josh Neff was also at the Club. This was the second of the two key nights in October 1980 when our all intersecting at the Club set in motion a dynamic of relationships and rivalries that would change—or perhaps sabotage—our lives. In such a way chance and fate combine or clash to transform our destinies, romantic and otherwise. The Club had at this point been open for nearly

two years, but for Alice and Charlotte this was its golden
age—the rest mere nondescript prehistory. Among our group
only Des and I had had much experience of the Club in its
initial period, before the jealousies within and without
started changing things.

Josh looked far more presentable than he had the week
before. What happened was that the Justice Department
attorney who acted as the federal counterpart to Josh's boss
had come to town with theater tickets and suggested that
they meet at the Harvard Club beforehand to discuss juris-
diction issues on an upcoming case. Josh's boss wanted him
to come along, as he was involved in the case, too. So Josh
had put on a suit to go to the Harvard Club. Then afterward
he went back downtown, where he and two other A.D.A.s
were preparing a series of cases set to go to trial on Tuesday.
For dinner they split a pizza (very carefully), and when the
others broke for the evening, as it was about the right time to
go to the Club, Josh decided to walk there directly from the
D.A.'s offices on Foley Square—not so far for someone accustomed to long walks.

Of course Josh's real reason for going to the Club was the
hope of finding Alice there. He just assumed that she would
be, and, by chance, she was—but it was actually her first time
back, too. When we go someplace infrequently, the conclusion we tend to jump to is that those we run into are there all
the time, or at least a lot, while we *know* we ourselves go only
rarely. This is part of the reason why people are always saying
that "*they* are not a something-or-other type"—such as Dan
saying he was "not a disco type," and Charlotte adding, "Nor
are we." Charlotte had been to the Club only once at that
point, so she was (partly) right to deny being a "disco type."

In any case, calling someone a "disco type" is obviously the sort of dismissive, pejorative, categorizing way of talking people get into that is actually quite aggressive and self-aggrandizing, even if the original impulse is out of defensive, inferiority complex–like motives—often justified.

At the other extreme there were cases like Josh who did frankly and openly love disco and would have been happy to consider themselves "disco types" if they could make the designation themselves, without the veiled sneer implicit when made by others.

Josh must have arrived at the Club an hour before Alice, or before spotting her there, and though it was terrific just to be at the Club, that night he felt like a bit of a chump wandering around watching and not dancing with anyone. This is a feeling a lot of us know well—the strong, overpowering sensation of "opportunities missed."

When Josh did spot Alice with Dan and Charlotte by the bar, it was also natural that he be a little apprehensive about approaching her. Once he had started toward her and then veered off to rethink his approach and fortify his courage. The possibility of abrupt rejection, no matter how unlikely, looms very large when the person in question is probably your only chance for happiness in life. Why wreck that, perhaps for all time, with an unthought-out, cloddish approach?

Josh might have reassured himself with reasoning along the lines of what's the worst thing that can happen? Why would Alice, who was obviously very nice, misinterpret and rudely rebuff a polite approach by him? Josh was almost the textbook definition of a "good guy," quite likable, and underneath the occasionally goofy veneer perfectly presentable—especially that night. He and Alice had already met before, and that meeting had been positive. Wasn't the reason people came to discos unescorted precisely to meet people and dance? What was there to be afraid of? (Of course, one answer was "Complete and utter humiliation.")

When Josh made his way toward Alice a second time, he did not veer off, but still hesitated a moment before breaking in.

"Excuse me," he said, "you're Alice Kinnon, aren't you?"

"Yeess . . ." Alice said tentatively. She had never seen him before in her life—as far as she could remember.

"We met at that party in . . . Sag Harbor, Labor Day weekend."

Alice drew a blank. All she could think of was the wonderful talk she had had with Tom that day. Even the kidding chat she and I had had was now relegated to oblivion.

"You were just coming in as I was leaving and you asked me where the kitchen was," Josh continued in a friendly and congenial tone. "Do you remember?"

Alice paused, thought, and finally had to shake her head no. "I do remember *getting* to the kitchen," she added, somewhat encouragingly.

Charlotte and Dan, drinks in hand, had turned in time to watch Josh's intervention, which both regarded very critically, though from opposite motives.

Charlotte slipped the whiskey sour Alice had ordered into her hand and then addressed Josh, very rudely: "Excuse us. We're here sort of as a group . . . If you don't mind . . ."

It could have been the gimlet talking. Alice and Dan were appalled, but before Alice could think of anything to say to counteract Charlotte's bizarre rudeness, Josh had gone.

"Excuse me," he said, and disappeared into the crowd.

"Why did you say that?!" Alice exclaimed.

"I didn't like the look of him at all," Charlotte explained, her tone reasonable. "Didn't you notice how he was eye-balling you?"

Alice shook her head.

"Creepy," Charlotte continued. "Frankly, I thought he might be the guy who bothered me on the subway. Sorry if I overreacted."

"Poor guy," Alice said, looking over in the direction she thought Josh might have gone.

"It's no big deal. This kind of thing happens all the time. Anyway, you've got Tom," she said, and took a big sip of her cocktail.

The disco version of "Knock on Wood" credited to Amii Stewart was an unusually good reworking of Sam & Dave's classic sixties soul hit of the same title and for the Club's dee-jays a reliable disco anthem, getting everybody up and danc-ing almost whenever it was played.

Alice, a little miserable, had returned to the dance floor, where "Knock on Wood" seemed to lift everyone's spirits except her own. As she went through the dance-floor motions, subdued and a bit maudlin, she was almost trampled by the Tin Man and the Cowardly Lion moving wildly to the song's heavy beat and incongruous lyrics ("knock on wood," etc.). Both were far too gone in the song's rhythm and clue-less how to express their enthusiasm in dance for the imme-diate safety of their neighbors. Heavy tie shoes sticking out from the bottom of their costumes flailed around the floor in dangerous disregard of those near them, like Alice. The lure of the shy and lovely exerted itself. Unconsciously, or not entirely consciously, they made Alice, attractive and dancing alone, the center of their circling dance, until the Cowardly Lion stepped left just as she stepped right, colliding into her with leonine force.

"Gahd!"

Tom Platt was just then pushing through the crowd on the rise overlooking the dance floor, searching for Alice. As soon as he spotted her, he stepped down to the dance floor and crossed to her. There were big smiles all around, though Alice couldn't entirely shake all the day's sadness.

"Sorry I'm so late!" he had to whisper-shout on the dance floor. "How did it go?!"

"Fine!" Alice said.

"You know they closed the airport?!"

"No!" Alice said, perking up.

"Yeah! The storm was terrifying!" Tom said. "We had to land in Washington until LaGuardia reopened! I was working on the plane, but finally was just praying over my legal pads we'd get in okay!"

"Wow!" Alice said. She actually couldn't make out everything he had said, but it did sound scary. Alice had entirely forgotten about the storm that had blown up during dinner—they had had to hurry around closing windows—and now had a guilty pang that she had not thought about Tom flying in, perhaps in jeopardy. It was odd, since she had been thinking about him constantly, but perhaps what she had been feeling was not an authentic selfless love but just some sort of self-indulgent, egotistical crush.

Then the music and joyous intensity of "Knock on Wood" reasserted itself—Amii Stewart worked her magic! For Alice the emotional coloration of the song was now entirely changed. Tom was a cool dancer, and as he and Alice moved to the music in free-style synchrony, the strobes came on and caught their images in time, and there seemed something Important and Romantic about it.

At the Club, above and along the far edges of the main floor, talking was not only possible but highly desirable. It was the primary way thoughts were communicated.

Tom had taken Alice up to the mezzanine balcony to talk over drinks. I could go into the whole sociology of who sat in this part of the mezzanine, as opposed to the ground floor or other parts of the Club—but won't. In any case, the sound speakers were below them, directed the opposite way, so there was no problem being heard. Tom did not know exactly where the conversation was going to take them but hoped it might, in a gentle and perhaps warm spirit, clarify or resolve the situation. Several alternating colored spotlights, arranged along the other balcony, illuminated Alice's lovely hair from behind, creating a beautiful aurora effect.

A waitress in one of the sexy Club outfits put their drinks on the little round mirrored table in front of them, so popular in clubs of that period. Alice, huddled with him on the banquette, reached for the fresh whiskey sour and took a long sip. She was so happy to be with Tom again and confirm that what she had feared might be a one-sided dream was, in fact, entirely real.

Suddenly she craved a cigarette—one last element of luxury to perfect the moment. From the couple smoking at the banquette behind theirs, she successfully bummed one. It turned out to be an elegant English Oval from Dunhill. For a moment she just cradled it in the palm of her hand, examining its exquisite architecture—more Neoclassical than Modern.

"It is oval," she said.

"And English," Tom added.

Suddenly Alice was overcome with the beauty of it all. "It's so beautiful," she said, and then wondered if that would make her seem a little drunk. Then she wondered whether she *was* a little drunk. But Tom seemed to smile and, taking a match from a Club matchbook, lit it for her.

He then began what he had to say quite carefully. This part he had thought through. How to get all the way to the end, he hadn't.

"Do you remember the conversation we had Labor Day weekend?" he asked.

Alice nodded intently.

"It had a huge impact on me," he said.

"Really?"

"You're in a relationship that's good, everything's fine— then you meet someone with whom communication is complete and total; and also is extremely nice—and very pretty . . ."

Tom looked at Alice significantly, then continued. "Jennifer and I had been talking all year about either acknowledging the permanence of our relationship and marrying or finally just breaking up . . ."

"I had no idea you were . . . even dating anyone."

"I thought you knew," Tom said.

Alice shook her head.

"No, we've been together since college. The week after Labor Day we had a long talk; Jennifer proposed a trial separation, which, normally, I'd have considered ridiculous—but I couldn't help thinking of you and went along, which surprised her a lot."

"Why'd she suggest it if she didn't really want it?" Alice asked.

"People do that all the time. It's very normal . . ."

Tom lost his concentration a moment and then continued. "Out of a sort of residual loyalty to Jennifer, I didn't call you immediately and instead started coming to the Club very late after work. I'm not a very good dancer—"

"No, you are—" Alice smiled in a lovely way.

"—but I like and find a huge release in it. I was also curious if the sexual revolution had gone as far as everyone said. It had. Much of September I felt as if I were living inside a porno film . . . Emotionally, though, I couldn't handle it. I got so . . . depressed. When I saw you that night, you were a vision, not just of loveliness, but of sanity and . . . virtue."

Tom, in a bleak funk, couldn't seem to continue. Alice sensed what was coming.

"What?" she asked.

"I shouldn't talk about it," he said. "I'll just sound like an idiot."

"No, what?"

"You're very sexy and modern and good-looking . . . and . . . hot. But what I was *craving* was the sort of sentient individual who wouldn't abandon her intelligence to hop in bed with every jerk she meets at a nightclub."

It was as if Tom, once started, could not stop and plunged into the kind of cruelties he could never have intended. "Why—why is it, when people have sex with strangers on their mind, their IQ drops, like, forty points?"

"It was not 'any jerk,' " Alice said. "It was *you*."

"That's irrelevant. It wasn't even a date. We didn't even have dinner, we just ran into each other in a nightclub. Please don't tell me that's not slutty. And then, all that affected sexy-

seductress-slinking-around? Is that how you are? Uncle
Scrooge is *sexy*?! My God, is there no limit?! Uncle
Scrooge?!—"

"No, that was to—"

"Do you think I'm an idiot? I'm sick of all the *lies* and
nonsense!"

Charlotte hurried after Alice as she ran down the stairs.
There was something terrible about how Alice moved which
frightened her.

"What's wrong?!" she called, trying to catch up with her.
"What happened?!" she asked.

I was still entirely disguised in the harlequin costume,
pushed up at the main bar next to Des, trying to get him to
intercede with Van or Berrie on my behalf, oblivious to what
had happened to Alice. In retrospect, I would give anything
to be able to relive that moment and have been able to comfort her then—not that she would have melted in my arms
and everything would necessarily have been different. I know
that the processes of human attraction are not quite so simple.

From the front door area we heard Van's voice as, accompanied by Rick, he entered the Club in a fury. One of his
flunkies met him on the inside.

"McGrath? Where is he?" Van asked him. The flunky
nodded in our general direction.

"Uh," Des whispered, "I'd say it's definitely not a good
idea to approach Van tonight . . ."

Together we started backing away from the bar area, as
unobtrusively as possible.

"McGrath!" Van called, looking for him.

Van plunged through the crowd toward where Des and I had been.

"You're through, McGrath! You're out of here. Right now."

"What?" Des said.

Van looked around. "Berrie! Berrie!" he called. Turning to the inside flunky, he asked, "Where is he?"

"He was around," the flunky said, looking in our direction.

"Here he is," Rick announced.

Berrie appeared, accompanied by the cute waitress Nikki, who kissed him before going off. I meanwhile tried to edge away unobtrusively and lose myself in the crowd. But the extravagant harlequin outfit, good for disguise, was not so good for blending in. Tassel bells on each tip of the starburst jester headgear jingled every move I made—even a head nod set them off.

Des, on the other hand, just stood where he had stopped, as if awaiting his doom.

"Berrie, this guy's through!" Van said.

"What?" Berrie asked.

"We had a public safety situation in the front," Van said. "This jerk comes out, trying to make it worse."

Des smiled sheepishly, a little embarrassed.

Berrie turned to him: "Is this true?"

"Public safety situation?" Des said. "Give me a break. It was a joke. I'm *sorry*."

Van glanced suspiciously in the general direction of the harlequin outfit.

"I tease him a tiny bit . . ." Des rationalized.

"No teasing, Des," Berrie replied firmly.

" 'No *teasing*?' "

"Either he goes, or I do," Van said, his voice almost qua-vering.

"Come on, Van, don't say that," Berrie said, and then turned to Des: "Des, grow up. Cut it out."

"Okay. Sorry," he said, as if repentant.

As in a blur came the sudden movement of a huge object toward me from the right. My view through the eye slots of the harlequin headgear was not at all good, which perhaps made what happened seem far more ominous and nightmar-ish, but in any case, the pent-up anger with which Van lunged toward me would, I think, have been pretty scary. I dodged back, trying to elude his grasp, but grabbing the tas-sels of my hood, he yanked it off with a sweeping movement of his arm.

I don't know if "cringing" or "cowering" would be a better description of the posture in which I was found. If it were not for the psychological disorientation of not being able to see properly, I would like to think that I would have handled the situation a little more bravely. Watching war movies as a child, particularly those of an older vintage, I had always imagined I would have been one of the brave fools fighting with at least a modicum of cinema courage. But you never really know until you're tested.

"*It's the ad guy!*" Van exulted.

"So—it's the '*dancing adman*'?" Berrie added.

Turning to Des, Van gloated: "You're finished."

Roughly held by Van and two of his bouncers, I com-pletely lost it, exclaiming, "*Okay, I work in advertising—is that a crime?! What's happening in this country?!*"

Meanwhile, out on the dance floor, the Oz characters

suddenly bolted for the back exits, Van's bouncers in close pursuit.

"The Tin Man!" Van called. The Tin Man had taken off in another direction and looked like he might get away. "Get him!" The Cowardly Lion, however, was caught up with and cruelly unmasked, revealing our client Jack.

Back where we were, Alice, Charlotte, Holly, and Dan had come up, attracted by the hubbub around my unmasking, and so were around to observe the pathetic denouement.

"Get this jerk out of the Club," Berrie told his thugs, indicating me.

Van, still furious, had turned to Des. "You're fired, Des! You're out of here!"

"You can't fire me, Van! Only Berrie can fire me!"

"Okay. You're fired," Berrie said. "And take this"—he indicated the Holly-Charlotte-Dan-Alice group—"*yuppie scum* with you!"

Rick and his cohorts yanked me toward the back. For the second time in a week I was being "ejected" from the Club. My entire social life passed before my eyes: the first coed birthday party I was invited to; then, in eighth grade, the first party with dancing—I had not yet shot up in height and there was a bitter competition between the five small guys in the class for the attention of the two girls actually shorter than us; at fifteen came introduction to Chicago's underage preppy bar scene of those years (perhaps mentioning the unhappy situation at home would make this seem more sympathetic) and the first trip (a bit of a downer) to a psychedelic disco where the women present preferred to dance with each other than some perfectly presentable, honorably intentioned fourth formers . . .

At least getting thrown out of the Club this time there was lots of company, including my clients, who again were really nice guys. That had been the worst part of my prior ejection—the solitariness of it all: ending up alone, outside in the dark, all dressed up with nowhere to go and no one to go nowhere with. Being ejected as part of a group was a far different and, frankly, far better experience; there was something almost joyous about it. This was one of the true glories of Group Social Life—sharing and, through companionship, ameliorating a bad, potentially almost traumatic situation—such as much of late adolescence/early adulthood itself.

12

The Ejected

In fact, there was something more poetical about leaving the Club the back way—passing through the darkened, prop-strewn corridors to the back door, which opened onto one of those mysterious downtown courts left from a prior period of lower density and real estate costs, now used casually for the overnight parking of some trucks, many of very old vintage. Those arriving for the great private parties usually entered the back way, too, but the feeling then was completely different—of glamour and anticipation, of groups of models and sleek climbers with invitations being ushered in while the occasional taxi or limousine leaving the wrong way clogged the alley. I doubt if they would have noticed the evocative details of the urban night.

Coming out this way late at night you did not immediately confront the crowds and street traffic of the front. It was deserted and actually quite pleasant and, for the metropolis, comparatively quiet. The Club was so close to the Hudson

you could hear the occasional calls of the seagulls flying over-
head. The night schedule of the garbage barges and trucks
had led them to have a more nocturnal existence, too.

Among the ejected we were nine in all—Alice, Charlotte,
me, Des, Dan, Holly, and, in the Oz costumes, the three
clients I had, with Des's help, been able to bring in: the Cowardly Lion (Jack), Dorothy (Wendy), and the Tin Man
(Harry; until this evening I hadn't realized he was gay, or perhaps it was an affiliation he was then just trying on from
within the safety—and anonymity—of a rubberized Tin
Man costume, which were becoming increasingly common
in the downtown club scene of those days, though not quite
so ubiquitous as they are today. What does it say about our
Society, this constant search for refuge in the images and
memories of childhood, cartoons, and films and literature for
children? Perhaps something not very mature.)

"Good riddance!" Van called from the back door area,
where he, Rick, and some of their more brutish bouncers
were gloating at Des's downfall and Van's final triumph in
their historic rivalry. This also was strangely suggestive of
childhood—the insult language we used when we were nine
or ten. The full expression was, I think, "Good Riddance to
Bad Rubbish!" (Not long after this, it started dawning on me
that Van, for all his mastery of the front door, was oddly inept
socially. There was something curiously "young" about his
behavior in many situations—such as the way his voice
wavered, as if he were about to sob or break down in invol-
untary tears, during the confrontation with Des in front of
Berrie. His behavior reminded me of my childhood friend
Bart Wilson, who grew up an only child the first eight years
of his life, until his little sister was born, which changed the

dynamic at home only in adding the adulation of a much younger sister to all the cooing and coddling by his elders. His behavior in relation to his contemporaries was always a little "off," which our constant teasing certainly helped ameliorate—but did not entirely correct. Des's needling must have hit a long-buried nerve of this kind in Van.)

Like Dan arriving at the Club, I had drunk enough that each step had that element of heightened drama, as the vibration passed upward from the soles of my big black leather tie shoes. The drinking was probably related to the intense stress of wearing a limited-vision costume over a long period in a darkened environment, but the result was that everything now seemed particularly significant and interesting, as it usually does when you are mildly ploughed.

Des was really shaken up by the confrontation, his firing, and all the hostility it evinced.

"Yuppie *scum?*" he repeated incredulously as the group walked away from the Club. "In college, before dropping out, I took a course in the propaganda uses of language," he said, looking around at the rest of us. "One objective is to deny other people's humanity—or even right to exist."

"In the men's lounge," I mentioned, "someone scrawled: *Kill Yuppie Scum.*"

" '*Scum?* ' " Des asked himself. "That's Khmer Rouge stuff: re-education camps. Mass executions and starvation."

We were walking as a group, a sort of posse, more fleeing than chasing, toward the alley that would take us to the street.

"Do 'yuppies' even exist?" he asked. "It's always the other guy who's the 'yuppie.' For a group to exist, I think someone has to be willing to admit they're part of it."

" 'Yuppie' actually started out as a magazine-advertising demographic term," I pointed out. "Magazines with weak circulations claimed the few readers they had were in a new category of affluent young people who bought disproportionate quantities of goods and services. It was just an ad sales gimmick—as sociology, ridiculous. No one thought such people actually existed."

"Of course yuppies exist," Dan pronounced from behind us, where he walked with Holly. "Most people would say you two are prime specimens."

Des and I looked at each other, dumbfounded.

"We're not yuppies!" Des exclaimed.

"You think we're yuppies?" I asked incredulously.

Charlotte snorted with laughter; later she told me she thought we were classic yuppies, too.

"You're seriously saying you're *not* yuppies?" Dan asked.

"No," we both said.

" 'Yuppie,' " Des said, "stands for 'young,' 'upwardly mobile,' 'professional'—'nightclub *flunky*' is not a professional category."

"Contrary to popular belief," I pointed out, "junior-level ad jobs don't pay well at all."

"I wish we were 'yuppies,' " Des continued. " 'Young,' 'upwardly mobile,' 'professional'—those are good things, not bad things."

Charlotte stopped. "Uh, where're we going?"

"Rex's," Des said, mentioning the name of a popular bar.

"Oh no!" Charlotte said.

"What's wrong with Rex's?" I asked. The actor in the movie did a very good job on this line, saying it just the way *I* would have. He put a break in his voice and slightly raised its

pitch on the word "Rex's," injecting a note of incredulity—
as if it were inconceivable that anyone could not like Rex's.
I think he got this from questioning me prior to shooting
the movie; I went off on a long digression about how great
Rex's was, waxing elegiac. It can be terrific the work that
actors do.

Charlotte's view of Rex's was the opposite. "Well," she
said, "you can't dance there—and it's full of boring preppies."

"Oh—and we're so interesting?" Des asked.

"You can dance at Rex's," I said.

"But why Rex's?" Charlotte went on. "Why not some
other place?"

"*Well*," Des started. "For one thing, everybody in the
Club knows I go there. When they come looking for me, I
want to be there."

With an incredulous smile, Charlotte asked, "Why would
they come looking for you?"

"What happened tonight was a mistake which, even now,
Berrie's probably very much regretting," Des said. "He's a
smart guy, not without some good qualities—even if very
few. I wouldn't be surprised if he's already called Rex's to
retract my dismissal."

"How can you be so sure of that?" Charlotte asked.

"Well . . . I'm not sure of it."

"Opportunity" by The Jewels was playing on the jukebox
when we entered Rex's. This was a great black girl–group
number from the mid-sixties at the height of the Brill Building period. Considered the inheritors of the Tin Pan Alley
tradition, the songwriters still working out of this legendary

structure on the northwest corner of Forty-ninth and Broadway, above Colony Records ("I found it at the Colony!" the store's logo, the image of a young woman in a fifties-style skirt jumping in the air, had it), churned out many of this period's great hits. One of the Brill Building writers, Carole King, went on to a great career as a singer-songwriter, though her biggest success near our period was her recording of the beautiful eighteenth-century hymn "Amazing Grace."

Des led the way into Rex's. "Hey, Rex," he called to him at the other end of the bar.

Fearing I might have neglected my clients sticking by Charlotte during the walk over, and trying to be sensitive to the awkwardness they might feel in costumes outside the club context, I held the door for them, blurting out, "Welcome to Rex's!"

But there was no cause for apprehension. They actually seemed to be enjoying the evening—the ejection having been less personal for them, more of a bonding experience, and on the way over they had hooked up with Dan and Holly, who were basically very nice despite whatever annoying little faults they might have had.

It was Alice I should have been more concerned about. All evening, lost in my own preoccupations, I had been stupidly oblivious to her situation.

While I hung back by the door waiting for the others to enter, Charlotte, concerned by Alice's red eyes and miserable look, walked on ahead with her.

"What's wrong?" she asked confidentially. "God, Alice, you look like you'd just seen the dark side of the moon. What did Tom *say*?"

"No. I feel much better," Alice said, though she still

sounded incredibly sad. "I love your idea of social life as a group—without all the ferocious pairing off. I couldn't have stood being alone tonight."

We found two tables that could accommodate us all at the back of the bar, not far from the jukebox. Rex was in fine fettle that night. He thought Berrie's actions incomprehensible. For Rex and others in the business, it was really Des who had made the Club a success.

"What a blunder," he said. "I can't believe it . . . I thought Berrie was smarter than that." Rex thought Berrie's actions could have been a product of the clouded judgment that comes from excessive drug and marijuana use. Rex despised the "weed" and its effects, and thought he was providing a service in offering young people wanting to get absolutely blotto a legal alternative.

"You really think that?" Des asked. "That drug use clouds your judgment?"

"Yeah," Rex said.

Rex praised Des for sticking up for what he believed in—even if that was only, in this case, the right to let friends in the back way even if they worked in advertising. In a larger sense, it was a question of loyalty to one's friends and one's self.

A former actor, Rex had a gift for recitation and a commanding presence that he could use to great effect, as he did now, while passing us our drinks, declaiming:

" 'It is not the critic who counts, not the man who points out how the strong man stumbled or where the doer of deeds could have done them better. The credit belongs to the man who is actually in the arena; whose face is marred by dust and sweat and blood; who strives valiantly; who errs and comes up short again and again; who knows the great enthusiasms, the great devotions, and spends himself in a worthy cause; who, at the best, knows the triumph of high achievement; and who, at the worst, if he fails, at least fails while daring greatly, so that his place shall never be with those cold and timid souls who know neither victory nor defeat'—Teddy Roosevelt," Rex finished with a flourish. The recitation was a tour-de-force, with Rex scarcely pausing for breath and correctly matching everyone to his or her drink order.

Des and, in fact, all of us were, I think, really touched. Perhaps it overstated the actual situation within the Club and the conflict with Berrie and Van, but there's something great about a friend who can make the struggles of daily life seem more dramatic and significant than they really are. Even in the objectively trivial and mundane, we like to feel there are elements of the epic and important, and getting fired from your job is certainly not trivial (especially from such a great job as Des's). Passing from "underboss of the world's most popular club" to "ex-flunky, thrown out the back way" is perhaps not so far from the transformation from "high estate" to "low estate" touched on in classical drama.

"Thanks, Rex," Des said, obviously moved.

"When Berrie does call, we'll get you immediately," Rex said before going. His confidence in Des's theory—that Berrie would call—was also inspiring.

After he left, Des said, "Rex is such a great guy."

I nodded. "Yeah," I had to agree.

Our table included Des and Alice on one side, Charlotte and I on the other; the Oz characters and Holly and Dan sat at the table behind us. Before Rex and Des's arrival with the drinks, Charlotte and I had picked up the thread of an earlier conversation. A theory she expounded seemed totally dubious to me but she was so convinced of it I wanted to get the others' reactions.

"Charlotte insists she can tell if a guy is gay or not just by looking in his eyes."

"I still don't get that," Des said. "How?"

"Maybe it's related to how they look at you," Charlotte said. "It's hard to define, but I think women can tell."

"I can't," Alice said.

"Are Jimmy and I gay?" Des asked.

Charlotte turned to examine us. Alice tried to interrupt. "Oh, come on. Don't . . ."

Charlotte scrutinized my face. "Uhhh . . . Jimmy, no . . ."

She turned to look at Des more closely. "Well . . . not your eyes," she said slowly. "But . . . you *do* have a gay mouth."

"A gay *mouth*? I have a 'gay mouth'? What does that mean?"

"Just what I said," she replied.

"It's true, Des," I said. "Your mouth does look gay."

"God, how *moronic* can you get? What nonsense."

"Don't . . . think . . . I . . . don't . . . know . . . your . . . whole . . . act," Charlotte said, speaking just that way.

"Excuse me?" Des said, as if he were hard-of-hearing.

"Pretending to be gay to get sympathy from women while cruelly dumping them—and to seem cooler than you actually are? I *despise* your whole pathetic act. You're not fit to lick the boots of my real gay friends."

"Well, I don't *want* to lick the boots of your real gay friends. You know, I *could* be gay."

"I see through you completely."

"Oh," he said, "you see through me completely."

"Yeah. I do!"

"That's the dark side of feminism—"

"What?" Charlotte demanded.

"That you have a kind of free pass to make any kind of derogatory, wounding comment you want—"

"I'm hardly a militant feminist."

"No, you're not," Des acknowledged. "A militant feminist would be a *lot* fairer. It's women like you whose attitudes to men are so *dehumanizing*."

Charlotte was incredulous. "Like what?"

"That men are swine, obsessed with large breasts and the sex act, devoid of any idealistic or romantic sensibility, when in fact we have that idealistic sensibility *in spades*."

Des took a big gulp of his whiskey, then continued: "For instance, you have no idea what men really think about women's breasts."

Alice hesitantly asked, "What do you think about women's breasts?"

Des seemed caught up a moment, temporarily at a loss for words, which was unusual for him. "It's not just something you blurt out," he said. "It's far more nuanced and complicated than that . . ."

He glanced around the table, looking for support, but in fact got none. Charlotte and one or another of us looked at him pretty skeptically.

"Okay, I'll tell you a story," he said expansively, as if trying to change the tenor of the discussion and get out of his defensive position.

"In college," he began, "there was a girl I had a crush on,

but she always had *older* boyfriends, invariably *some senior.* Finally, they all graduated and, one night, we went back to her room alone. Suddenly her shirt was off and I was confronted with her breasts, which turned out to be . . . completely surprising and, frankly, disconcerting. They were . . ."

Des gave some sort of representation of the breasts with his hands, but pretty inarticulately.

In the background one of the great soul songs of the late sixties came on the jukebox. This one had a very danceable beat and inspired several couples to get up to non-disco dance, including Dan, Holly, and the Oz characters. I glanced at Charlotte, as this was sort of a vindication for me—people *did* dance at Rex's—but she was focused on Des's story.

". . . rather large and not ugly nor especially strange-shaped, but in all the time I'd thought about her, these breasts had never figured. She took her shirt off so quickly, there was no time for adjustment. And I sensed something arrogant about it, as if her abrupt unveiling of her largish breasts was going to slay my swinish male self, as if I hadn't already been slayed on a much higher level . . ."

He thought a moment and looked at Alice. "Her name was Alice, too—"

"Oh come on, Des: you know that isn't true!" I interrupted.

"What do you mean, it isn't true?"

"Her name was not Alice," I said.

"Well, I'm not going to use her real name!"

I turned to Charlotte: "Would you like to dance?"

Charlotte turned to Alice and said, "Would you mind?" But before she could reply or react in any way, we were on our feet headed for the dance floor.

This was one of those points when, watching the film, I noticed something I had never seen or known before. Had I noticed, I think my life could have taken an entirely different path. Most of us like to believe that the way our life transpires, the path we follow is inevitable, fated, and ultimately "for the best." "Whatever IS, Is RIGHT," as Pope wrote, simplifying quite a bit. It would be comforting to accept that view, and there is certainly an advantage in not getting excessively bent out of shape about facts and events one can't change. But it is not true. Had certain things happened differently, had we done some things and omitted others, the later outcome might have been much better. Ultimately we accommodate ourselves to the way things did happen because we have no alternative to that accommodation, so it becomes hard to imagine that not being "for the best," but it is not really true.

What I didn't notice until then was Alice's expression when I asked Charlotte to dance. For the actress who played Alice, it was a beautiful moment. Alice really did mind. She started to say something—though what could she really say?—but Charlotte and I had already taken off for the dance floor and only Des saw it. Later she kept her eyes glued on us as we danced, her expression not happy.

Des looked at Alice, disconsolate—first Tom, now this— with concern and affection. He tried to both distract and, in his way, comfort her.

"If whatever's bothering you relates to Tom Platt, I wouldn't take it personally," he said. "Did you know Tom and Jennifer had a trial separation, which was to end tonight?"

Alice nodded yes, though, in fact, the timing—that it was to end that night—she had not known.

"What you might not know is that, about a week ago,

they started seeing each other on the sly, cheating on their trial separation."

"How do you know that?" she asked intensely.

"Working at the Club you find out all kinds of stuff."

Meanwhile, I got to dance with Charlotte to the wonderful 1968 semi-hit, "The Oogum Boogum Song," with its delightful nonsensical oogum-boogum lyric, by the male soul vocalist Brenton Wood, the only recording artist of the 1960s to take his name from a monetary conference (Bretton Woods, 1944; another, less interesting, theory had it deriving from "Brentwood," a Los Angeles neighborhood).

I loved the giddy romantic excess of this song and its great beat in the tradition of popular R & B dance music, which would, in a sense, ultimately flower in Disco.

Many of the regulars at Rex's were very good dancers of an older school. They had all the steps and dance tricks of early-sixties or pre-sixties vintage smoothly down pat. Near us, Holly, Dan, and the Oz characters also danced enthusiastically. There was an element of the bar version of a sock hop from the television show *Happy Days*, or something of that ilk. It was the ideal version of how one would imagine dancing in bars if one had never experienced such a thing.

Simply recounting Charlotte's talk, which tended to the funny-bitchy side, gives no indication of how appealing she could be "existentially"—dancing, walking around, a trip to a store or a cab ride, cooking a meal, brushing her teeth. Everything became a fun event, though such enjoyment was essentially nonverbal and thus harder to set down afterward.

After we had been dancing this way awhile, I observed, admittedly nostalgically, "This must have been the way people used to dance in bars in the old days."

"Did people ever really dance in bars?" Charlotte asked. "I thought that was a myth."

"No. People my brother's age—they did."

"Your brother must be a *lot* older," she said between steps, "because before Disco, at the end of the sixties and the beginning of the seventies, this country was a dancing *wasteland*. You know the 'Woodstock Generation' of the 1960s, who were so full of themselves and conceited? None of those people could dance."

"Huhn."

Then Charlotte broke into some ultracool moves which took all my attention to follow. Unlike some people on the dance floor, when you looked Charlotte in the eyes, she smiled right back. She was very cool without having to officially act "cool."

Des's tendency, once he got started, was to pick over what had happened that night years ago, the way the people pick at the scab of an old wound that has not entirely healed—which in a sense it was.

"I think she noticed that, for a moment, I 'flinched.' Do you know what I mean? I hesitated, and—the moment was over. I made her feel self-conscious. She threw a robe over herself and stood up."

"What happened then?"

"That was it, really. She dropped me like a rock. It was really bad . . . I was crushed. I dropped out of college, came to New York, and got into the nightclub business early—thanks to which I probably owe my success today."

With the excuse of feeling "bushed," we had stopped dancing and were all thinking of going home.

"Let's share a cab," Charlotte suggested to Holly and Dan.

We shuffled back to the table, where Alice and Des still talked.

"We're thinking of going," Charlotte said when we got there.

"You're all going?" Alice asked.

We nodded. My preoccupation at that time was to get Charlotte off alone somewhere. If Alice was upset, I was in little condition to see that.

"Have they called yet from the Club?" I asked Des.

Des shook his head. "I don't think they will call," he said now. "Berrie'll probably send some emissary. That's more his style."

"What should we do with the Oz costumes?" I asked. "Drop them by the Club tomorrow?"

"Actually, those costumes are mine," Des said. "Just get them back when you can."

Then, looking to Charlotte, Alice blurted out, "I thought we were here as a group. You talked about the tremendous importance of group social life."

"Well, it's really late," Charlotte said.

"Yeah, Alice, it's really late," Holly added.

"We'd better be going," Dan put in.

" 'Bye," we said.

"*Ciao*," Charlotte added.

"Thanks again, Des," I repeated.

There were more " 'byes," "thanks," and "so longs" from the others. I went off to say "so long" to Rex.

Des waved us off with a simple "*ciao*" and, as we shuffled off, turned back to Alice, who was still apparently very upset.

"All week Charlotte's been talking about the importance

of group social life—opposing this ferocious pairing off.
Then tonight—"

She broke off and shook her head in chagrin.

"Well, group social life has its place," Des started slowly
and quite gently. "But at a certain point, other, biological,
factors come into play. Our bodies weren't really designed
for 'group social life.' A certain amount of 'pairing off' was
part of the original plan."

Des's mistake was to say all this—it did have the "defense
of truth" and a certain comedy value—without really looking at Alice and seeing what effect it was having in her then
extremely vulnerable and humiliated state.

At first she said nothing, just looked down at the empty
glass with that sort of emotional catatonia we get when we're
very upset but it's impossible or very embarrassing to explain
why. When she did speak, it was barely audible, just under her
breath.

"God, I can't believe you'd say that."

"What?"

Alice, upset, just continued looking at her glass.

"What did I say?" Des asked.

Alice stood up to go, looking like she was about to break.
"What you mean," she said, "is that they've all gone back . . .
to . . ."

She paused a moment.

"Screw Their Brains Out!"

"Don't go," Des pleaded, standing up and chasing after her.
"I didn't mean to say anything anyone could be offended by!"

Pushing through the doors heading out of Rex's, Alice
crossed with Adam and Victor, Berrie's sleek office flunkies,
who were on their way in.

"Oh thank God!" Adam said. "He's here—"

"—Des, Berrie regrets what happened," Victor said. "It was a mistake. He wants you back—"

Des—thinking only of Alice—nodded and edged past them out the door to the street. Alice was still waiting under Rex's awning in the rain, trying to flag down a cab.

"I'm sorry," Des said. "I know why you're so upset."

Alice looked back at him.

"I mean," he said, "I know what really happened with Tom."

"What do you *mean*?" Alice said, her voice breaking.

"That he thought you were really slutty or something. God, that's so stupid."

A cab had swung in toward the curb. Alice looked at Des with an expression he could only describe as very sad, then ran through the rain to the cab and opened the door, while Des followed her.

"You can't worry about what misinterpreters think!" he called. "That's so unfair!"

Alice looked back at him, eyes watering, a lot of emotion bottled up.

"Come back to my place," he urged. "We should talk . . ."

Alice turned wordlessly and closed the cab door behind her. As the cab slowly got under way, Des paced alongside it, pleading: "Nothing will happen! I just really need someone to talk with, and maybe you do, too."

Adam and Victor had come out of Rex's to see what was going on, both opening their umbrellas simultaneously as if choreographed. Des finally gave up trying to keep up with the accelerating taxi and stood mutely watching it disappear, letting himself get soaked in the downpour. Then he turned back to Berrie's waiting henchmen.

As the cab headed uptown, Alice sank back into the seat—

wet, bedraggled, and very unhappy (what would today be called "desperately unhappy"). All her hopes were collapsed while something sordid and evil approached. She closed her eyes and shook and shivered for a moment as if having just had a close brush with Beelzebub.

13

Unhappiness Anatomized; or, The Apartment

Alice, still dripping from the rain, entered the former tenement building and climbed the two flights to her floor. The bedroom that had fallen to her was really more a sleeping alcove between the living room—which Holly had volunteered to take—and the larger bedroom (with doors) next to the kitchen, which Charlotte felt she had to take as it was the only one big enough for her bed to fit in.

Alice went straight to the entrance on the living-room side of the apartment but had some trouble with her key—only later did we learn that the lock had a catch which was much easier to open if you pulled the door hard, toward yourself. In the living room she found Holly and Dan sitting next to each other at the far end of the sofa, slightly mussed and breathless, as if startled in the midst of an intense make-out session, which was in fact the case. The room was dimly lit by a single lamp and still furnished mostly with unemptied cardboard boxes. It later turned out that Holly was one of those attractive women who are also a bit slobby. (When the cardboard boxes remained unemptied for several weeks, Charlotte finally gave her the choice between unpacking them or having them dumped on the street. She then did unpack them and was actually relieved to finally have it done.)

Alice and Holly exchanged "hi's," Holly a little awkwardly, sitting forward on the sofa. Dan took a swig from his beer—not in a rude way, he just didn't know what to say at first in this kind of situation.

From Charlotte's room Gwen Macrae's slow, sexy, disco-era ballad "Rocking Chair" filtered through the closed door—rather loudly for the middle of the night, which was apparently not a problem for this building. The recording was very much in the female soul vocalist tradition that Alice loved, but the relentlessly sexy lyrics were a little depressing in her then mood.

With the briefest glance in the direction of Holly and Dan, Alice passed quickly through to her bedroom. There was no door on the living-room side, which she considered a bit of a problem. Though a prior tenant had extended the partition with wooden two-by-fours and plywood, it was still essentially a sleeping alcove that people walked through, or a bed in a passageway. Looking for a more secluded spot to change, Alice walked through her bedroom to the closet passageway leading to Charlotte's room. The music pouring through Charlotte's closed door seemed to offer a sufficient impression of privacy for changing purposes—Alice wanted to be as far out of earshot of what was going on in the living room as possible. But the sound of us laughing it up in Charlotte's room next door wrecked that illusion.

I had the chance to read the raw interview Alice gave about the events of that night and it was pretty affecting. She was completely in the grip of that horrible emotional single-mindedness when the pain seems to be within each cell of our bodies and nothing anyone says or does can lessen it. There are short-term and long-term healing processes. When we're rejected romantically, a typical strategy is to find another person on whom to project our romantic hopes and desires, even if we know that really nothing is likely to happen, or perhaps should happen, in that direction. But even that avenue was closed off to Alice as, under her nose, Charlotte and I quite ferociously "paired off." Perhaps if she had been less sunk in despair and withdrawn on the walk to Rex's, she and I would have talked and everything could have ended very, very differently. But events conspired against us, and the conscious author (she was sufficiently feminist to reject the word "authoress") of that series of events was Charlotte Pingree.

While slipping out of the tight pants she had worn that night, Alice retreated from the sound of Charlotte's and my giggling to return to the middle of her own room. Earlier that day, in happier times, she had propped a snapshot from the party Labor Day weekend in Sag Harbor up on the bookcase next to her bed. In the image, Alice, Tom, and I— standing by the grill behind Kate Preston's house—look toward the camera, smiling inanely (which was actually the indicated smile for occasions of that kind). It looked like the sort of happy, perfect moment you always wish you had a photo of and rarely do. But noticing it now, Alice abruptly turned it facedown and put a book over it.

Next, the living-room light, already dim, was switched off.

As much as she might have wished to have them entirely blocked out, Alice couldn't avoid hearing Dan and Holly's whispering, snuggling, cuddling, and smooching. At one point Dan knocked over his empty beer bottle, which rolled across the bare floor, making quite a racket and provoking a giggling fit from Holly which she did not at all try to muffle; it just went on and on. (I guess it should be admitted that, at times, Holly did act like a bit of a moron.)

In principle, to get to the bathroom to brush her teeth and complete her ablutions, two routes were available to Alice. She could open the closed door to Charlotte's room, where Charlotte and I had at least temporarily grown quiet (doing, from her point of view, who knows what), and tiptoe through to the kitchen to reach the bathroom. Or she could walk back through the living room, go out the door to the exterior hallway, walk down it, and—with her keys—open the exterior entrance to the kitchen to reach the bathroom at its far end. She chose the latter route.

Bathrobe on, keys and bathroom kit in hand, scuffling loudly to warn them of her approach, Alice cautiously entered the semi-darkened living room. Only some light from the street filtered through the windows. She tried to keep her look strictly ahead to respect their privacy, but this turned out not to be necessary.

"Alice," Dan's voice came out of the dark, "what would your dream book to publish be, if you could publish any book?"

Alice stopped and thought. "Anything that might become a bestseller," she said.

"Aside from that," Dan persisted, as if they were having

some chat over coffee at Currier, Harvard's dating library. "Your dream book?"

Alice thought again. "I'd say—a collection of new J. D. Salinger stories, but in the direction of 'The Laughing Man' or 'Raise High the Roof Beam, Carpenters,' not 'Hapworth 16' or 'Seymour: An Introduction.' "

"Huhn . . ." Dan responded. "Did you know that, in his own day, Mary McCarthy and Alfred Kazin wrote devastating pieces on Salinger?"

"No."

"Yeah, they really destroyed him . . ."

Alice left for the exterior hallway, shaking her head in extreme irritation. After shuffling down the grubby exterior hallway in her floppy slippers, she fortunately had an easier time with the lock of the kitchen entrance. Once in, she let the door swing shut, but Charlotte and I frankly never heard it. According to the movie, Alice paused in the kitchen to cast a look of hatred in the direction of Charlotte's door, from which our voices and laughing could again be heard over the music, now a sexy sixties bossa nova from Brazil. Charlotte knew just the right music to put on in such situations.

Alice shuffled to the bathroom and closed its door, with one last pathetic look in the door's direction just as I laughed at the conclusion of some joke.

Alice lay in bed wrapped in covers, on her side, facing the wall, with her eyes wide open. A shaft of light entered the room from the uncurtained windows. The music had long since stopped. By then it must have been well past four in the morning—more than an hour after what Fitzgerald called "3 a.m. in the dark night of the soul."

A nearby door could be heard closing, followed by a man's footsteps in the hallway and on the stairs; then the more distant sound of the door to the street slamming shut behind him. Then footsteps on the street outside.

Alice could hear Holly whispering to Dan in the living room. "I'm sure it was him. It's very quiet . . ."

"Why don't we go the outside way, like Alice did?"

"No, I'm sure it was Jimmy. It's very quiet."

From the living room, Holly and Dan apparently couldn't hear everything Alice could—the rhythmic squeaking of bedsprings and low sighs coming from Charlotte's room.

Alice now heard the approaching steps of stockinged feet.

"Don't worry," Holly whispered to Dan. "It's okay."

Holly peeked around the corner. Alice remained completely still—the last thing she wanted was for them to know she was still awake. Holly nodded the all-clear to Dan behind her. Their shadowy forms—both in a state of some *déshabille*—scurried tiptoeing through Alice's room and the closet passageway, the floor creaking in several places, before quietly opening the door to Charlotte's.

Suddenly a weird and terrible shriek, like that of a stricken animal, shattered the quiet of the night.

"Get out!! Get out!!" a woman's voice screeched.

Later Charlotte said that the fact that they had entered at that particular moment was excruciatingly embarrassing for her. I had not left, as Holly had thought—far from it. There are few more embarrassing experiences in life than to be caught in precisely that situation.

The astonished forms of Holly and Dan scurried back through to the living room beyond, tiptoeing as if there were someone still in the apartment they were concerned about not disturbing.

Alice closed her eyes and pushed her face into the pillow. From the next room the rhythmic bedspring sound resumed.

Running water splashing into the bathroom sink mixed with blue toothpaste and swirled down the drain. It was morning. Alice looked in the mirror while finishing brushing her teeth. She rinsed two final times, then turned off the water and dried her face on a towel.

Wearing sweatpants and a T-shirt, she stepped out of the bathroom and sat on a kitchen chair to tie her sneakers. Though it was a sunny Sunday morning, for Alice the day already had a forlorn quality: a stupid TV show played loudly in the apartment next door and from outside came the voices of children calling to each other in whining tones; besides which, she felt a little strange physically, maybe something akin to hungover, though she hadn't really drunk that much.

Upon getting up she had cleaned all the dishes, pots and pans, and kitchen mess left from dinner the night before, admittedly a little resentful of her two roommates sleeping late after their nights of *amour*. Now, besides the unpacking and apartment-arranging she still had left to do—the prospect of which was not very encouraging in view of the rooming situation—she had promised to read and write reports on two manuscripts for different editors as well as those she'd rescued from the slush pile on her own initiative. Normally she would have looked somewhat forward to that, but tasks that are almost joyous when conditions are right become "impossible burdens" when the joy goes out of life.

Abruptly Charlotte opened her bedroom door, looking a little the worse for wear in her wrinkled sleeping clothes and acting oddly aggressive.

"What's the matter now?" she asked, her expression pained. (During the night Charlotte and I had slept little. She had found it hard to calm down after the walk-in but finally got some sleep after I slipped out around dawn.)

"What?" Alice asked, completely surprised.

"All the noise: clomping around, banging pans—"

"Sorry—I didn't realize it."

"You obviously intended it."

"What do you mean?"

"That's very aggressive. You don't clomp around banging pans for no reason."

"Like what reason?"

Charlotte crossed over toward the bathroom. "You know perfectly well . . ."

"Because I only bang pans?" Alice inquired.

Charlotte semi-gasped and put on a look of being flabbergasted, then recovered.

"Well, frankly, that's not what I heard," she said pointedly.

For a while they just looked at each other with something like hatred, while from the next apartment a Jordache jeans commercial played loudly. In those days, Jordache commercials (". . . *You've got the look that's right—Jordache, Jordache Jeans"*) saturated local commercial ad time—Channels 5, 9, 11, etc. It was pretty depressing.

Alice got up and went to the chair where her long wool overcoat lay folded over the back. She put it on over her jogging clothes—the look was a little incongruous—and headed out the door.

Charlotte scrambled to follow her. "Okay," she conceded. "Anything I did that was wrong, I apologize for.

"But," she added, addressing Alice's receding form with

increasing volume as Alice got farther down the stairs, "anything I did that was *not wrong*, I don't apologize for!"

Holly, in a bathrobe, popped her head out the doorway with a worried look. She hated disagreements of any kind, having lived through a parental divorce during her last months at Pine Manor.

Charlotte turned to go back inside. "God, Alice is such a Scorpio . . ."

She gave Holly a significant look, the exact meaning of which Holly, as with most things, could only guess.

Alice's objective was to jog around the bridle path in Central Park, near the Central Park reservoir. Just getting to the park took a lot longer than she anticipated but gave her time to think and make decisions. (In the movie the mood was set by the beautifully poignant Techniques' recording "Queen Majesty," their 1966 Jamaican version of the song Curtis Mayfield recorded earlier as "Minstrel & Queen.")

Jogging down Ninetieth Street in her incongruous overcoat, Alice passed the austere limestone walls of the Heavenly Rest Episcopal Church before starting across Fifth Avenue. In so doing, she almost stepped on a tiny terrier—I think it was a Yorkie—which immediately retaliated, snapping at her feet and barking excitedly.

"Sorry," she told the owner, though she hadn't hurt the dog at all, merely startled it, and continued on her way. The owner—a blond guy in his thirties, pleasant-looking and reasonably nicely dressed, someone whom in other circumstances she might conceivably have dated—shouted an obnoxious, complaining comment at her as if she were some kind of hit-

and-run driver. The anger, self-righteousness, and dispropor-
tionality of it were stunning. That kind of behavior—making
obnoxious, complaining, often very aggressive comments to
strangers, ruining their quiet enjoyment of the city and
invading what little privacy it afforded—infuriated her. It was
so "New York." It had already happened to her a couple of
times before. And what was more disturbing, she often felt on
the verge of saying things like that herself.

Fifth Avenue had little traffic at this hour on Sunday. Alice
jogged partway into the street before stopping, even then not
really focusing on the beat-up station wagon barreling down
the avenue a block away. Instead of rushing to cross ahead of
it, Alice just stood as if in some kind of daze, watching the
car's approach. For a few seconds it looked like some weird
subconscious death wish. Then she snapped out of it, dashing
across the avenue ahead of the car, reaching the other side just
as it shot past.

Immediately after, Alice came to the park "loop" road and
carefully waited for the light to turn green before crossing—
"on the green, not in between," as the traffic safety slogan
had it. The Ninetieth Street entrance was the big uptown
mouth to the park—non–New Yorkers might recall it as the
entrance nearest Frank Lloyd Wright's exotic concrete snail-
shell design for the Solomon R. Guggenheim Museum.

Once across the park road, Alice turned right to jog along
the broad tree-lined bridle path that was one of Central
Park's glories, respecting the counterclockwise direction the
runners had established. She had already made some decisions and resolutions. She did not want to play the part of a
victim, but in avoiding that, she did not want to turn into a
de facto victimizer either—as so many did. The horribleness

of the situation with Charlotte would be easy to exaggerate. Now that she knew what to expect, she felt little further harm could be done. In her heart, she had never really trusted her, though an undeniable comradeship had grown up since the bad old days at school and would often reassert itself.

There is an image of everyone graduating from college and then congregating in the big city en masse, surrounded by friends and acquaintances of long standing, but that, in fact, is not the way it usually is. After a few years, such a mass of friends and acquaintances might so congregate, shortly before starting to disperse to marry or relocate elsewhere, but that's not often the case to start. None of Alice's real friends, nor even the acquaintances she most liked, had come to the city with her. They had either not yet graduated, gone straight to graduate school, won fellowships, or found other opportunities to study in Europe; one, Kate Dryer, semi-radicalized by her elder sister, had gone to Latin America to stir up what trouble she could; others went to Los Angles or even Washington—Manhattan was no longer everyone's Mecca. Even the New Yorkers she knew were elsewhere this year.

In the circumstances, with her and Charlotte heading from the same college to Edward Riley Publishers' prestigious training program together, it was logical, almost inevitable, that they would end up rooming together. Intrinsically, neither the apartment nor the neighborhood was so bad. From what she had heard and, briefly, seen, it could have been much, much worse. But the rooming arrangement, sandwiched between two individuals with whom she felt little affinity, both dating guys she knew, one snatched out of her own romantic reveries (not conceit on my part—it was acknowledged; more like stupidity), discouraged her greatly.

Originally it was the lack of hallways she had most minded; now she would add another—the lack of doors. Except for Charlotte's room and the bathroom, there were none. If she were living alone, or with just one roommate, such as Holly, this would not have posed much of a problem. It was the prospect of no privacy combined with the likely constant presence of Charlotte and various boyfriends such as Dan and me that discouraged her so. But she resolved not to let it.

Instead, her decision was this: to make the apartment a stronghold where she could advance the only aspect of her life she had much control over—her work, and not the highly pleasant but basically insignificant work of editorial "secretary" (in her case as a normally *over*-appreciated, only occasionally disgraced office slave of a quite kind Senior Editor), but the more important job the company did not pay or even expressly ask her to do, only allowed and encouraged. She was going to make herself an "editor" in her free time and the apartment her base. Every plausible manuscript she could lay her hands on she would read and, whatever was of value, appreciate, unless the first twelve pages were so hopeless going further would be mere self-indulgence. The company had its democratic aspect: any manuscript she could get an editor to co-sponsor, she herself could then "bring up"—or propose for publication—at the regular Wednesday editorial meeting.

These resolves were bolstered or perhaps triggered by the serotonins, endorphins, and whatever other advantageous naturally occurring biochemicals that steady, rigorous aerobic exercise such as long-distance jogging (First Avenue to Central Park and onto the bridle path) stimulated the body and/or brain to produce (an effect I believe vigorous disco dancing can also achieve, especially when combined with an effective program of Dewar's Scotch).

Her thoughts were interrupted by the rapidly approaching growls and yaps of a small, quickly running dog.

"Rufus. Ru-fus! Here, boy!" the young dog owner called from where he jogged twenty yards behind.

Rufus did not obey. The man was evidently one of those dog enthusiasts who pride themselves on unleashing their pets at every opportunity, on the premise that they have trained the dogs so well leashes are not necessary for obedience—which in this instance turned out not to be the case.

"Ru-fus!"

Rufus had reached Alice and was nipping and growling at her feet fearsomely, for his size. Alice did a little dance, trying to shake him, but Rufus-boy did not know when to halt, nor did his master know how to control him. Alice lengthened her stride, but Rufus kept up, finally baring his tiny terrier fangs and lunging at her sneakers. After one long stride Alice kicked back her leg and caught Rufus mid-lunge for a smart *thwack* in the chops. Little-dog yelps and whimpering followed as he scampered back to his obnoxious master.

"Never do that!" the man called. "How dare you!"

He bent down, comforting the dog. "Aw, poor boy. She hurt you?"

Rufus continued to moan and whimper but, as his master checked his muzzle, appeared uninjured by Alice's love tap.

"Aw, poor Rufus," he went on, then turned back toward Alice, calling after her at the top of his voice: "Bitch!"

Alice jogged onward, a determined, somewhat grim set to her features.

Over the subsequent weeks things arranged themselves in such a way that Alice and Charlotte interacted less and less, and then more at the office than at home, where Alice had retreated into her makeshift privacy. Partly it had to do with Charlotte and me continuing to go out a lot, sometimes to my place and often to the Club, to which Alice had ceased going entirely. (I still had the problem of not being able to bring clients in the front way, but Des promised he could soon get me back on the list, which would be a big relief. The situation at the agency was not good. A trendy creative "shop" called Ad Nauseam—famous for its bad-boy creative types—had been acquired by the same British multinational that owned us, and now the two agencies were to be melded into a single frightening unit. So far, the bad-boy loudmouth egomaniacs always seemed to come out on top. I had been relegated to doing a series of venereal disease–related "Public Service Announcements," make-work for the agency. Anything else I could do to be "useful" to the agency's new powers that be seemed highly indicated. The positive situation with Charlotte helped to compensate for, and distract from, the tense situation at work. In fact, during this period Alice and I were on opposite tracks—she seeking sanctuary in work while I sought it in decadent social life.)

Coinciding in the Xerox room was a typical occasion for interaction between Alice and Charlotte. One afternoon several weeks later Alice was at the copying machine duplicating a set of readers' reports for her first book proposal when Charlotte came by to pick up the Title Information sheets ("TIs") she had just had duplicated. Charlotte liked to leave copying behind to be done by the stockroom staff she was very friendly with, while Alice preferred to do it herself, unless the job was very big.

"I've decided to go ahead with the Tungsten Odzal book proposal," Alice said.

"Who?"

"The Tibet book."

"Oh."

Alice placed another report on the glass and closed the machine's lid, prior to pressing the copy button.

"I'd like to bring it up at Wednesday's editorial meeting," she said.

"You really liked that?"

Alice nodded.

"Other people liked it, too?"

Alice opened the lid and handed Charlotte the set of reports, the top one of which Charlotte started reading intently.

"David said the account of the Dalai Lama's escape from Lhasa was one of the most exciting things he's ever read."

Charlotte looked up from the report. "Escape from where?"

"From Lhasa."

Charlotte drew a blank. "*Lhasa?*" she said unfamiliarly. "I'm not sure I got to that part."

She looked down at the reports again. "Is mine here?"

"Yeah."

Charlotte found her report and pulled it from the pile, handing the others back to Alice.

"Okay," she said, "I'll take another look . . . You know, it's considered self-indulgent to read too much of a manuscript if it doesn't seem to be going anywhere."

␣␣*␣*␣*

Favorite jaunts to break up the daily editorial workday at Riley Publishers were to the canteen for beverages and snacks, or outside to the nearby Chock Full O'Nuts lunch counter on Madison Avenue for coffee or, at lunchtime, its "nutted cheese" sandwiches. In those days Chock Full O'Nuts also had soups, a hot meal in a cup, priced at an incredible 43 cents—a sort of Publishers' Row editorial-secretary special. Another popular destination was the manuscript room, but that had the disadvantage of requiring work beforehand (reading and reporting on a manuscript). The best available jaunt not involving food was to the art department on the spacious twenty-second floor. A typical errand would be to pick up new book jackets—often the editor or the author would express an interest in seeing them and it was an easy task to pick up a few to please them. Art departments always seemed to get the best real estate at such companies, with good views, etc., or perhaps it was just that their open-plan layouts made them seem that way. At Riley Publishers it was in the art department that you got the most spectacular midtown-skyscraper feeling.

Alice and Dan coincided at the counter where sets of the flat newly printed book jackets were stacked. As she looked at those for the books she worked on, Alice let a sigh of disappointment escape. Dan took a look and nodded, too. Most of the jacket designs were drab and unaesthetic, part of a larger problem at the company—never going the extra distance to make things right—that, Alice felt, ultimately sank it. Already having a reputation as too critical, she rarely said anything. That was a little bit the atmosphere at Riley in those days: if you didn't say how wonderful everything was, you were considered a pain in the neck and faintly ostracized.

She and Dan picked up the samples for their or their editors' new books—most were still without the last "varnish" coating that would make them shiny and seemingly more resilient—and walked back down the corridor toward the elevator bank.

"Have you—uh—known Holly long?" Dan asked.

"Just since we found the apartment. Why?"

"She's very—uh—quiet, isn't she?"

Alice thought a moment. "I would say, not more than normal."

"But your standard of normal could be different from other people's?"

"How do you mean?" she asked.

Dan made a face, signifying who-knows-what.

"I don't understand that," Alice said.

"I guess what I'm asking is—"

"You do like Holly, don't you?"

"Yeah, of course . . . But . . . she is intelligent, isn't she?"

"Well . . ." Alice left him hanging. "Sometimes I question her dating judgment."

"God, you're tough."

"I'm not tough in the least."

They had reached the elevator bank. Alice pressed the Down button. For a moment both waited silently; then there was a soft *ding* and a down arrow lit by one elevator door, which they approached.

"No," Dan said, "you're really tough."

14

The Decade of Envy

In retrospect those were magical months—the first socially great ones of adulthood. It's surprising how many people seem to judge decades based on who was President. But does the nature of a whole country really depend on who holds national office? Every time a governor is elected, does the heart and soul of that state change?

Elections were taken gravely during this period, as if civil war threatened, with large numbers of people vowing to leave the country if the opposing candidate won ("If he wins, I'm going to leave the country"), but rarely if ever, so far as I know, actually doing so. Months later you would still see them around, conducting their lives just as before, nothing seemingly different. It reminded me of going as a child to Princeton football games with my father and of the terrible emotions unleashed if Princeton lost, the angry shouts of "Wait till next year!" while everyone stumbled around drunk in the dark.

Were the 1980s really the Decade of Greed? There were stories of some people making lots of money, but did that make them or all of us a lot more greedy? Is resenting the success of others a reaction that people of goodwill should have? As Des would say, isn't prosperity—even if it's other people's—a good, not a bad thing? Certainly during the eighties there were cases of behavior that looked "grasping" to an antisocial degree, but was this so widespread—was it in all our hearts—that the whole decade deserves that obloquy?

Perhaps the notable feature of the decade was not that some people made money but that so many others were so bent out of shape by that. If some yuppie got a bonus, what was that to us? Rather than the Decade of Greed, wasn't it really the Decade of Envy? Or the Decade of Envy, Jealousy, and other resentments there was no reason for those afflicted to sound so proud about?

Subjectively, far from being a Decade of Greed, the early 1980s were years of hard work and maximum productivity, better in my opinion than any period that has come since. For me and a lot of other people, the eighties were the young-adult Wonder Years, when autonomy came to the fore and we could finally do the things we were in uncomfortable preparation for all the years before that. At that precise moment, my situation at the agency was, admittedly, not so good, but I felt I had done good work in the past and hoped to again one day.

In any case, how much do those Wider Trends so beloved of newsmagazines really affect our daily lives? Factors much closer and objectively more important than national trends or politics, such as how badly we are treated at the ad agency where we work, can be negative, while we nevertheless continue to enjoy life, just as sometimes, though everything is objectively wonderful, we descend into funks of the most terrible cast. The truth is that we have a lot of leeway about which aspects of our lives we decide to consider important, and that we can shift our thinking based on what bears thinking about. A lot comes down to the biochemistry of our bodies—not the biochemistry that goes into the external medicines people take (also an area of great activity in the 1980s) but the natural, internal biochemistry that can put us in fine fettle or a total funk with little regard to external factors, hence the obsession with "aerobic" exercise during the period: all the good-feeling chemicals the body releases in response to it. A case could be made, Des said, to consider exercise fanatics "healthy" drug addicts, dependent on all those sweat-related body chemicals. Alice said she often experienced such an effect while jogging and that it was in a sense the reward.

Sorry for going on at length about all this, but it's not as if we have *so many* decades available to us that we can afford to go around trashing them for no very good reason. As one gets on in years, the realization begins to dawn that there is actually a bit of a *decade scarcity* in life.

All this was by way of prologue and apologia for a brief description of the great situation I found myself in that fall and winter. Through no effort of my own, which was part of the charm, I had fallen into a combined living situation with Alice and Charlotte that was as close to the ideal as any I had experienced up to that time. When she was not creating a scandal of some kind, Charlotte was actually a lot of fun and very interesting, as well as beautiful and tremendously extroverted.

But although I was officially "living" with Charlotte, because of the apartment layout and a natural affinity that grew up between us, I also saw Alice *a lot*. She had sort of set up office in the apartment and worked there after hours, bringing home lots of reading. On evenings when Holly and Charlotte were going out, Alice would take over the kitchen table and read manuscript after manuscript over tea or, later in the evening, whiskey sours, then use the Olympia manual typewriter she had brought from Hampshire to write up the reports. After rescuing the Tibet book from the reject bin, she started doing a lot of the related research at home at night—books on Tibet and Tibetan Buddhism that would have to be mentioned in her report for the editorial meeting.

Often, after getting back from work or while I was waiting for Charlotte to get ready to go out, or just while doing chores in the kitchen, Alice and I would talk over the day's events. From my side at least, the feelings of mutual comprehension and understanding were overwhelming. Alice sympathetically followed my accounts of the twists and turns of agency politics as those of us from the Old Regime were marginalized and hung out to dry, while the pretentious filmmaker types and creative bad-boys took over. Over time, a great friendship developed between us, underlined by a growing romantic interest. That it was completely impossible and out of the question relieved any feelings of guilt about inconstancy to Charlotte.

Des asked about Alice often, which I found surprising—usually his romantic preoccupations were not especially long-lasting. To extract information, his approach was quite oblique, which I usually fell for. One night we were coming back from the deejay booth when he spotted a patch of vomit that had not yet been cleaned up near a balcony banquette. While looking for someone who could take care of it, Des asked me how things were going with Charlotte and I opened up—far too much, as it turned out.

"It's the first time I've had a relationship of this kind—really living with someone. It's different and really, well, very pleasant."

"Didn't you and Laurie live together in Cambridge?" he asked.

"Well, I wouldn't call that 'living together.' We were still in college—it was more a 'liaison.' There was no stove or refrigerator."

"Okay," he said. "Fair enough."

"The odd thing is, I can't remember ever really deciding to go out with Charlotte." I glanced at Des; he was listening but signaling a busboy to get a mop. "Usually you're obsessed or very interested in some girl and finally manage to go out with her, and then get her to like you. There's a lot of back-and-forth, an emotional seesaw, lots of strategizing and nail-biting. But with Charlotte, it all just happened naturally. Maybe this is the way things should happen and the other way a mistake, dooming things from the start."

"Huhn," Des said. "And in a railroad apartment, too. Phew . . . tough."

It was well known that Des had a phobia of some kind related to railroad apartments and even a rule—later broken—never to date a girl who lived in one.

"How's . . . uh . . . Alice? She hasn't been around at all."

"I think I was wrong about her."

"Yeah."

"I thought she was irritating. I guess she just doesn't make a good first impression."

"She made a good first impression on me," Des said.
"Maybe you're just kind of obtuse."

"I've thought of that . . . Yeah. I think what happened
was that I interpreted what she said as cynical or sardonic
when she was just being *honest* . . . Actually, she did make a
good *first* impression—that was at Sag Harbor. It was the *second* impression that wasn't so good. In any case, now it's
completely different. We're pretty close; we talk a lot. She's
almost always at the apartment. Alice never goes out on
dates—"

"Alice never goes on dates?"

I shook my head. "Maybe she's a little judgmental and
critical, but you want that: you don't want to spend your life
with people with no judgment or criteria whatsoever.
There's enough of that at work."

"Why doesn't Alice go out on dates?"

"I don't know. Maybe no one's asked her. Also, she could
be one of those great people doomed to be alone all their
lives, through no real fault of their own. These patterns, once
they get started, are hard to change."

"What nonsense!" Des said. "I mean, I can't believe that.
You look at Alice, and all her qualities—"

While he said this, Des looked at the palm of his hand, for
some reason.

"—and you have to say that this person is extraordinarily
well prepared for a happy and productive life—though probably not in the company of any of us."

At Riley Publishers the Wednesday Editorial Meetings
brought together a large group from various departments,
though mostly editorial. Representatives from the business side

joined the editors around the conference table, while more junior staff such as Charlotte sat along the wall. Normally only one secretary or assistant—the individual designated to take that week's meeting notes—sat at the conference table, but this week Alice was positioned there, too.

Carol, the department's Editorial Director, a very bright woman of middle years, ran the meeting benignly from the head of the table. Alice admired her "extravagantly," and one of the good parts about her experience at Riley had been her happiness working in a department run by someone she respected. This did not make her any less nervous when Carol finally called upon her to present her first book proposal to the Meeting.

In fact, Alice did begin speaking too quickly and inaudibly before finding her meeting "voice."

"The elder brother of the Dalai Lama of Tibet has written a memoir of their childhood and youth," she explained, with the focus on their "escape from Lhasa during the early years of the Chinese occupation . . ." She recounted the whole dramatic story and then went on to mention sales estimates from the relevant departments and all the other information apparently required in a book presentation of that kind.

"So far," she concluded, "I've had seven reader's reports: one mixed, one negative, and five positive."

"Good goin', Alice," Bob, the nice-guy publisher, threw in as encouragement. "Nice work."

Bob was sort of the Alan Alda kind-boss figure at the company and, though Alice never was quite sure what he really did, he was probably partly responsible for the good atmosphere at Riley Publishers.

Carol looked down at her paperwork—a photocopied

Meeting Agenda setting out all the relevant information, sales histories, and projections—before calling, as she usually did, on the young editor to her right for comment.

"David?" she asked.

"It's good," he said. "The story of the Dalai Lama's escape from Lhasa is very exciting. He actually wouldn't go until an 'oracle' told him to. It's all a little weird, but I suppose if at age three you were told *you* were God, you'd be a little weird, too . . ."

"Thanks, David," Carol said.

"Good, Alice," Bob added.

Carol turned to Andrea, an attractively dressy woman of fifty-two. "Andrea, what about the clubs?" she asked—referring to the company's affiliated book clubs.

"Well." Andrea hesitated, reluctant to dampen enthusiasm for Alice's project but having to represent the best interests of her division. "Asia, Communist oppression, celibate monks—they don't exactly scream sales. If the Chinese were to *evacuate* Tibet so the Dalai Lama could *return in triumph*, that would be different, but they haven't, so the book ends on quite a . . . *down note*. I'd have to say, probably not for the Guild."

Carol looked down the table toward Frank, the well-dressed subsidiary rights head. His arms and legs, draped in Savile Row fabric, were crossed: the body language could not have been clearer.

"I'm sorry," he said. "I don't think Tibet is commercial."

Betsy was next. She supported the project, but focused on the aspects relating to sibling birth order, a subject she was actually developing a book on. "Oldest children tend to be the focus of their parents' aspirations, the highest achievers, often at some cost. The youngest are petted and spoiled, the family favorite or 'baby,' self-absorbed and conceited. Middle children are the responsible, self-effacing 'good citizens,' dedicated to the well-being of others but often, frankly, with serious drinking problems." Her feelings on the subject seemed unusually strong. It was no secret in the world of book publishing that the autobiographical concerns and preoccupations of book editors often played a very large role in the projects selected.

"What if the despised younger sibling turns out to be not just the family pet but the reincarnation of God?" Betsy asked. "The birth-order issues raised could hardly be more dramatic." Looking down at the conclusion of her report, she read: "It's a fascinating story, and Tungsten Odzal tells it well."

Carol next called on Dan.

"Thank you," he began. Dan was not a spontaneous, ad-lib talker, as some with college theatrical training such as David might have been. What he said was prepared and perhaps rehearsed, but did not make less impact on those gathered in the conference room.

"Tibet's a small, almost comically backward country which—despite its current vogue—is in itself of virtually no importance whatsoever," he started.

No one was offended, as Dan's role as the truth-telling contrarian was understood and well tolerated in the affable confines of Riley Publishers. He also had a quality of personal likability that ameliorated the inevitable obnoxiousness of his behavior and comments. (Alice had to be more careful about making critical remarks as what she said tended to be taken more to heart. Dan, as a political "character," had more leeway.)

"That Tibet was occupied by the PLA and there were the inevitable massacres and terrible incidents might be true, but it is not terribly interesting," he said. "Many countries have suffered similarly but, as we know, that doesn't mean there's a book in it.

"I see its real subject as Tibetan Buddhism, which, if you look into it, I think you'll find is not only thoroughly reactionary but . . . quite silly."

Alice had been led to believe that Dan was going to *support* the book and was stunned by his negativity—she saw her proposal going down in flames. It certainly got everyone's attention. Meetings at Riley were normally dull affairs, with little conflict. The main drama usually involved editors who wasted the Meeting's time talking indiscriminately about a lot of projects unlikely to see the light of day; this was called, dismissively, "opening your mail at the Meeting." At any time there were normally one or two editors in such a state of advanced dysfunctionality. When they were finally replaced or moved on, there always seemed to be some other, formerly competent editor who would metamorphose into a bowl of jelly to take their place. Rarely was there as much conflict in an entire meeting as Dan seemed to find within himself in a single paragraph.

". . . which is partly why I think it's so important we publish this book," he concluded unexpectedly. "It's about as eloquent an explanation of Eastern religious thought and Buddhist mumbo-jumbo as we're ever likely to get. Time and again we've seen the public's hunger for undemanding religioso pap of this kind. If we don't occasionally publish titles like this one, we'll never be able to publish those we really want."

Coming out of the editorial meeting, Alice was warmly congratulated all around. "Good goin', Alice" . . . "Your first book" . . . "Great," etc.

Zenia was especially enthusiastic: "Eet could be a best-seller."

That someone so recently out of the training program would already be proposing a book at the meeting, let alone having it approved, seemed unprecedented—at least in the company's modern, more bureaucratic era. These were the Envious Eighties, when premature success was often the source of fierce resentment, but Alice managed to dodge that. She and David, from an earlier training program, were the "company pets," but so basically likable and helpful in their attitude to others—with readings and reports or whatever was asked—that their apparent fast-track progress went unbegrudged even by those contemporaries who might have felt entitled to begrudge it. When at the start of her time there Alice had seen some of her comments questioning company policy taken as personal criticisms by those involved, she had quickly backed off and learned how to present them less offensively or just shut up completely and find another way around the problem.

"Smart, cheerful, and hardworking"—qualities which Alice exemplified—were in fact those most valued by the late Edward Riley, the company's dynamic founder and namesake, whose career partly overlapped those of the other giants of American publishing—the great F. N. ("Effendi") Doubleday, the older Charles Scribner, Alfred Knopf, and in later years Cass Canfield and Bennett Cerf, Random House's wry chief. When Edward Riley, who was unmarried and childless, died unexpectedly, control of the company passed to his nephews, who—though less talented and dedicated—at least kept the company going and autonomous, which was emphatically not the case with all of Riley's historic competitors, many of which were submerged in the frantic merger waves of the 1960s and after.

Charlotte was also attracting favorable notice within the company. In the corridor as they were leaving the meeting, one of the editors, Betsy, still moved by something Charlotte had said during it, approached her.

"Uh, Charlotte," she called. Charlotte turned to her.

"That was so moving," Betsy said, "what you said about our obligation to writers—"

"Thanks."

"—and how often we fall short of that."

"I don't know, though," Charlotte said. "Let's face it: most authors are still conceited dopes."

"You can't say that!" Betsy said in a quit-teasing tone.

"Well, you're an editor—you don't have to deal with them on a daily basis. When you're an assistant, it's harder to dodge their calls."

The affable publisher, finishing up a chat with Dan on an unrelated matter, stopped in the hallway to congratulate Alice, too.

"Good goin', Alice. I'm really glad we got this book." Bob spoke enthusiastically. "By the way, I've heard you know people at the Club. Do you think you could get us in some night?"

"Yes. Certainly," Charlotte, overhearing, put in. "We'll arrange that."

"Great," he said, "thanks," and with Betsy turned to go back down the corridor where the higher-ranking staff had their offices.

Meanwhile, Dan edged by Alice and Charlotte, en route
to the bay.

"Thanks a lot, Dan," Alice said.

Dan smiled and nodded but, sensing the situation, decided
not to stop.

Once he had gone, Charlotte pounced on Alice, her tone
not at all congratulatory.

"Do you have any idea why Jimmy's suddenly so interested in your social life?" she asked.

"No . . . He's interested in my social life?"

"Haven't you noticed? Jimmy's always wondering why
you don't go out or go to the Club."

"He is?" Alice asked, very surprised.

"You know, Alice, you've been hanging around the apartment a lot. You've sort of set up office there. None of the rest
of us has any privacy."

"How can you say that?" Alice said. "The railroad apartment wasn't my idea."

"That's true. But it's odd you're *so* much friendlier to
Jimmy now he's with me . . . I just think the situation's kind
of awkward."

For a moment they just looked at each other in silence.

"What do you want me to do?" Alice finally said.
"Promise not to talk with him anymore?"

"Would you?" Charlotte first asked, as if relieved. Then
she said, "No—but I'm sure you know perfectly well how to
subtly get a guy to cool it, if you really wanted to."

15

The Tortoise and the Hare: A Fluke

I had resolved to push Des as hard as I could to resolve my situation with Van and Berrie. Since Des's rehiring I was tolerated inside the Club but needed to get back into Van's good graces to be able to get clients in. Nearly everyone from the agency's Old Regime had either already gone or was on the way out and I knew my continued employment could not be justified under the general rubric "nightlife ambassador" much longer. I was also a little keyed up as Charlotte said Alice would be making her reappearance at the Club that night.

Pounding on the steel door at the back, I jumped in place and flapped my arms, trying to keep warm, while waiting for someone to respond. When the usual back doorman—I knew him as "Shad"—finally opened up, his only greeting was a shrug and: "Oh. You."

Great. "Oh. You." What a punk. I hated the smugness and "cool" that since the sixties had come to infect nearly everything trendy and overly popular. What had happened to the old idea of gracious hospitality and deferential service—not to mention the Golden Rule? "Oh. You." Sometimes it seemed as if the world had turned into an enormous junior high school, and not a very friendly one.

Walking down the back corridor, I couldn't help thinking how sadly our nightlife culture had deteriorated since the glory days of El Morocco, the Stork Club—on some nights the likes of J. D. Salinger, Gloria Vanderbilt, and Oona O'Neill could have been spotted there—and other truly great nightclubs of the past. Maybe the early eighties were tremendously better socially than the early seventies, but maybe that's setting the bar pretty low. *Excuse me* if this contradicts anything I argued earlier about not maligning decades!

The door to Des's office was open and the lights on. I entered and sat on a beat-up metal chair near his desk. A lit cigarette burned in the ashtray, suggesting he had not gone far.

His office was a small, nothing room improved with a few "homey" touches—shade lamps, a poster by a French cartoonist showing a funny beach scene at St. Tropez, a black-and-white line portrait of the poet Alexander Pope, an old sofa for sacking out on, and a fairly good stereo Des used off-hours for checking out new record releases. A couplet from Pope's *Essay on Man*, among the many drilled into us in fifth-form English class, came to mind while I waited: "Hope springs eternal in the human breast: Man never Is, but always To be blest." Pope's wisdom and insight I admired. But I rejected the pessimism.

✳✳✳✳

Des came in looking preoccupied, then noticed me.

"Oh, damn," he said.

" 'Oh, damn'? Thanks."

Des went to the desk and emptied his pockets, mostly the plastic poker chips being used that night as the Club's free-drink chits as well as some wads of crushed Kleenex.

"You're here to see Van . . . ?"

I nodded. "You don't mind, do you?"

Des took a drag on the cigarette while making the kind of equivocating grimace supplicants in my position dread—I knew it well from the agency business.

"Well . . . I sort of do," he said. "I hate asking that guy for favors."

"They're not going to keep me on much longer if I can't get clients into the Club."

"It's that important to you to stay in advertising?" he asked, rather ludicrously.

I nodded emphatically.

"Okay." Des checked his watch. "We'd better see him while he's still on his . . . 'upswing.' "

He took a last pull on the cigarette, smashed it out, and gathered up a handful of drink chits.

As we walked down the back passageway, maybe sensing my down mood, Des offered me some of the chits.

"Thanks," I said. He was a contradictory guy, nice and not nice at the same time. Always doing favors, but at the same time complaining about it. Maybe part of it was that, inside the Club, our friendship was entirely unequal: Des was in a position to do endless favors for me; I, on the other hand, could do nothing for him. The idea that he was basically a good guy and a friend, despite the occasional gruffness or excessive candor, took hold of me as he was giving me the drink chits. That warm glow you get when you realize that, even if they are occasionally obliged to eject you, there is true friendship in this world and we are the beneficiaries of it. Often when drinking I get sentimental this way.

From the other end of the corridor, Shad appeared.

"Hey, Des," he called, and nodded toward a bedraggled figure emerging from the dim passage behind him. It was Josh Neff, looking really scuzzy, smudged with grime, one side of his ill-cut blond hair matted with dried blood.

"God. What happened to you?" Des asked.

"Hi," Josh said in a friendly way.

"Jeezus, Josh—you're a mess," I said.

"I'm a mess," he agreed.

Des nodded to Shad, who relaxed and headed back to his usual spot by the back door.

"I need an interview," Josh said.

"An *interview*?" Des asked.

"I've got to talk to you."

"Don't you want to clean up a little?"

"It's kind of serious."

"I'll look for Alice and Charlotte," I said, excusing myself. "See if they've come in."

As I went through the door leading to the main bar area, Des led Josh back toward his office.

"You don't want to clean up a little?" Des asked.

Josh shook his head no.

"You know, you look *really bad*."

"I know," Josh said as they got to Des's office. "That's actually good in my work. It puts people at ease. With me looking like this, they feel frankly superior and say things they ordinarily wouldn't."

Josh glanced down at his disgusting clothes. "It's very disarming," he said, settling into the overstuffed couch, careful not to dirty it.

"Phew," Des said, reacting to the smell. "What happened?"

"I was having drinks with some friends in the Village. There was this terrible guy really bothering a girl, so I decided to intervene—but it turns out they were married."

Des nodded.

"What's this now?" he asked. "You're not here on official business, are you?"

"Actually, I am . . . Knowing that we went to college together, they asked me to talk to you."

"Who is 'they'?"

"I . . ." Josh hesitated, ". . . can't tell you—"

"You can't tell me?"

"I couldn't believe you'd be involved in the kinds of things that've been going on here and told them so. I consider you a person of some integrity . . . except, you know, in your relations with women."

Young women in a low period or trough of their social lives and with apparently no prospects should not feel as alone and discouraged as they sometimes might be inclined to. They are probably being observed, thought about, and appreciated, even when they don't realize it. Not all their admirers are terribly direct.

That night I intercepted Alice and Charlotte as they came in the front way, before they got to the main bar area. Charlotte was one of Van's pets and never had any problems getting in; this had actually helped me, too. The chits Des had given me went to buy our drinks, though Alice only ordered a Coca-Cola. Charlotte noticed her atypical abstemiousness and looked puzzled. I assumed it was only part of Alice's spartan new work regime, though in fact she often had a nightcap when she worked at home.

Charlotte had once confided to me that she felt part of Alice's intense campaign at the publishing house was actually anger directed against herself. She felt that underneath the façade of somewhat bland "niceness," Alice was a classic, very controlling, passive-aggressive personality—though she said (for what it's worth) she did not mean this in a negative way and actually compared Alice's approach favorably with her own modus operandi, which she characterized as "hell-on-wheels" and considered far worse. With me Charlotte was always sweet, but I had witnessed her occasional ferocity and the rapprochements, also sincere, that would follow.

As we approached the platform, the occupants of one side of the nearest booth left for the dance floor. "Here's a booth," Alice said, moving for it. We didn't mind sharing booths at all—it was part of the convivial spirit within the Club—and were happy to grab the vacated seats.

Charlotte had her eyes on a group in a booth along the near wall.

"There's Audrey Rouget," she said, nodding in her direction. "She's the youngest person ever to be made an editor in the history of Farrar, Straus."

We all looked toward the booth. Audrey Rouget, whose story was told in an earlier movie by the same people who did the one on us, sat with an elegant Eurasian man, while another friend from earlier days, Nick Smith, sat with them, and an exotic, wild-haired young woman in a tight dress.

"How do you know her?" Alice asked.

"She interviewed me."

"How did it go?"

Charlotte thought a moment. While they were watching them, the group Audrey was in got up to dance.

"Have you ever been in an interview and gotten the impression that they see through you completely?" Charlotte asked.

Alice looked as if she understood.

"I didn't get an offer," Charlotte concluded.

They both looked toward Audrey and her friends as they joined the dance floor.

For me it was around this time that my enjoyment of the ambiguous living situation I was in stopped and the yearning for Alice started in (painful) earnest.

When Des emerged from the back later, he was accompanied by Josh, who had clearly spent considerable time in the backstage washroom. He was cleaned up, hair slicked back wet, and wearing the shirt from the harlequin costume. They both scanned the dance floor and found where we were dancing.

Alice had left Charlotte and me to ourselves, dancing slightly apart, stealing an occasional glance at Audrey Rouget, who moved gracefully to the music, elegant and self-possessed, someone who seemed to have life figured out and under control.

Josh edged boldly onto the dance floor to join Alice, who smiled at him either in welcome or just amused by his get-up. At this point they knew each other only slightly. Somewhat like Dan, Josh's awkwardness in real life disappeared on the dance floor. He danced surprisingly well, with slow movements which seemed more depressive than manic.

Des, who, it was well known, never danced because he felt it looked silly—and also because Berrie was already on his case for mingling too much with the clientele—took out a cigarette and smoked while observing the action.

We were all at the banquette farthest from the dance floor, along with Holly and Dan, who were also at the Club that night. Victor, one of Berrie's flunkies, huddled over the back of the banquette talking in low tones with Des.

"No, I'm sorry," Des told him. "I don't want to play that stuff."

"Okay. I'll tell him," Victor said, and took off.

Josh was then expounding his thesis that a lot of what passes for wisdom in literature is just the flattering of popular prejudice, and that this audience-sycophancy goes back to ancient times.

"If you examine fables closely—Aesop's, for instance— you'll notice there's often something a little contrived about them, a little dishonest," he said. "Take 'The Tortoise and the Hare.' Okay, the tortoise won *one* race. But do you think that hare is really going to lose any more races to *turtles*? *Not on your life*. By limiting the fable to an absurdly small frame— one race—a bogus lesson is learned, and then for centuries taught young people the world over."

"I liked that tortoise," Alice said.

Josh stopped, a little taken aback—saying anything that might annoy or irritate Alice was the last thing in his mind. On the other hand, he was not going to lie, even in a sensitive pre-dating situation. (I would have. Desirable women are normally full of strongly expressed opinions which you might disagree with but should hesitate to immediately contradict. There will be plenty of time for that later.)

"So do I," Josh replied to Alice's comment that she liked the tortoise. " 'Virtue rewarded' and all that. But if you were a betting person, would you say, 'That turtle won against the hare—in future races, I'm backing him'? No. It'd be absurd. That race was almost certainly a fluke. Afterward, the tortoise is still a *tortoise,* the hare still . . . a *hare.*"

Des gave Josh a hard look. He saw where the threat was coming from.

Behind them, a waitress came up and took drinks orders.

"A vodka-tonic," Holly requested.

"Domestic beer," Dan said. "A Bud."

"I'll just have a, uh, Coca-Cola—thanks," Alice said.

Charlotte looked at her curiously. "You're not drinking?"

Alice shook her head.

"Alice is not having a cocktail? I can't believe it," Charlotte said.

"Well . . . I'm not."

"What is it?" Charlotte persisted. "Do you have strep throat or some . . . flu you're taking antibiotics for?"

Alice, looking a little concerned, shook her head again. Suddenly Charlotte seemed to burst with excitement.

"Omigod . . . !" she exclaimed. "You've got the clap, don't you?! You're on antibiotics and the doctor told you not to drink or something?!" "Clap" was the slang term for the venereal disease gonorrhea.

We were stunned, embarrassed—except Charlotte, who acted thrilled and amused, as if it were a clever joke.

"That's why you haven't been drinking," she continued. "Usually there's no coming between Alice and a cocktail."

Alice could barely speak. "How . . . could—"

Alice stood up and, almost tripping over everyone's legs, bolted out of the banquette. Holly went after her. Josh stood up, too.

Charlotte misunderstood our shocked reaction as skepticism. "No, I'm sure I'm right: the bottle of tetracycline on her bureau top—tetracycline's specific for the clap."

"How could you say that?!" I asked, an incredulous whine in my voice.

"Oh, come on," Charlotte said. "Everyone gets something."

Alice ran up the main staircase, with Holly just behind her. Josh followed, but too late to see where they went. Searching the mezzanine for her, he went out onto the darkened balcony, picking his way through the shadows strewn with amorous couples and drug consumers. As he went by, some gay guys with their shirts off—a "look" popular in the Club then—gave him the twice-over. (To be honest, in my opinion, the dandy fashions of the good ol' repressed days made a better case for the gay lifestyle.) Josh found his way back to the lighted corridor, passing the Tiger Lady coming the other way with a younger man. She, too, turned to watch him. Until that night it never occurred to me how handsome Josh might be considered by women, not to mention other men. With his hair slicked back wet and the harlequin shirt, he too looked like he might have stepped out of a Visconti movie. Getting him to clean up, Des had done Josh a life-changing favor. It seemed like everyone was going through big, positive changes in that period, except me.

What Josh did not know but Charlotte instinctively did was that Alice would immediately seek refuge in the ladies' lounge. After staying behind justifying herself, she arrived just as Alice and Holly were heading out again.

"Alice," she said, intercepting them, "I'm so, so sorry! I should *never*'ve said that. I've . . . some sort of *sick compulsion* to say everything that occurs to me."

Alice, with Holly behind her, stopped and turned to her just before leaving the lounge area's foyer. "I just wanted to let you know that as soon as I can find another rooming situation, I'm moving out," she said, her voice controlled but on the verge of breaking. "I can't take it anymore. I'm sorry."

"That's not possible," Charlotte said.

Alice just looked at her, saying nothing.

"You're not serious," Charlotte repeated.

Alice nodded.

"Let me know when you're ready to go," Holly whispered to Alice supportively, darting a reproachful look at Charlotte before leaving.

"Please, Alice," Charlotte continued, a little distraught. "Rooming with you and Holly has been the most important thing to happen to me in my life. You're the first women friends I've ever had . . ."

Alice watched Charlotte intently, but did not give her the comfort of any particular reaction.

"The anger you're feeling now is actually more justified than you know. When we were at Hampshire"—Charlotte paused for a moment, then continued quite emotionally—"I really hated you. You seemed so moralistic . . . I had no idea how you really were. When guys wanted to ask you out, I talked them out of it. I can't believe how *evil* I was. But I've *completely* changed. If you'd give me another chance, I'll be the best friend you've ever had."

"If the apartment situation weren't so impossible, I'd move out now," Alice said, trying to sound resolute but with her voice on the verge of something weaker.

"I can understand how you'd feel that way," Charlotte said, a lot of emotion in her voice, too. "You're right to. But things aren't always as they seem. Bad and inexcusable as what I said back there might have been, I think you'll find that it'll actually *improve* your reputation with these guys enormously. You'll be more popular than ever. Watch. VD's not all bad. You'll find there're positive aspects to it."

"What?!" Alice asked, incredulous.

"You know that 'please inform all previous partners' thing? Well, it's actually a *terrific* way to get back in touch with guys you might've liked but've lost contact with. Just in my own experience it's twice led to renewed relationships that lasted quite a while and were really . . . sweet."

She paused and then continued more quickly: "I'm not talking about herpes infections, which are far more serious and apparently incurable—just standard VD and other conditions easily treatable with antibiotics."

Des came out of a stall in the men's lounge sniffling and futzing with his nose—obviously he'd been snorting—and went to a urinal without apparently noticing that I was at an adjacent one.

"Gahd, are you following me around or something?" he complained.

"You said you weren't taking anything."

"Well, I'm not," he said. "It was a gift. I never buy the stuff, and anyway, it hardly affects me."

He wiped his nose again.

"Oh, no."

"Actually what I'm high about is the situation with Alice," Des said, worrisomely cheerful. "This makes her seem much more accessible. She's not operating on a plane so far removed from the rest of us."

I really loathed Des at that moment. Flushing the urinal, I shot him a look full of daggers, though he was facing the wall and didn't seem to notice.

"There's hope for me," he concluded optimistically while I washed up at a nearby sink.

I thought it best just to change the subject. "What did Josh want to talk to you about? Is everything okay?"

"Uh, no," he said, flushing. "Not exactly."

Disgusted at the idea of Des's preying on Alice in her psychologically vulnerable state, I hated to have to still pester him for favors, but felt I had no choice.

"I'm sorry to bug you about this," I mentioned as we walked down the stairs toward the main floor, "but I'd be really grateful if we could talk with Van or Berrie soon."

Des nodded.

"The way it's going," I went on, "if I can't get people in here, I'm going to lose my job."

As we headed down the last flight of stairs, Des's former girlfriend Nina—in the film beautifully played by the actress

Jennifer Beals—looking distraught but still gorgeous, bolted from the crowd.

"Des!" she called. "You . . . *lied* . . . to . . . me . . . ! I thought you were a wonderful *man* . . . but it was all . . . *lies!*"

"No!" Des replied, using his compassionate voice.

"You *said* you *loved me*! Then you said you were *gay*! But you're Not Gay! Everyone knew, but me . . . You completely *humiliated* me! *Why*, Des?! *Why?!*"

It was a little scary. Nina had been hurt so badly she had apparently lost all pride and self-restraint. (Des had thought it was "kind" to tell women the story about being "gay," taking the onus for breaking up on himself, rather than just doing it the usual mean "let's be friends" way.) For someone in his position, this was the most dreaded nightmare—an ex-girlfriend going berserk and making a spectacle of herself in front of everyone one knew and everyone one didn't know. It was as if the next step would be Nina pulling out a gun and shooting either us or herself. It was that bad.

"I, uh, *could* be gay . . ." Des offered weakly.

"*Bullshit!*" Nina screamed. "You're saying *again* you're gay? Tell me, honestly: have you ever had . . . *SEX WITH MEN?!*"

Her shrill voice, rising above the disco din, attracted a large crowd. Des looked around, noticing both straight and gay friends awaiting his reply with a certain expectancy.

"Well . . ." he started. "That's defining it rather . . . narrowly . . ."

"*Bullshit!*" Nina sobbed. "You *bastard!*"

Continuing to shout "Bastard! Bastard!" she abruptly charged up the staircase, slammed Des against the railing wall, hard, and fled up the rest of the stairs. Des looked completely stunned.

So ended what we called "Meltdown Night" at the Club. Rarely afterward would our group constitute itself in the same way again.

Certain Generalizations Are Unmade

16

The Wet-head Was Not Dead

"The key to finding the right person is not marrying—or getting heavily involved—with the wrong person first."

"Definitely don't marry anyone who tries to pressure you into it. Marriage is not the puppy in the window."

"It's always the people you can't stand who later approach you for favors."

These were aphorisms Des and I generated in the period, often while sitting around his office in the back of the Club. Though the third—about favors—was really Des's, he insisted it was not directed against me. What got him were all the people he detested from former lives who would show up at the Club expecting to get in because of their past acquaintanceship.

I was with Des the night when "Thad," someone he knew from his school in Washington, appeared at the back door with a group of his friends and appealed to Des to get them in. Des was amazed because he said this "Thad" had made his life miserable in seventh grade, beating him regularly.

"He beat you regularly?"

"Well, at least once, but the threat was implicit."

"I thought 'Thad' was a friend of yours—wasn't he the guy with all the brothers?"

"That was the New York 'Thad.' He was fine. It was the Washington 'Thad' I couldn't stand."

Des was always telling stories about people he had known, often fictionalizing their names to protect their identities, but then forgetting the names he had fictionalized them under, making it sometimes very confusing. Though at first it was virtually impossible to keep track of everyone he talked about, after a while you got in the habit of referring to them as if you had long known them, too. People always thought Des and I had been friends far longer than we actually had, just because I had grown so familiar with the cast of characters he talked about, his acquaintance with whom went back to kindergarten or earlier. Actually we had first met not in Professor Bate's course but in the freshman dining hall, the Union, like everyone else; it turned out that Des had been in preschool with a Dobbs girl I had long been obsessed with and let me grill him for details for the duration of one of those open-ended dinners so common then. This was the mythological past of our friendship that made it seem we had known each other much longer than we had.

The good Thad, the one from New York, had studied to be a geologist and ended up in Alaska. He had sent a snapshot of himself in the snow with his girlfriend, a cute blonde in a mukluk, and a dogsled pulled by his own dog, a Chinook, which Des had posted in his office. To kill time while waiting for Des, I often examined it and sometimes fantasized about the girl, the dog, the snow, and the sled—in short, about the possibility of having a different identity far from the tensions and unhappiness of New York. Sometimes I tried to imagine how it would be if the girl were Alice. I am quite sure she is the sort of person who could have been very good with sled dogs and tough near-arctic conditions.

On a subsequent night, the bad Thad, the one from Washington, ended up getting thrown out of the Club and during the hubbub shouted out what was apparently Des's old school nickname, "Puff"—not in this case a reference to smoking but to the fey Peter, Paul & Mary song of that period, "Puff, the Magic Dragon." Des was strangely upset about it—in the realm of school nicknames, there are far worse, I can assure you. Perhaps it was because, once you leave a bad school experience behind, you dread any whiff of it infecting your masterful present existence. Should you ever participate in one of those alumni fund-raising "phonathons" you'll see how widespread this phenomenon goes—a lot of people really don't want to hear from the ol' alma mater at all. But they could at least be politer about it.

*_**_**_**

In the five months that had passed since "meltdown night" at the Club, District Attorney Morgenthau's office had won convictions against eleven executives at six commercial real estate brokerages as part of what was described as "the first in a series of investigations forming part of a countywide crackdown on white-collar crime," which can be quite significant when the county is New York (i.e., Manhattan in its governmental form).

In the television coverage of the press conference where Morgenthau congratulated his prosecutors in the real estate probe, Josh could be seen standing with some of his colleagues against the wall in the back. Later he was surprised how many people said they had seen him on the evening news. Josh's self-presentation had improved considerably since the previous fall. He now wore a dark suit, clean shirt, slicked-back hair, and even a not-bad haircut. Hair tonic was part of the solution for Josh. The goofy, unkempt look had really emanated from the top of his head. "The Wet-head Is Dead!" an ad campaign of the seventies had announced, seeking total conformity to the terrible blow-dry look of those years, but it was typically just when the "wet-head" look was being derided in mass-market advertising that quite a few of us decided that it was in fact not so bad; that it was in fact quite cool. This is how style changes come about. Though often condemned, "fashion" can indeed be exhilarating when it seems to be going in your direction or somewhere you want to go also. The emerging New Wave look of those years fit in with this.

Leaving the press conference as the last questions were being fielded by one of the D.A.'s associates, Josh slipped unobtrusively out of the room past the TV reporters already doing their "stand-ups" for the cameras atop the court building's beautiful red-yellow marble staircase. He let his legs carry him rapidly down it like the well-oiled working parts of a machine gun and then continued along the marble corridor to the unprepossessing office he shared with another A.D.A. Once inside, Josh shut the door and dropped into his chair. On the wall behind him, a poster showed a sprinting tortoise tearing past a feckless hare. The tortoise was a cult figure in the D.A.'s office—the public prosecutors tended to be less experienced (and, maybe, less smart) than the top attorneys (the hares) they were up against in the big cases, yet they still prided themselves on occasionally winning one.

Josh stared for a while at the phone, trying to build up his courage before dialing the local number he had written on the pad before him. Ultimately nearly all people, women as well as men, sometime or another, find themselves in the same romantic predicament—trial by phone call. For a while Josh had thought he could rely on running into Alice at the Club, but the times he had gone there she had been nowhere around—in fact, she had not been going at all in this period. To see her he had realized he would ultimately have to call.

Semi-subletting my apartment turned out to be a real mistake. I had told a cousin from Cincinnati he could stay there while he was on assignment in the city. But the inconvenience of not having easy access to an apartment of one's own became pretty acute. What Charlotte had said about not really having female friends was, it seemed, essentially true— all the people who called or passed through town wanting to see her were guys, generally ex-boyfriend-types, almost all tall, handsome, and dressed as if they had just come from doing forestry work in the Great North. Charlotte would usually have them over to catch up and reminisce about old times and mutual acquaintances. They were generally perfectly friendly to me, but it was not a friendliness I relished. By the time they showed up or, even beforehand, I tried to be out of there. That I not be around for a few hours seemed pretty clearly indicated.

Temporarily homeless, I got in the habit of walking through the Yorkville neighborhood, savoring what re-

mained of its "Germantown"—i.e., Central and Eastern
European—atmosphere. Weekend days this became an excuse
for leafing through the *Times,* the *Post,* or even the revved-up
Daily News (the legendary Clay Felker having briefly taken
its helm) over a coffee and pastry at the Heidelberg, or if later
in the day over a beer and bratwurst somewhere else. The
central worldwide fact at mid-century and for many years
thereafter was Communist Oppression, and the fallout from
it was particularly dramatic in Yorkville, which received
waves of refugees following each failed uprising, notably from
Hungary in 1956 and Czechoslovakia in 1968. Local shops
included in their inventory postcards honoring Cardinal
Mindszenty and other national heroes of the opposition. I
remember being struck by a window display in a combined
travel agency–bookstore featuring a book with an intriguing
title: *The Lean Years: Hungarian Calvinism in Crisis.* To me
there was something ineffably poignant about the whole
panorama of human experience these words suggested.
Finally, I bought the book—sometimes there are objects
you feel you must own even if you do not understand
exactly why.

By the time I returned to the apartment, the old
boyfriends would usually have left. Charlotte was always
especially warm in welcoming me back. On a couple of
occasions, though, I couldn't help noticing that the bed in
her room looked either slightly mussed or more neatly
arranged than it had been when I left. I was beginning to
sense that Charlotte was one of those people with a problem
"closing the door" on past relationships. But I did not feel
entitled to obsess about this too deeply, as by then I was pining pretty intensely for Alice.

The big news at Riley Publishers was David Novak Productions' acquiring the TV rights to Alice's Tibet book for one of the networks, NBC—astounding everyone, since foreign topics, except an occasional romantic intrigue set in the Caribbean or the French Riviera, were considered "ratings poison" in network television circles.

"Alice, congratulations on the TV sale," Helen said as she returned from one of her quick trips to the canteen.

"Thanks," Alice said with an awkward smile as she finished attaching her readers' reports to a pile of manuscripts prior to taking them to Zenia's domain. For Alice the TV sale was very encouraging and led her to feel she could breathe a little easier about the book's commercial fate and concentrate on just making it as good as she could, within the traditional limitations of Riley Publishers.

"Could you watch my phone?" Dan asked the assistant nearest him, and then took off down the bay with a manuscript box under his arm.

"Hi," Dan said as he pulled up near Alice in the corridor.

Alice hi'd him back and, typically friendly, slowed a little until he could catch up.

"How's Holly?" Dan asked.

"Fine."

"Is she, uh, going out with anyone?"

"Yeah, this really nice guy who went to Denver—University—and works in real estate."

"D.U.?"

"Yeah. He found her this incredibly cheap apartment."

"She no longer lives with you?"

Alice shook her head no.

"You hold what happened against me?" Dan finally asked a little uncomfortably.

"Not that you broke up," Alice said, "just that you go out with people based primarily on looks."

"Holly's also very nice."

"A lot of people are nice," Alice said, stopping and turning around before entering the manuscript room. "You only asked out the fabulously good-looking one."

"You hold that against me?"

"Well . . ." Alice paused. "Pretty shallow."

"You know, Alice, except for politics, we've got a lot in common. We're both pretty serious and, I think, respect each other's bases for judgment. . . . Occasionally, I get reactionary thoughts, too. . . ."

"I'm not reactionary," Alice replied, finally entering the manuscript room.

"Well, aesthetically," Dan offered, following her.

"Oh, well . . . Aesthetically . . ."

That didn't seem to bother her at all.

An influence in Alice's life not previously mentioned was her close, admiring relationship with her Aunt Janet—the youngest, prettiest, and most glamorous of her mother's sisters (also the most stimulating to have long lunches with). At thirteen Alice had emerged as her aunt's favorite younger relative, and Aunt Janet and Uncle Jack were themselves the most popular members of the Parker clan (her mother's family). The big question regarding any Parker family gathering was whether Aunt Janet and Uncle Jack would be there, because, if so, the fun was virtually assured. From the way Alice talked about them, I imagined the characters played by Cary Grant and Carole Lombard in the original *Topper* films, though Alice said that her aunt more resembled the warm and demure Jane Wyatt character from the old *Father Knows Best* television series. Up to then her aunt and uncle had been childless, and undoubtedly much of the love and attention that would have been absorbed within the confines of a nuclear family they instead directed to their younger relatives, a wide circle of friends, and a colorful social life.

When visiting New York, they usually stayed at the old Gotham Hotel on Fifth Avenue in the Fifties (occupied now by the luxurious Peninsula Hotel), where the petite, very quiet sixties discotheque L'Interdit had been. Her aunt would meet Alice's train coming in from the Hudson Valley and take her for lunch and a movie, or shopping, starting from her early teens. Often they would go to the Brasserie restaurant, which again became a haunt for Alice during her early publishing days. After a while, the afternoon movies and shopping were dispensed with and they would linger over lunch for conversations lasting almost until dinnertime.

Aunt Janet and Uncle Jack were the only couple of her parents' generation who struck Alice as truly romantic, an ideal relationship and match-up, though in most respects they were opposites of the "opposites attract" variety. (Sorry to bring this hackneyed phrase—and the hackneyed concept behind it—up again, but the idea that "opposites" in some perverse way belong together has, though delusional, a direct relevance to this story as well as being the source of an appalling array of social problems.)

Alice loved hearing Aunt Janet's stories of how she had

first met Uncle Jack, of their first rendezvous and courtship, and of the amazing adventures Uncle Jack undertook in pursuit of her, so different from the way guys act today. (At the time they met he was "seriously" involved with three other women, one of whom was married and aimed a revolver at him when she learned that he had proposed to someone else; apparently earlier, when she had wanted to leave her famous husband to marry him, he had said he was adamantly opposed to marriage on moral grounds—something which later turned out not to be true.)

Against all logic and expectation, except those of the trite "opposites attract" kind, Aunt Janet and Uncle Jack's romance had flourished; once again the skeptics were confounded. For Alice, their relationship seemed a sort of ideal, a model she could use in her own life. I wanted to mention it because I think it was this idealization of Aunt Janet's experience with Uncle Jack, despite all the logic and everything the naysayers claimed, that influenced Alice to start accepting Des's dinner invitations that spring. Infatuation in its earliest stages loves opposition and skepticism, even if these later will exact a heavier cost. Passion is the hare, conformity the tortoise. Maybe the hares do win most races, but that doesn't mean tortoises don't remain a major pain.

The inevitable took longer than expected, but finally in March the agency's new management informed me, and not exactly in the nicest of terms, that my services would no longer be needed.

This could have been seen as the inevitable consequence of the agency takeover and larger trends within the advertising industry, not to mention the new administration's and

Federal Reserve's preoccupation with squeezing inflation out of the economy, even if it meant a severe economic slowdown that would hurt millions of wage earners such as those around me on the unemployment line. But, on the other hand, to be honest, if I had paid more attention to my work and done a better job, maybe I would have been kept on— i.e., perhaps I was just too distracted and frazzled to focus on my work at the agency in the intensive way that might have preserved my employ there. Late nights at the Club had been compounded by late nights and some early mornings trying to write. A short story originally intended for *Harper's* magazine—someone I met at the Club was an editiorial assistant there—appeared two years later in *The Beacon*, a Cambridge, Massachusetts–based literary magazine. Then a casting director I knew, who was friendly with the producers of the television show *Hart to Hart,* encouraged me to write a script to propose to them, though that fell through, too. Finally, I had drinks with an agent at ICM—actually someone's assistant but in training to become a full-fledged agent—who told me that the best way into the business from New York was writing for the children's television show *Sesame Street.*

"Do you think you could write for Bert and Ernie?" was the question she was posing to all the young New York–based would-be television writers. Looking around, it struck me that the swank midtown cocktail bar we were in was an incongruously worldly setting for the children's television subject matter. I didn't realize then that this was often the way things happened.

Of course I immediately said yes, but even as I did so I realized it was going to be a bit more complex than that. I knew *Sesame Street* was considered a good show, though ostensibly targeted at subliterate tots, and that Bert and Ernie were considered pillars of the program, but I honestly didn't know if I could write for it unless I tried, and if that didn't work out, material originally written for two puppets—or "Muppets," as they were called—would be hard to recycle at *The Beacon*, which was edited by a former Harvard "expository writing" instructor of mine whose taste I knew ran more to the "serious" and mawkish. The times we—or at least *The Beacon* and I—then operated in were still very much pre–"Post-modern."

By mid-April I was in my fifth week of filling out forms at the New York State Department of Labor's unemployment claims office, along with everyone else. To burn up some of the anxious energy the humiliating unemployment office experience tended to stir up, I resolved to make the long march uptown from Centre Street on foot. The route passed through TriBeCa and the Village to the city's overrated Chelsea neighborhood, which in those years was still a semi-deserted quasi-industrial nowhere land—or at least seemed so to a nonlocal such as myself.

The drab Apex Technical School building—one of the few in the area to remain unrenovated in the succeeding decades—stood on a northwest corner of a lower stretch of Sixth Avenue at something like Nineteenth Street. After passing it, I veered east down a side street; that brought me, a half block in, to a Chelsea-style loft building with a characteristic, though now rare, "streamlined" stainless-steel storefront on the ground floor. I stopped at the doorway, examined the names on the intercom, then pressed the buzzer marked *McGrath*.

After the inevitable "Who is it?" I answered and waited for the buzzer to sound as the door-lock mechanism was released. This was then called "being buzzed in." But the door was slightly tricky, not so simple to open on the first pull. After getting it, I climbed the narrow, sloping wooden stairs up three flights to a large light-gray painted steel door typical of lofts in that era.

Evidently Des was just getting up. He opened the door without comment. He was barefoot, with a faded blue-plaid wrapper pulled around him, and carried a cereal bowl in one hand. He turned back to the main room of his somewhat grubby semi-loft apartment. A parking garage across the street was the principal sight through the broad expanse of window, helping to give the space a certain amount of authentic "Chelsea" atmosphere. Des flopped into a beat-up old easy chair covered with a cheapo brown-and-tan Indian cotton print—in most of our places, the furnishings were still essentially college-dorm surplus. He flicked on the TV with a primitive wireless remote control, and the show he often described as his favorite, Mutual of Omaha's nature documentary series, *Wild Kingdom*, came on. We joined the show already in progress.

But I was a bit distracted and stayed on my feet, glancing around his apartment.

"What, uh, exactly are you looking for?" Des asked, without looking up from the TV. "Alice isn't here."

"I didn't think she was."

I looked around anyway, examining various things Des had left strewn about. Some of the objects were interesting. I guess it could have been considered "gawking."

"Wha's tha . . . occaziun fah yah visit?" Des had filled his mouth with Cheerios, and the effort not to let any of the milk and fragments spill out made his pronunciation a little weird.

"I was just on my way back from Unemployment," I said. "My eight weeks are nearly up. I've got to get more serious about looking for work."

"Eight weeks?"

"Yeah," I said, and stopped, unsure about confiding in Des any further, but then deciding to risk it. "I just think it's a little immoral to take unemployment for more than eight weeks unless you're seriously looking for work—the excuse for that period being that it takes a while just to recover from the shock of getting fired."

"Huhn," Des responded. At no time did he take his eyes off the tube. For a little while I watched, too. *Wild Kingdom* wasn't as good as I had remembered it. The photography, music, narration, etc., were all fairly dorky—at times veering pretty close to the ridiculous.

"It's ironic that now Van and Berrie like me, it doesn't matter anymore."

"I woooldn't say they 'like you,' " Des replied, his mouth jammed with cereal.

"Well, anyway . . . Has Alice ever been here?"

"None of your beeswax."

"It *is* my beeswax. Alice's a friend, and I know what you're like."

"I've changed," he said.

"Oh sure."

"No. I have," he said, looking away from the TV for once. "You didn't notice that? You're not very observant."

"I don't think you can just be sitting around watching *Wild Kingdom* reruns some afternoon and decide that you're going to be virtuous for the rest of your life—and have that stick."

"Well, it's been seven weeks," Des said. "I think that's a pretty big, pretty massive start and that, as a friend, you could cut me some slack."

"Not when it concerns Alice."

"You're with Charlotte," he said, exasperated.

"Okay. That's my problem."

17

Tom

During this period when Alice was starting to see Des for dinner, chats, etc., Tom also called. That's often the way it happens. When something new starts going, something old starts back up again, after perhaps weeks or months of nothing happening at all. Sometimes it tempts one to reconsider one's blanket dismissal of all astrological portents and signs. Perhaps Venus had re-entered Scorpio, Alice's sun sign, or something of that kind.

After their awful last encounter, Alice had not known what to think about Tom's call, so she just said yes, accepting his invitation to have drinks. There was a big curiosity factor involved. But she didn't want to build it up in her mind beforehand or think about it, she was just going to go. Inevitably of course, it went beyond that. She started wondering whether he would retract everything and apologize as a sort of prelude before getting back together again. She knew that this kind of thing happened often—very often, in fact. Definitive ruptures were hardly ever really definitive. If trial separations sometimes did not work out, neither did permanent reconciliations.

What was seriously perilous for Alice's heart was that there would be over two days until their rendezvous. As she walked to work or did her laundry or the dishes, she started letting her imagination indulge in reveries of a risky kind, thinking, What's the harm? If Tom and Jennifer's relationship had been destined to be permanent, they would not have been having trial separations in the first place. When people stay together six years without marrying, it means something, and not something especially positive. It would be reasonable to assume that for most of those six years, at least one of the two was deciding that they did *not* want to marry the other.

Alice felt she understood the morbid guilt feelings that underlay Tom's despicable screed the night they broke up. In fact, realizing that, she found Tom almost more sympathetic for it. She was subject to the same sort of morbid guiltmongering and manias herself—it had been one of the problems she had relating to those at Hampshire who were happily immersed in the dubious "I'm okay, you're okay" cant of those years.

In this way Alice started allowing her reveries to go far, far beyond what might have been reasonable or prudent, in directions absurdly romantic and even amnesiac.

They finally had cocktails in the quiet back room of Trader Vic's, still nestled in its traditional location in the basement of the Plaza Hotel. Alice ordered a rum-based drink called a Gardenia, served in a bowl-like goblet, while Tom eschewed the traditional Polynesian guy's drink, the Samoan

Fog-Cutter, served in a tall ceramic flask, to stick with a simple whiskey-and-soda.

"You mean," Tom was saying, trying to keep his voice very quiet, "you think *I* gave it to *you*?"

Alice nodded her head emphatically.

"How can you be sure?" he asked.

"I'm sure," she said.

"Well . . . you were a lot more . . . active than I was."

Alice made a face.

"You were obviously very experienced," he persisted.

"No."

"Oh, come on . . . How did you know all that?"

"Well"—Alice paused—"I read a lot."

"You must've been with *some* guys—it's nothing to be embarrassed about."

Alice didn't respond.

"You weren't a virgin," he said, beginning to lose the thread of what he expected to say.

"I didn't consider myself a virgin, but—"

"What?"

"I don't know. Technically . . ."

"What?" he asked, sounding concerned.

"Well . . . If, when making love, the man . . . spurts . . . outside the woman, does that count as sexual intercourse?"

" *'Spurts'?* "

"If it squirts outside, without getting in. Does that count as losing your virginity?"

"No part of the guy got in at any time?"

"I don't . . . think so."

"I think part has to get in to be considered . . . sexual intercourse."

"So then I *was* a virgin."

"I can't believe that . . . The first time you make love, I give you both—"

Noticing a couple entering the back-room area and taking a table not far from them, Tom dropped his voice even further. "—G. and an H. infection . . . ?"

He paused before continuing.

"You must really despise me," he said.

"H.?"

✳ ✳ ✳ ✳ ✳ ✳

Sometime after midnight I was in the bathroom hurrying to finish shaving while Charlotte and Alice, dressed to go out, slouched on the chairs around the kitchen table in waiting mode.

"I don't know," Alice said, "I'm beginning to think that maybe that old system of people getting married based on mutual respect and shared aspirations, and then slowly, over time, earning each other's love and admiration, worked the best."

"Well," Charlotte said. "We'll never know."

I pushed open the bathroom door and crossed quickly to the bedroom.

"Almost ready," I said.

"Gahd," Charlotte said, "waiting around all night for the unemployed guy to get around to shaving—" She called to the other room: "You're so busy you can't shower until midnight?"

This smarty-pants needling really got to me. I returned, pulling on my sweater but really irritated. "Excuse me, 'unemployed' is not who I am. I'm a fully employed person who just happens not to have a job, largely because of structural problems in the advertising industry."

Charlotte was really wonderful, immediately contrite. "I'm sorry," she said, her tone clearly sincere. "That was really inconsiderate. Please forgive me."

Her apology I accepted with a nod, but out on the landing, while Charlotte and Alice were putting on their coats, I still felt the need to explain further. "I did shower earlier, I just didn't shave, because I didn't need to, since I don't have a job, and one of the few real advantages of unemployment is, precisely, not having to shave all the time."

Perhaps in consideration of my employment situation, Charlotte insisted that night on paying for the cab. The trend among dating couples for the woman to occasionally pay for something—normally whatever did not cost too much—actually started in those years.

18

A Little Sociology of the Night

In that period it became normal among those who still had occasion to wear evening dress—whether for formal dinners, Monday nights at the Metropolitan Opera, evening weddings, or actual deb parties—for someone, or a group of people collectively, to have the brainstorm: "Let's go to the Club; dressed like this, we're sure to get in!" This was not entirely true, but though not all succeeded (which was not so tragic—most were by then "feeling no pain"), as a rule they did get in at a much higher ratio than others, affecting the mix inside the Club in ways that were occasionally very noticeable—bunches of people in evening dress grouped in various parts of the Club, giving the whole place a different feeling. This was an aspect of life in those times which is rarely discussed or even mentioned today.

Among those from this crowd who went to the Club often was Sally Fowler, the blond late-night socialite whose early story was partially recounted with those of Audrey Rouget and that whole Manhattan crowd in the movie *Metropolitan*.

In the early seventies she and her friends had gone through the usual long-hair, druggie phase that so marked that generation—many wrecked themselves pretty badly, some died (though not anyone in the "Sally Fowler Rat Pack" itself or the "S.F. R.P.," as they were sometimes styled). But as the seventies ended and the eighties began, there was a tendency to return to former traditions among this group, too. This tendency was taken advantage of on a national scale by Ronald Reagan's presidential campaign, with its famous "Morning in America" advertising spots, though in this particular group the return to tradition involved more late, late nights.

In the late sixties/early seventies period, Sally had begun her first tentative steps toward a recording career—which in her case meant dating a not very impressive record producer who had offered to make a "demo" for her. This initial contact went nowhere, and she cannot be said to have ever really established herself as a singer. But despite her lack of success thus far, those years of striving (when her friends were in college and just after) had given her a wide circle of acquaintance in the music business, which made visiting the Club much more interesting than if her attendance had been purely social. She still hoped to break through someday, and even if this hope was not very realistic, it gave her a rudder and a compass which made her life more purposeful and interesting than if she had not.

That particular night Sally had come with another member of the old group, Fred Neff, after one of those "Let's go to the Club" exoduses from a junior committee event at the Whitney Museum. She and several of her friends still often relied on Fred as a sort of "date substitute." He had once complained about this as being "dehumanizing," but now—

after having been through several intense, failed relationships—he had come to rather like and, in fact, rely on it. He was not especially oriented toward making plans in advance, and he had come to consider being called up this way one of the positive elements of his life; it had gotten him through some bad times, too. Fred still had an exhausting day job and was one of the few people I heard of who often actually slept at the Club, and he was always looking for a banquette spot where he could do so comfortably and unobtrusively.

There were many such circles within the Club, occasionally overlapping but rarely entirely merging. Whatever dynamic originally caused groups to form also preserved them from the sort of permutations and combinations that might have radically changed their nature.

On the mezzanine, one level above them, isolated from the downstairs hurly-burly in the quasi–"conversation pit" formed by two semicircular banquettes arranged to face one another, we were all gathered en masse that evening. It would be one of the last such gatherings we would have at the Club, but of course we did not know that then.

Among the semi-newcomers were Skip, Holly's new nice-guy boyfriend who had, in fact, as previously mentioned, been to Denver University, or D.U. (sometimes pronounced "duh"—even its own students considering its academic reputation less than stellar; according to one lame campus joke, *Archie* comics formed part of D.U.'s Great Books series), and Josh Neff, whose infiltration of the group, while unobtrusive, had been surprisingly successful.

(Josh and Fred Neff were distant cousins, but did not know each other, at least at that point. Both had the ability to insinuate themselves into groups where they might not normally have fit, and perhaps this was some hereditary Neff family trait. They certainly didn't look alike.)

Meanwhile, Des was up at the nearby mezzanine bar, or "mezz-bar," as it was sometimes called, getting house drinks for a lucky few of us.

All I can remember of how the conversation started that night is that I had gotten into a sufficiently self-confident mood to engage in some jocular industry-related self-criticism. "Of course," I was saying, "if you talk enthusiastically about your work in advertising, you sound like a total cretin."

"No," Charlotte insisted, "your enthusiasm is actually enormously appealing. In fact, I used to think not so well of people who worked in advertising—but that's one of the great things about getting out of college and into the Real World, how experience *improves* and *modifies* your views . . ."

While Charlotte was talking, Des arrived and handed out the drinks, finally sliding into the banquette next to Alice, who edged over to make room for him. Someone said later that, observing this, Josh looked pretty depressed—not clinically depressed, just the discouraged and deflated kind we all get into on occasion.

I did not then notice Josh's reaction, as I was following closely what Charlotte was saying, which seemed increasingly to implicate me.

"During college, I remember seeing couples with crying babies and thinking, How horrible," she recalled. "Recently I've spent a lot of time with my niece and nephew; Saturday I took my niece, who's seven, to see the Disney movie *Lady and the Tramp*—she *loved* it; she was *so* cute."

She glanced at me. "I'm beginning to fall in love with the whole idea of having kids," she concluded.

I just took a big sip of my drink.

"I hate that movie," Alice said.

"What?!" Charlotte responded.

"It's so . . . tacky. Not to mention . . . depressing."

"This *sweet movie* about *cute cartoon dogs*"—Charlotte, incredulous, looked around to the rest of us for support— "you found *depressing?*"

"There *is* something depressing about it," Josh answered, defending Alice's comment from the other side of the booth, "and it's not really about dogs; except for some superficial bow-wow stuff at the start, the dogs all represent human types—which is where it gets into real trouble. Lady, the ostensible protagonist, is a fluffy blond cocker spaniel with absolutely nothing on her brain. She's great-looking but— let's be honest—incredibly insipid."

It might not have been mentioned previously but Holly, with her fluffed-up butterscotch hair, compact size, and small, regular features, did somewhat resemble what we might think of as the pretty human version of a cocker spaniel puppy. I'm afraid several of us stole covert glances at her while Josh spoke.

"Tramp, the love interest," he continued, "is a smarmy braggart of the most obnoxious kind—an oily jailbird out for a piece of tail, or whatever he can get—"

"Oh come on," Charlotte said.

"No. He's a self-confessed chicken thief and all-around sleazeball."

I glanced at Des and could see the color draining out of his face—he already saw where Josh's analysis was taking him. I tried to interpose a question: "One thing," I addressed Josh, "if what you're saying is that the dogs in the movie represent people, then who do the people in the movie represent?"

"It doesn't matter," Josh replied, taking a swallow from his drink and then continuing.

"What's the function of a film of this kind? Essentially it's a primer on love and marriage directed at very young people—imprinting on their little psyches the idea that smooth-talking delinquents recently escaped from the local pound are a good match for nice girls from sheltered homes. When in ten years the icky *human* version of Tramp shows up around the house, their hormones will be racing and no one'll understand why—films like this program women to *adore* jerks—"

"Gahd, you're nuts," Des interrupted.

Josh glanced at him, clearly vexed; his voice was growing a little strained. "The only sympathetic character, the little Scottie who's so concerned about Lady, is mocked as old-fashioned and irrelevant and shunted off to the side."

Everyone had been reacting somewhat differently to what Josh was saying. Alice was sympathetic, Charlotte skeptical and faintly disgusted—she hated lengthy analogies—and Des firmly opposed.

"Isn't the whole point that Tramp *changes*?" Des argued. "Okay, maybe in the past he stole chickens, ran around without a license, and was not always sincere with members of the opposite sex. But through his love for Lady—and the beneficent influence of fatherhood and matrimony—he *changes* and becomes a valued member of that, you know, rather idyllic . . . household," he concluded, rather moved.

"I don't think people really change that way," Josh said. "We can change our context, but we can't change ourselves."

"What does *that* mean?" Charlotte asked.

"Well, you've changed," Des said pointedly.

"Come on, Des," I put in, sensing the implicit threat.

"That's a little different," Josh said.

"I agree with Josh," Alice said intently. "The Scottie *is* the only admirable character. It would have been a much better movie if Lady'd ended up with him."

"I'm really surprised," Des persisted. "I think Tramp really changed."

"Maybe he wanted to change, or tried to change, but there's not a lot of integrity there," Josh said. "First, it'd be hanging around the house drinking and watching ball games—and maybe knocking Lady around a bit—but pretty soon he'll be back down at the town dump, chasing tail."

"Oh, give me a break!" Des blurted out. "Have you been taking your medication, because what you're saying is completely nuts—"

"God, Des," I said, trying to stop him.

"No! People should know that our friend has a certain condition—"

"*Shut up*," I told him.

Looking directly at Josh he said, "How can Morgenthau employ you? He knows about Mass. Mental and all the looney tunes junior year?!"

"Of course he knows about it."

"Gahd!" Des said, and then bolted up and away with an angry exasperation that seemed really excessive and out of place.

Josh, tense yet exhilarated, looked toward Alice as if for support.

Later that night I was climbing the stairs back to the mez-zanine, in a slight funk, thinking about my employment and romantic situations, when a still-revved-up Josh caught up with me. On the dance floor below, Don Ray's incredibly dynamic "Got to Have Loving" had the crowd in its rhythmic grip. I think the ferocious beat propelled us up the stairs at a faster than normal rate. Also, at this point in the evening, having had access to free drinks through Des, we were both probably somewhat bombed.

"Have you seen Alice?" Josh asked, quite winded.

I shook my head no; he nodded and went on ahead looking for her.

A voice coming from one of the nearby banquettes at the top of the stairs held me back. "Excuse me, were you at Leo Burnett, in Chicago?"

Perhaps I should explain that I am a native Chicagoan with all the crazy pride that implies. Summers and one year after college I had worked at the great Leo Burnett Agency there. Turning to the sound of the voice, I recognized a friendly face from the past. The man—I could not immediately recall his name—had worked for one of our clients, IHSMOCO, as the Illinois High-Speed Motor Company was then known. He was a sort of protégé of the company's president and had been quite helpful to us when it looked as if we were about to lose IHSMOCO as a client.

"Omigod, how are you?" I said, sincerely pleased to see him. "Ted Boynton," he was saying almost simultaneously, to reintroduce himself. This was one of the great things about the Club—the way people you knew from elsewhere were always popping up.

A pretty young woman with dark natural-blond hair, demure in pearls and a "wrap" dress (like one I had bought Charlotte for her birthday), smiled at us.

"Do you know Betty?" Ted asked.

"Jimmy Steinway—hi."

"Hi."

"You're still with IHSMOCO?" I asked Ted.

He nodded. "There's a sales conference at the Americana this week. I'm actually on the international side now, based in Spain—Barcelona . . ."

"How's that?"

Ted paused before replying and looked to Betty. "Well, I've only been there a couple of months. The city's beautiful but, in personal terms, pretty cold . . . How about you?" he asked.

"I was at McCallum, but just got sacked."

Ted nodded in a way that thoughtfully minimized the ignominy of it all, as if to say, "Someday all of us will be sacked from McCallum or its equivalent."

"Have you found anything else?" he asked.

I shook my head.

"Any leads?"

Again, I had to nod in the negative.

"You know," Ted said, "there are a lot of agencies in Spain looking for people with experience from here. There's one in Madrid some Burnett people have affiliated with—I could give them a call."

"That would be terrific."

"Madrid's really great," he added.

Des had Alice up in the deejay booth with him, standing together, looking out on the whole Club, and especially the dance floor action below, seeking to impress her and largely succeeding.

Michael, the Club's top deejay, was not the cool jerk one

might imagine in such a job but a rather quiet and serious-minded enthusiast of the music. Des, in his work at the Club if not in every aspect of his life, tended to raise everything quite a few notches above what might have been expected.

"Michael, 'Good Times,' " Des requested.

The young deejay nodded and immediately laid hands on the vinyl disc in one of a dozen sturdy wood boxes the Club's top records were organized into.

"I don't identify with Tramp at all," Des explained to Alice. "I was just sticking up for him because no one else was."

Alice smiled at this malarkey.

"I actually identify with the loyal Scottie, too . . . I've changed."

Des leaned toward Alice as if about to kiss her.

Josh had been on the main floor overlooking the dancing when "Good Times" came on. As the crowd shifted to the new beat, something prompted him to look up at the moment Des kissed Alice, which at least as seen from afar looked reciprocated by her. As much as such activity can be judged by external observation, Alice seemed to know how to kiss "very well." Theoretically, such knowledge could have come from reading—the book-club edition of the classic *The Art of the Kiss* had been widely available at Riley—but it was more likely from audiovisual media—film and TV—coupled with some firsthand personal experience, that she might have developed such a skill. Or maybe she was just "a natural."

Exactly what her relationship with Des was—and what she saw in him—remained a mystery, subject to considerable speculation then and since, and not just among those of us who felt we had a direct stake in the answer. The conversation Alice had overheard in September—during which Des "declared his homosexuality"—made an enormous impression on her and so far as she was concerned had never been fully refuted. While, as Charlotte said, the evidence pointed to its being a pathetic ruse, there was always a more compassionate interpretation, and Alice was invariably more prone to compassionate interpretations. Perhaps Des did suffer from some sort of sexual-identity confusion for which his hyper-heterosexuality was a kind of "mask." This was a dangerous habit of thought for someone of Alice's vulnerabilities to get into; it's precisely when you are governed by compassion in a romantic relationship that your own emotional annihilation becomes almost certain. (Better to keep such compassion for yourself because, chances are, you're *really* going to need it.)

Josh, for example, had saved little or no compassion for himself. His far-fetched Lady-and-the-Tramp analogy was prompted precisely by his concern at someone like Alice getting involved with the likes of Des. As he talked, he'd felt the bond between Alice and himself, which was already existent, greatly strengthened. But confronted with the truth of the balcony, he could no longer ignore all the other evidence, previously accumulated, pointing against himself.

Josh gazed longer than he intended or had any right to, then turned away and propelled himself out of the Club and all forty-five blocks home, scarcely realizing the geography he was walking through. Many people get depressed for romantic reasons—it's not all Byron and Shelley. Nor was the manic-depressive tendency to which Josh was prone in any particular way involved.

Early the next morning, as he went downtown on the subway and then walked to the Hogan Building, Josh's state of mind was not greatly changed—the discouragement continued unabated. After desultorily making calls and trying to tackle some paperwork, distracted and depressed, Josh finally went to the office of his immediate boss, Justine Prashker, and reported to her as she reviewed the relevant file.

"I can't continue on this case," he concluded. "There's a conflict."

"Well, we know that," she said. "You told us. You know this guy . . ." She leaned forward, checking the paperwork on her desk. "*Des McGrath*," she read. "That's okay."

"No, but now there's a real conflict."

During my period of unemployment I got in the habit of visiting friends in order to get out of the apartment—and have the illusion of an independent life. Though Josh himself had written his address down for me, when I got there I doubted I was in the right place. It was a claustrophobia-inducing tenement-style dump—trash spilling out of cans in the downstairs hallway, incredibly depressing decor, noise, and that terrible "hundred years of dust, dirt, rodent feces, and unopened-windows" low-rent-building smell.

As I went up the stairs, the bad-air atmosphere was so oppressive I felt I was going to have a gasping asthma attack— and I don't *have* asthma. Touching the banister, grime stuck to my hand, which, not having with me the red bandanna I normally kept in my pocket as a handkerchief (snot-rag) and all-purpose cleaning instrument, I finally wiped off on the inside of my sweatshirt—at least something which could easily be thrown in a washing machine.

Josh himself had earlier commented on what unbelievable conditions people in the city had gotten used to living in. In his work he saw a lot of apartments and he said smallness was not the half of it. Nor was the problem just bad landlords or the then-strict rent regulations that made buildings uneconomical to properly maintain; a lot of the tenants themselves were just, he had reluctantly concluded, amazing slobs, too lazy or addled to clean and evidently willing to live in pigsties if of their own design. The cool waitress at the local pub was apt to live in some dump stinking of cat pee and strewn with clutter of unimaginable proportions. Where it would all end, no one knew.

According to Josh, the terrible, not quite classifiable sour smell in many buildings was that of long-term cockroach infestation—decades of rotting insect feces and carcasses filling the walls and every cavity and crevasse. The standard-issue former-working-class tenement housing the girls lived in, though admittedly scant in amenities, was a cozy bed-and-breakfast in comparison.

Outside Josh's third-floor apartment, several strands to the overwhelming bad smell could be distinguished: discount insecticide, the inevitable cat pee, and undisposed-of garbage wafting from the floor above. A Harold Melvin & the Blue Notes album playing inside suggested that Josh was was *in*, and momentarily he opened the door in standard shabby weekend wear—shirt with a collar frayed like capellini, trousers with paint smears and holes near the pockets, etc.

"God, what a dump," I said as he led me inside.

Looking around his apartment, Josh agreed. "Yeah."

"No, I don't mean your place—outside." With my thumb I roughly indicated the hall and stairs of the building behind me.

"Oh yeah," he agreed. "Phee-yew."

Josh's place was microscopic but well arranged. Of course, the music improved the atmosphere. The previous tenant, a girl, had scrubbed every inch with baking soda, and Josh had built on her work, leaving the furnishings very spare. The overall effect was appealing. It gave you the impression Josh could have been a designer of some skill. Still, the gantlet of the building outside was not something to expose Alice or anyone like her to. The relationship would have to be very, very far along to risk that. Better dates at some safe restaurant—or nightclub. People thought a lot about this sort of thing in the New York of those years.

On Saturdays I always bought the *New York Post* and now carried a copy with me. It was a quick read and often quite informative. I found some edge space for it on the table and sat down on a wooden chair next to it.

"You iron your own shirts?" I asked.

An ironing board was set up at half-height in the middle of Josh's tiny kitchen, with a chair in front of it and a pile of clean but unironed laundry on the kitchen table pushed against the corner. Painted a high-gloss yellow, the table was the room's bright spot.

"Well, if I'm going to court, I wear a laundry-ironed shirt," he said, "but otherwise, yeah, I do it myself . . ."

A can of Niagara Spray Starch rested on the ironing board, and as Josh sat down to his work, he applied it liberally. "Starchy" is one of those adjectives that has been widely misused in our society. Starch, properly applied, keeps us looking sharp and trim even when, basically, we're not; it has been given an undeserved negative connotation, probably because literature—and especially social commentary—tends to be written by the slobs.

Steam spewed and sputtered from inside the hot iron, which was one of the good new chrome-and-steel models that had glass along one side to reveal the interior water level. This was the first time I had ever seen anyone iron sitting down, though I suppose there was no reason not to do so, especially if you were as slow and painstaking about it as Josh and most guys were—not that the results ever looked very good. It reminded me of my own laundry experiences.

"That's a great moment in life when you can start sending all your shirts out for laundering," I said. "At the agency, after my last promotion, I briefly had that."

"Yeah," Josh agreed. "In any case, I doubt I'll be working there much longer."

"What?"

"I'm thinking of quitting."

"You can't do that . . ."

"Why not? What's it to you?"

I couldn't quite believe what he was saying.

"You assured me that if I helped you, you'd be around to protect Des!"

"Well," he said, "the situation's changed."

"How's it changed?"

"I can't say . . ."

He stood up and put the shirt he had been working on on a hanger. I still awaited his reply.

"Maybe Des is more involved than I thought."

"Or more involved with someone you know," I said. "That's it, Josh, isn't it? That's a conflict."

Josh took another shirt. "I can't believe Alice is really serious about Des."

"Why not?"

"She seems so smart."

"That doesn't matter," I said. "It's something deeply ingrained in human biology. Women prefer 'bad' over 'weak and indecisive'—and 'unemployed.' "

"I don't know about that . . ."

"You think they do prefer 'weak, indecisive, and unemployed'?" I asked hopefully.

19

Past Perfect

Well past 4 a.m., after the Club's bars had stopped serving, it still took quite a while for all the stragglers from the Club's several floors of lounges, balconies, nooks and crannies to gather themselves up and go. There were usually a few found asleep or passed out by the cleaning crew, and occasionally someone would wake up or return to consciousness long after the Club was closed and dark, in which case they could only get out if they found their way downstairs and a watchman unlocked the doors.

But it was not yet that late. The close-down had just begun on an early Saturday morning, i.e., very late Friday night. The house lights had not yet been brought up for the cleaning crew, though some, using gray Rubbermaid tubs, were already collecting the dirty glasses and empty bottles with the consequent clinks and clunks. A short line remained at the coat check as the last stragglers made their way to it. Above the dance floor the glitter ball spun slowly, dragging beautiful bits of refracted light along the walls of the nearly empty Club, as if timed to the music, now a slow and mellow Dean Martin song, "Everybody Loves Somebody Sometime."

"Wrap beer" for the staff was sort of a Club tradition. I had gone to the main bar to get some Rolling Rocks for Van, Rick, and Bobby outside. The main bar's managers, Jay and Alexis, were doing their count for the last two cash drawers and there was a discrepancy that really worried Alex (as he was also known).

Meanwhile, Charlotte and Alice lounged on a banquette they had to themselves, as relaxed as if they had been in their own living room, which, in a sense, they were. Josh was also lurking around the Club somewhere.

"It's one of the aspects of the sexual revolution they don't like to talk about," Charlotte was saying. "Men have gotten very, very weird." She darted a look toward me at the bar, where I was joking around with Jay, who was sort of the club clown. "Jimmy's terribly closed off now," she said, the concern in her voice unmistakable. "His previous girlfriends weren't very nice to him. But I'm still confident I'll be able to break through to him emotionally at some point."

Victor was just then crossing the main floor, on his way from Berrie's domain upstairs to Des's office in the backstage area. He knocked perfunctorily on Des's closed office door before entering. Des was at his desk, looking as if he might have just snorted some cocaine—which was in fact the case.

"Berrie wants to see you."

With an apprehensive look, Des got up and followed him out, staggering slightly on the stairs—not necessarily the effect of the coke, probably more from the booze before that. Also, it was very late and everyone working at the Club tended to get really tired at some point.

Crossing the main floor, Des veered over to the girls' banquette to say something to Alice while Victor waited impatiently a ways off.

"Could you wait for me until I get off? Let's have breakfast together—there's something I want to talk with you about."

"Come on," Victor said. Des turned and followed him up the stairs, as if to his doom.

After they left, Charlotte leaned in toward Alice. "You know, I think I could have been wrong about Des," she said. "You might have really changed him."

Alice didn't look especially reassured, though.

Next to Berrie's third-floor office was a large space he used as the counting room for the nightly take. It was actually the superstructure behind the Club's interior dome, all steel and raw concrete, with just a few lamps and wooden tables and chairs where the front-door cashier, coat-check operator, and bar managers completed the nightly count under his supervision, assisted by Victor and Adam.

Berrie was in the process of getting an inexpert back massage from Nicole, a sexy black waitress in one of the revealing Club outfits, as, vodka in hand, he monitored Alexis's recount at the table next to him. When Alexis lost his place, Berrie interjected the count so far— "Twenty-three thousand eight hundred twenty-six"—a bit scarily. Alexis nodded, wrote it down, and continued counting.

Victor led Des past the echo-y sound of vacuuming in the Club's upper reaches into the sanctum sanctorum of the Club's operations, an area Berrie normally kept him out of.

"Berrie—you wanted to see me?" Des asked.

"Yeah. I do," Berrie said, but then took a long, thoughtful sip of his vodka while monitoring the count and letting

Nicole work on the tense muscles bunched up below his neck. Des was left just to stand there looking on. Finally Berrie said, "Sometimes I get the feeling you hardly know me, Des," glancing up in his direction only once. "I care about ideas. I care about them *a lot*."

Des opened his mouth as if to say something affirmative, but no sound came out. He tended to be more awkward and nervous with Berrie than anyone. It was a "new Des" for anyone who had not seen him that way before.

Sick of the useless massage, Berrie turned to Nicole and gave her a kiss. "Thanks, babe," he said in the soft tone he reserved for "babes" as she crossed out of the room.

"Des, do you know that old Caribbean song—calypso, I guess—that goes, 'If you want to be happy for the rest of your life, why not make an ugly woman your wife'—or something to that effect?"

"Uh, yeah, I know it."

"Funny, isn't it? Cute."

"Yeah. Funny."

"They play it on the oldie stations *a lot*, Des. Really. A lot."

"You want us to play it here?" Des asked. This seemed really odd—normally Des was fiercely protective of the Club's playlist, which was his domain. This song would have been pretty inappropriate for play at the Club.

"No," Berrie said, shaking his head. "I'm not talking about music now, Des. I'm interested in the ideas. The ideas as embodied in words. That's my interest. Have you ever thought, Des, how much time people spend listening to the words to a song like that and thinking, *How true*?"

He turned to Des for emphasis. Des shook his head.

"The amount of time is almost . . . unimaginable. But the song is . . . *not true.*" He glanced at Des again. "The truth is, Des, if you make an ugly woman your wife, you probably *won't* be happy for the rest of your life.

"Do you know why?" he asked.

Des shook his head.

"No one likes to be considered ugly, Des. Everyone likes to be considered attractive in some way, in someone's eyes. If a woman thought someone had married her just because she was ugly, she would be very resentful—and resentfulness doesn't lead to marital happiness, Des, so far as I have seen."

This was new. Usually Berrie just talked about how much he hated people in advertising and law enforcement. He was a big repeater, but Des had never heard any of this before.

He found Berrie watching him, as if waiting for a response.

"That song's a lie, Des," he insisted. "A stupid, moronic lie."

"I didn't know you'd been married," Des said.

"I haven't," Berrie replied. "I'm not speaking from personal experience, Des. I've never jumped off a building, either, but I can imagine what it feels like to hit the ground."

Des was a little weirded out by all this. He did not know what to say—so in fact he said nothing and just nodded as Berrie started up again.

"I'm sure many ugly people are . . . *fine,* Des. Maybe they would be . . . *fine* to be married to, but it's not their ugliness that makes them so appealing. You cannot be *certain* someone would be a good spouse just because she's ugly. That's absurd."

Berrie sipped at his vodka thoughtfully, then looked at Des.

"Marriage, Des, is far too important a decision in life to make on the basis of physical attractiveness of whatever sort."

Des nodded. He, in fact, agreed with what Berrie was saying—in theory.

"I know you think I'm a bad person, Des—"

"No—"

"I've committed some *infractions* in my day. I'll admit that. But I've never done anything *really bad*. I've never written *lying song lyrics*, for instance. I've never made money by spreading ideas that are *completely untrue* and could wreck people's *lives* if they should actually believe them—which they *normally do*. I'm not a bad guy of—*that* kind.

"Oh, I know," he continued, " 'It was just a joke. A *novelty song*. I didn't expect them to take it seriously.' Give me a break! That's not a defense, Des. That's rationalizing crap and I don't buy it for a second!"

Des kept quiet, nodding occasionally and keeping his eyes down, which just seemed to incite Berrie more. Everyone else in the counting room had pretty well cleared out.

"Did you know that I went to Catholic schools, Des?" Berrie continued.

Des shook his head.

"Yeah. Parochial schools, here in Manhattan. I was a choirboy, too. Pretty cute. And don't feed me that crap about priests bothering kids. For high school, I went to Regis. Have you ever heard of it?"

Des shook his head.

"I'm surprised. It's considered one of the best schools in the country. I thought you would have heard of it. For college, I went to Loyola, though I ended up at Bard . . . I can't believe how little you really know about me, Des."

Berrie shook his head as if in disbelief that two people

who had worked together over such a long period should not know each other better.

"In college, my senior paper was on Ernest Hemingway," he added, looking up at Des for emphasis.

Around then Victor came up and put the night's takings in bricks of cash on the table.

"Forty-eight thousand six hundred fifty-four," he said, holding the work sheets from the count. Berrie nodded, not looking especially pleased.

"Leave it—I'll take a look," he said.

Victor nodded and left. Berrie and Des watched him go. Des was starting to feel pretty lonely by now.

"Did I ever tell you about my first job, Des? It was at one of these big ad agencies—Y & R, maybe you've heard of it?"

Des nodded.

"I'm reluctant to talk about it. In fact, I've never told anyone. What really bothered me about working at one of those big agencies was how you had to pretend to be 'nice' to everyone—to the secretaries, the media department, the copywriters, the art department . . . *the Client* . . ."

Berrie shook his head in disillusionment and repugnance. Des listened intently, trying to avoid giving any impression he might have heard all this before.

"I'm not a 'nice person,' Des . . . But some things are important, such as . . . loyalty. Loyalty's not eyewash, like 'niceness.' I've been loyal to you, Des. I could have fired you, lots of times, but never did—"

"Well—"

"I'm not 'nice,' Des. But I'm not . . . a thug, either. I'm not Mafia. If you slip up, I don't promise to ruin you. I've never threatened to cause anyone *'bodily harm'*—"

Berrie lit a joint he had in his jeans jacket and took a drag, continuing as he exhaled: "I hate that sort of thing. I'm not the kind of person whose former associates are found in trash cans, or floating in the river . . ."

He gave Des a sharp look. "Maybe you're not aware of this, Des, but there's some kind of *investigation* going on here. I think to myself, How could this happen? How could they get this information? Has some disgruntled employee—former or current—informed on us? Is there some sort of *spy* here?"

He let Des hang a moment. Des allowed himself to look mystified.

"How could agents even get in? They'd really stand out in this crowd and, normally, not get past the door . . ."

Des looked as if he were trying to think how they might have gotten in.

"Do you know how they got in?" Berrie asked.

"Uh, no," Des said. "Could Van be letting them in?"

"They're coming in as ad agency clients."

"What?!"

Berrie nodded.

Des thought a moment; then a flush came over his face.

"I can't believe it! . . . After all I did for that guy!"

"So you don't know anything about this investigation?"

"No . . . Well, a sort of . . . acquaintance who now works in Morgenthau's office approached me. But I didn't tell him anything."

"You didn't tell me about that."

"Well . . . I didn't think it was important . . . It only just happened."

"When?" Berrie asked.

"Tonight. Just now."

"Why did you use the past perfect, then?"

Des was stumped. "I used the past perfect?"

"Yeah, 'approached me'—it sounds like a while ago."

Des just looked blank—maybe he had slept through that grammar class. Was it *really* the past perfect, anyway? In any case, Berrie had made his point.

Des descended the stairs in clumps. The cleaning lights were now on throughout the Club, but Alice and Charlotte were sacked out, dozing on two main-floor banquettes. Josh, tremendously fatigued, rested his head on his arms folded across the back of an adjacent one while obliquely keeping his eyes on Alice. The cleaning crew was in full swing in different parts of the Club, vacuuming and collecting glasses and bottles.

As Des crossed the room, Josh scrambled up to intercept him.

"Des!"

Des looked back, very angry, but did not stop. Josh followed him.

"Get away," Des said. "Don't talk to me—"

"Berrie knows about the investigation," Josh said.

"I haven't told you anything!" Des snapped, and pushed through the doors to the backstage area. Josh followed.

"There was some leak at the precinct level; Berrie had an informant; but it's been fixed. It's not a problem any longer."

"It's a problem!" Des said, very emphatic, turning to confront Josh. "I've never said anything to you. Nothing. You've got to make that clear to everyone."

"That doesn't matter."

"What?"

"When everything comes down, Des, it's going to be very rough. Your whole life'll be open for examination and—it might not look so good . . . Cut out the drugs, Des."

"What?!"

"Stop making such a spectacle of yourself as a drug user. Don't receive them, don't consume them, and don't . . . 'pass them on' to others."

"What are you talking about?"

"You could be charged with dealing," Josh said.

"Dealing?! Those were gifts!"

"*Well* . . ." Josh interjected skeptically.

"Who's accusing me of this? It's you, isn't it, Josh? That's a conflict—we both like the same girl."

At this point they heard a chilling cry from the front of the Club, and both rushed out toward the sound to see if there was anything they could do to help.

I had brought a supply of cold Rolling Rocks out to the front of the Club for Van & Co., as well as one for myself. We joked and chatted with the last stragglers as they streamed out or sometimes lingered with us by the velvet ropes. Many had over the last months become Van's friends—so there were lots of "*Ciaos*," "G'byes," "G'nights," or "Hey, get some sleep."

Freed of the necessity of getting clients into the Club and the conflict of interest that posed, I had gotten in the habit of hanging out with Van quite a bit and was beginning to understand the tremendous pressure he was operating under—and how (basically) well he handled it. It turned out that Van was not a bad guy at all—I don't think he could have been and still made the Club such a great place. I started to develop a lot of respect for him. While I did not question the role Des had played in creating the Club's success, I now saw that Van, too, played an important part.

As a corollary, I had to acknowledge that, before, when I thought he was such a monster, I was mostly in the wrong. Sure, there were problems with how Van conducted himself at the door, but I couldn't use that to let myself off the hook. My behavior had been cynical and narcissistic. When I was trying to get all those out-of-town clients into the Club "by any means necessary," it was really all about "me," "my needs," "my clients," "my job," not the objective conditions Van faced.

Even Van's explanation of the Club's notorious "door policy" rang partly true. Van said that because the publicity job initially done for the Club had been so fabulously effective, turning it into a phenomenon (Des was partly responsible), all sorts of people wanted to come who ordinarily wouldn't have, who really weren't suited to it, and probably wouldn't even enjoy it that much. He said that if he let in lots of people not cut out for the Club, they probably wouldn't have a good time and would end up complaining, "Oh, the Club isn't so good. I went there once and didn't really like it; it's nothing special." That's how places' reputations were trashed.

This rang true. I had found that the clients who had been the hardest to get into the Club often became its toughest critics, sometimes scathingly negative, once we got inside. It could be a little exasperating, after the trouble of getting them in, to have them immediately start badmouthing every-thing, sometimes going on and on about some defect I frankly had never noticed. I don't know what they expected.

On the other hand, it was logical that people who did not feel comfortable in the Club, or were lost on the dance floor and unrhythmic, or perhaps did not even particularly like or value dancing or Disco itself, should have not enjoyed an evening at the Club. There is an old saying that the girl who complains that the orchestra can't play is generally the one who can't dance. This explains a lot—for instance, the entire anti-disco movement.

What happened outside the Club that night I can recon-struct better from what others said later than from what I saw myself. A group of three thuggish guys—one of whom car-ried with him a thick piece of doweling wood—were appar-ently approaching where we were at the Club entrance, but still quite far off. A big wide-bodied Pontiac rolled just behind them, so slowly as to seem basically parked.

"You really should go to Ibiza," Van was telling me, pro-nouncing it the lisping Castilian Spanish (*ee-bee-thah*) way.

"Uh-bee-thuh?" I asked mispronouncing.

"Ibiza."

"Ibiza?"

"Yeah. It's great. The women go topless there."

Rick stepped over and whispered something to Van out of my hearing. It turned out that he was alerting him to the approach of the three suspicious-looking guys. As later reconstructed, the sequence of events appeared to have been as follows: One of the thugs, called Bruno by the others, pointed Van out ("the tall guy") to his pal carrying the stick (which no one had noticed at that point). The stick guy nodded, and when they got close to the stanchion, all three rushed us. Rick and Van dodged back just as I turned to see what was going on and caught the stick—*thwack*—hard across the face. A jolt of pain such as I had never experienced—and hope never will again—engulfed me before I lost consciousness, or something close to losing consciousness while still feeling excruciating pain.

The Pontiac gunned forward and the thugs scrambled to climb into it, with much shouting as they did so, one of them briefly hanging on to the swinging passenger door as the car pulled away.

"Bastards! We'll get you!" Van called after them.

Rick chased the car a good thirty yards before giving up and resignedly watching them take the corner, tires squealing.

Alice and Charlotte said they could hear the shouts and squealing tires from inside the Club. They sat bolt upright as some of the remaining Club staff ran outside, followed by Josh and Des.

"Rick!" Van called. "Jimmy's hurt! . . . Call an ambulance!"

Alice said the last thing she heard was an eerie, high-pitched cry like a wounded animal, "It's my *no-ose!*"—that she found absolutely chilling.

20

A Meteorite Does—or Does Not—Head for the Club

A gurney carrying a young man looking quite a bit like me—his face bloodied—was rushed by two scared-looking orderlies into the pre-dawn emergency room. Only his eyelids fluttered, as if he might have lost some brain function and descended into a coma.

The doctor who treated me said that if the blow had struck at a less deflecting angle I might have ended up the same way. But, luckily, all that was required was some stitches and bandaging. Perhaps if I had been more severely injured it would have done more to assuage Des's anger.

We were sitting in the emergency room's waiting area, which was pretty quiet at that time of night, except for the occasional bloody admission. Charlotte lay stretched out on a row of seats next to us, sleeping. She looked beautiful, innocent, beyond reproach.

"I didn't know anything about it, Des," I said in reply to his insistent questioning. "The agency just funneled everyone they wanted to get in through me. Usually, before getting in the car, I wouldn't even know them. I just assumed they were clients from out of town . . . That the IRS was our largest client didn't occur to me—then."

My voice was very nasal, almost absurdly so. I knew it made me sound like a whining liar as well as feel like one. I tried to enunciate, but occasionally had to almost gasp for breath, unused to having my now-blocked nasal passages unavailable for respiration. Pieces of cotton wadding jammed each nostril, with cotton gauze covering the whole nose area to sop up additional bleeding but fairly suffocating nonetheless.

"I swear, Des, I didn't know anything about it . . ."

I really hated the way I sounded—such a liar.

"*At first,*" I added.

"You scumbag."

"Josh *promised* me you'd be protected."

"Oh great," Des said. "What's a little shocking," he went on, nodding toward my injury, "is that they'd do something so obvious and clumsy—and move so fast, no matter how *richly* you deserved it."

"No," I said, "these were just some creeps mad Van'd turned them away before. It's scary how much anger's out there, Des—this kind of thing's happening all the time. Van's operating under tremendous pressure out there. I'm beginning to feel a lot of sympathy for the guy."

"Oh great," Des repeated. "That's priceless. You and Van! I love that."

Meanwhile, rummaging in his pockets for cigarettes, he located something else.

"Look," he said, pulling out one of those tiny plastic bags cocaine is usually represented as being packaged in. "Want a snort?" he asked cynically. "Sorry. Guess not," he added.

I was, in fact, getting a little concerned about the amount of cocaine Des was consuming and mentioned something to that effect, which he did not take well. The irritation was unmistakable.

"I've a really bad feeling about the Club, Des," I said. "It's like a meteorite is headed straight for it and is going to destroy everything. The best nightclub the world has ever seen is going to be smashed to smithereens."

"Well," he said, "I don't think it'll be a meteorite."

Josh and Alice had returned from the hospital comptroller's office, where Josh had offered to take care of the paperwork. He handed me back my ID cards and gave me the receipt.

"Everything's set," he said. Des gave Josh a withering look, which Josh ignored.

"Are you feeling better?" Alice asked me, with a wonderful concern.

I nodded, grateful for her sympathy.

The sun was already up when Des put Charlotte and me in a cab to take us back uptown to the—I hoped—less violent precincts of Yorkville. He then rejoined Alice and Josh on the curb in front of the coffee shop near the hospital—which was not the Acropolis, our usual pit-stop place, but in fact closely resembled it. Des immediately put his arms around Alice's shoulders in that awful, possessive, braggadocio way I frankly can't stand, a pretty vulgar touch even for Des. It really bothered Josh, too.

"Alice and I are having breakfast together," Des informed him brusquely. "It's a date. You can't come."

"That's not for you to say, Des."

Des looked around, exasperated. "Has everybody gone crazy?"

"Sorry," Alice told Josh. Despite having seemed very much "with" him all that morning, she felt obliged to prevent any kind of altercation. Des was also correct—they did have a breakfast date.

Josh, craning his neck, looked in the plate-glass coffee-shop window—as if checking if the atmosphere were sufficiently good for Alice. He was experienced enough to know that wars were not won by having to win every skirmish. "Try to get some sleep," he told her before taking off, with a proprietariness which in this case she did not mind.

"So long," she called. " 'Bye."

" 'Bye, Josh!" Des added facetiously.

"What's with you and Josh?" Des asked once everything had calmed down and they were settled in one of the old-style coffee shop's classic burgundy vinyl and fake wood booths. "Are you two *dating* or something?"

"Not really," Alice said.

"In what sense, 'not really'?"

"He just invited me to lunch to discuss a book idea."

"That's what guys do who want to date you?" Des asked. "Say they have a book idea?"

"Maybe," Alice said.

"Did he say what it was about?"

"He said he had some crazy ideas for a book on the criminal-justice system."

"Of course. That makes sense. *Crazy* ideas are the kind that Josh would have."

Des sipped his coffee before continuing. "Be careful with

that guy. I was there when he flipped out. *Really scary,*" Des said, and sort of quaked, as if thinking back on that night. "He got up on a table at this cafeteria off Harvard Square and started weirdly singing this hymn . . ."

In a strange voice, Des started mock-singing, " 'Once to every man and nay-yay-tion comes the moment to-oo decide . . . ' "

From across the room, some patrons eyed Des askance.

"Apparently religious mania is highly typical of manic depression entering its 'manic' phase," he said. "Josh is not just your garden-variety 'loon' or freakazoid but a serious nutcase. What gets me is that this serious nutcase now pre-sumes to judge others."

The waitress came around and, a little warily, topped up Des's cup with coffee before moving to another table.

Des looked down at his cup and then up at Alice. "Do you really think the neurological effect of coffee is similar to that of cocaine?" he asked.

"That's what I read somewhere."

Des contemplated his coffee cup for a moment. Suddenly he plunged his nose into the lukewarm brew and seriously tried to snort it. There was a loud, liquidy, snorting sound. Coffee splashed into the saucer and onto the tabletop. Nearly everyone in the restaurant stared, not knowing exactly what was going on, but Alice laughed.

A few days later, in another part of town, coffee was being poured into a different cup, a nicer one. Milk was added, then Alice raised it to her lips. In addition to being the restaurant of choice for her lunches with her Aunt Janet, the Brasserie (in its nicer, older incarnation) served as commissary for the more economy-minded of the midtown publishing crowd— the high-rollers might be at Four Seasons on the other side of the Seagram Building, but the non- or modest-expense-account crowd tended to congregate here.

"In addition to amazing stories, there're a lot of entertaining prosecutors' anecdotes," Josh said. "Then there's the whole culture of the downtown legal district."

"It could be good," Alice said.

For a moment they both pondered how good it could be, vague smiles on their faces.

"Of course," Alice added, "like anything, it all depends on execution."

"This is sort of related," Josh said. "It's an article I wrote for *Harper's* during law school."

He handed her the photocopied article, which Alice examined with interest, rather impressed. In those days *Harper's* was still very well-considered, and serious magazine publication lifted a book proposal up from the usual impossible/vanity-projects bin. Though, later, it would be easier for people to dismiss—"Oh, it was basically a magazine article."

When the waiter left the check, Josh took it. Alice did not even pretend to start the typical sharing wrangle. Meanwhile, she looked over Josh's article with interest, then folded it up to take with her. "Did you really just want to have lunch to discuss a book proposal?"

"Uh, no . . ." Josh replied. "How serious are you and Des? Is it absolutely, completely, irrevocably serious?"

Alice did not respond immediately, so he continued: "Did he tell you the story about how he was traumatized by a

Radcliffe girl suddenly taking off her shirt—revealing her largish breasts?"

Alice, surprised, nodded.

"He tells that story all the time," Josh said, "to get sympathy and justify himself, as if he were the victim of female
aggressiveness and duplicity."

"That wasn't true?"

"No, it was true. He *was* the victim of female aggressiveness and duplicity—but so was everyone else. Not everyone
else then went on a rampage exploiting the opposite sex."

Alice said, "He thinks his problem is just that he falls in
love a lot."

"Well"—Josh smiled a little skeptically—"everyone falls
in love a lot . . ."

He stopped and regrouped. "I'm really surprised you'd
be . . . taken in by him."

An awkward moment followed. Josh feared he had over-
played his hand: generally, it's not a good tactic to accuse the
object of your affection of foolishness on the first date, or
even semi-date business lunch. There'd be plenty of time for
that later.

But Alice seemed to take it pretty well. That, incidentally,
was typical of her. She was not the sort of person who always
looks around for some reason to get offended.

"You should notice," she said, "I didn't answer your original question."

"My original question?" Josh thought a moment.
"Whether you were absolutely committed to Des—you
didn't answer . . . ?"

While Josh pondered this, Alice finished her coffee, tip-
ping the cup up to taste the last sweet, caffeinated drops.

After lunch they walked back from the restaurant along Park Avenue in front of the impressive spare international-style Seagram Building and the intricately decorative, almost Babylonian St. Bartholomew's Church (familiarly "St. Bart's"), where some of New York's most beloved couples have been married (including my brother and sister-in-law, Linda). Some trees and a garden planted alongside it, now in bloom, brought some color to an otherwise austere stretch of Park Avenue.

"What does 'loon' mean?" Alice asked.

Josh smiled. "Des calls me that."

Alice nodded.

"I sort of like it," he said. " 'Loon'—it's short for 'lunatic,' and also the lake bird with the eerie call—"

Josh did his loon call, which really was eerie.

"It's the other terms Des uses for me—'nutcase,' 'freaka-zoid,' etc.—I kind of mind."

Josh had a pretty weird way of making himself interesting to girls but, unfortunately, it worked.

"A lot of people like to say they won't take 'no' for an answer," he continued. "I just wanted you to know I'm not one of them. I can be easily discouraged. I *will* take 'no' for an answer."

Alice thought about this for a while.

"Okay," she said, " 'No.' "

"You don't mean that?" Josh asked, worried.

"No," she said.

21

The Tiger Lady Has a Name

After parting from Josh, Alice entered her building with an enigmatic but essentially happy expression, as if rethinking the recent events. She walked quickly to the back elevator bank and was able to just slip into an up car before its doors closed. Even for someone working in book publishing, notorious for its "long lunches," it had gotten pretty late. Alice transgressed this way so rarely she thought that it should be okay, or at least hoped so (her editor tended to be pretty indulgent about such things).

Passing through the reception area on her floor, she nodded to Nancy the receptionist, who was on the phone and did not see her. Heading toward the bay, she ran into Helen, whose problems concentrating on her own work (which was deskbound) had led to constant errand-wandering, making her seem ubiquitous at times.

"Alice, sorry," she said, in a worried tone.

"What?"

Helen hesitated. "You'd better see Bob," she said.

When Alice got to the bay and was nearing her desk—Charlotte was not around—she was further disconcerted at the way Josephine looked up at her approach.

"Bob wants to see you right away," she said.

"It's something . . . bad?"

Josephine nodded.

"The author of your Tibet book . . . doesn't exist. The whole thing's a fraud. Carol thinks it could be more serious than the Clifford Irving case."

All that day Charlotte had been at sales conference at the Barclay-Hotel Inter-Continental—salesmen from all over the country were in town to hear presentations and get revved up about the books on Riley's next "list," excitement that they would then communicate, or not, to the booksellers and wholesalers in their territories—so she and Alice had not had a chance to talk about the emerging book scandal until that night at the Club. They were in the ladies' lounge, as mentioned, a bit of a misnomer, since there were often plenty of guys around, too.

"Carol thinks it's as bad as the Clifford Irving case," Alice said as they approached the washstands. "It turns out the author is *not* the Dalai Lama's brother but a Los Angeles writer named *John DeSimio*. It's a shame, because it's a really good book. Dan thinks it's one of the best things ever written on Tibetan Buddhism."

"I'm sorry I haven't been more of a help," Charlotte said, looking at Alice through the mirror. While speaking she could not help noticing that she herself looked extraordinarily beautiful that night. Often her own good looks surprised her—she wondered whether the biological changes taking place within her body might be involved, giving her the "glow" she had heard others speak of.

"I've been a little preoccupied myself," she added.

"What?" Alice asked.

"I'm late for my period."

"How late?"

"A day," Charlotte said.

"A day late—and you're worried?"

"I'm sure I'm pregnant."

"But . . . isn't that what you wanted?"

"What do you mean?"

"You said you wanted to 'have Jimmy Steinway's babies.' "

"Yeah . . . But . . . not this way."

Meanwhile, Des and I were just leaving his "office" at the back of the Club. It was really a raffish sort of living room with stereo equipment for screening records the Club might play and only a small table and some chairs added to make it at all office-like.

"I'm not an 'addict,' " Des insisted, quite angry at something I had said. "I'm a 'habitual user.' "

None of us, no matter how bad our habits might seem to others, especially likes having them misrepresented as something even worse. This was evidently Des's posture. When we got to the doors leading to the main Club area, he stopped and turned to harangue me further. "I'm sick of you and that *nutcase* going around judging everyone—'Oh, he's an addict . . . Oh, he's basically honorable, except in his treatment of women.' I'm not a womanizer. In fact, I *hate* womanizers. In any case, Alice completely changed all that."

He pushed through the doors and we re-entered the main part of the Club. I followed Des to the edge of the dance floor, where he stood looking over it as the scene unfolded. Not far from us the sexy, attractively older Tiger Lady was dancing with a handsome younger guy.

"God, is she here every night?" I asked, not intending to be controversial or anything.

"Who?"

"The Tiger Lady."

"Don't call her that," Des said sharply.

I looked at him in surprise.

"That's so dehumanizing—'the Tiger Lady.' She has a name."

"She does? What's her name?"

Des did not say anything for a while; he just stared out over the dance floor, wiping his nose once quickly with his bandanna.

"Francesca, I think," he said finally.

"You know her well?"

"No. But there's nothing wrong with her. She's just very sexy. Big deal. It's what everyone aspires to."

Des was very odd that night—sentimental and sappy and reflective. Maybe he sensed that it was going to be our last night at the Club as a group. Sometimes there is an odd precognition of that kind which is not Nostradamus or astrology or clairvoyance, just the not-quite-conscious sensors in our minds or Greater Intelligence putting together all the hints and sensations within our ken and coming up with a conclusion in fact justified by observable phenomena.

There was a sudden commotion on the dance floor as Francesca's partner collapsed and started having a seizure of some kind. The guy jerked around, his eyelids fluttering, then puked.

"Get an ambulance!" Des called.

I intercepted Charlotte and Alice coming down the main staircase.

"Des had to leave—there was an emergency."

"What?" Alice asked.

"The young guy Francesca was with o.d.'d. Des's accompanying them to the hospital."

"Francesca?" Charlotte asked.

"The Tiger Lady," I clarified.

One of the revelations in this period was that Des had been keeping a terrible sort of private "journal," narrating in detail his sexual encounters and the events leading up to them, though it wasn't until the next week that I actually discovered it. The following account is partly based on a non-pornographic passage from that narrative.

Dawn was already in progress when the cab Des was riding in with Francesca—his jacket covering her semi-naked dancing outfit—approached the modern high-rises along the East River. They were returning from their vigil at St. Vincent's Hospital, where it seemed that Francesca's young friend—she called him "Paco"—was going to recover from his near-o.d. comparatively satisfactorily.

"No one has died in the Club," Des said. "I'm really proud of that."

"Is that so remarkable?"

"Yeah. It's pretty remarkable. Clubs are dangerous places, not so much in themselves as for the behavior people tend to get into there. Often, when someone's hurt at another club—and sometimes it's the bouncers themselves doing the hurting—they just hustle the person out the back and leave them there, where they might bleed to death or slip into a coma. It's really terrible. I always have an ambulance called, or get a doctor to check them out completely."

At this close range Des couldn't help occasionally noticing aspects of Francesca's see-through outfit and what lay under it. Francesca noticed him notice. Des shifted his look forward, out the front window again. The cab slowed and pulled over to the curb before her building, one of the pricey cracker-box high-rises.

Francesca leaned forward and rested her head on her arm. "I feel so weak . . ."

"You must be tired."

"No, I'm afraid I . . . took some of the same stuff Paco did."

She exhaled, making a *phuffing* sound, which did seem to express a state of extreme tiredness that could have been a consequence of drug involvement.

"Do you think you could see me up to my flat?" she asked. "I don't really trust the elevator man on this shift."

"Yes, certainly."

"Could you stay for a drink?"

"Certainly . . ." Des said. "What, uh, do you have?"

22

Des McGrath's "Wild Kingdom"

In the Animal Kingdom, all was not work. The animals also played, especially with their young. Zebras played with baby zebras; elephants with baby elephants; giraffes, similarly, with baby giraffes.

Then Man entered the Kingdom. His hair was white and he wore a trim safari outfit. A baby chimp gamboled playfully into the arms of Marlin Perkins, curator emeritus of the St. Louis Zoo and host of Mutual of Omaha's *Wild Kingdom* television series. Passing the chimp off with a smile to Jim, a handsome, younger, rather muscular colleague also wearing safari khaki, Perkins turned to directly address the camera and the television audience. Risk and danger are endemic in nature, he observed, but unlike our counterparts in the animal kingdom, Man has the means to make provision for his young—the comprehensive insurance coverage available from . . . *Mutual of Omaha*, he concluded with a euphonious flourish.

It was a little comical to see the grave expression Des, sitting in his comfortable chair, wore while taking all this in. He was glued to the set, nothing else mattering, engaged in the ritual of the "favorite TV show" in all its absurdity, what one critic has called the "ceremonial overvaluing of mediocrity." It was still breakfast time for Des, though chronologically midafternoon, and his watching was interspersed with the crunching of loud mouthfuls of Cheerios cereal. Eating was often part of the "favorite show" ritual.

I was sitting on the sofa, still wearing my raincoat, aware that I was not especially welcome but not especially concerned about my transgression, either—that was, in fact, my state of mind in this period. I would avoid using a trite expression like "quiet desperation" only because my "desperation" was not entirely quiet at this point. I had taken to plowing part of my weekly unemployment insurance stipend back into the New York economy in the form of discounted Happy Hour cocktails at such East Side watering holes as The Raveled Sleeve on Third Avenue in the upper Seventies, popular with young financiers and their banking jargon–spouting femme friends, and the legendary Dick Edwards' at Lexington in the Sixties, which drew an older, if-they-were-wood-they-would-have-been-mahogany crowd smelling of Bay Lime and old smoke but who were much more simpatico to premature failures.

I guess, without fully realizing it, I was looking for some way to subvert my life, unwilling just to sit back and let it be subverted solely by forces over which I had no control. The problem was, unless you were a totally out-of-control lunatic, subverting your own existence could not be achieved so easily. You had to wait for ways and means and, often, the passage of time.

Watching Des watch *Wild Kingdom* was a little dull even
for me, so I started looking around the jumbled clutter of
books and papers on his coffee table for something to glance
at, finally extracting a leather-trimmed (just the corners)
notebook of some kind full of his handwriting. Maybe I
would have shut it immediately had I not noticed Alice's
name written there, which I felt almost gave me the obligation to look further. Her involvement and the possible danger she was exposed to obviated any qualms. Written in a
compressed, somewhat frantic version of Des's handwriting
were other names I recognized—Nina, Diana—and notably
that of Francesca, the Tiger Lady. I had just started intently
reading when—

Whoppp!

—the book was slammed shut in my face, practically on
my nose. Des pulled it out of my hands and threw it onto the
table, also disorderly, he called his desk.

"Don't feel that every time you go to unemployment you
have to pass by here on the way uptown," he said.

"This is the last time anyway."

"Why don't you really look? I thought that only applied if
you weren't sincerely job hunting."

I stood up. "It's not just about finding a job anymore.
I've got to make some *radical changes*, Des. Staying on unemployment would just postpone the . . . radical changes I need
to make."

I nodded toward the mysterious notebook. "What was
that? There was some really weird stuff in there."

"None of your *beeswax*."

"Some kooky novel? I hope you haven't gotten the literary bug . . . Ugh."

This was a little disingenuous, since I was then also trying to write on the side myself.

Des turned back to *Wild Kingdom* and his breakfast—no reply was to be offered.

"Why all the mystery?" I persisted.

"Gahd, you're nosy!" he exclaimed. "As a matter of fact, I've been thinking," he said, getting up and going to where the notebook was. "Basically you know all about this."

He looked down and opened the book. "Sometimes I feel I see too many things that you really shouldn't see if you're going to be a . . . 'good person.' For instance, you have this idea that women *dislike* being exploited."

He looked toward me. "No. In fact, they like it," he said. "This isn't something I thought up. It's a, frankly, disturbing insight, based on experience, which has actually caused me lots of problems."

In my facial expression I tried to register a complete rejection of everything Des was saying—a "*rechazo total.*" My contemptuous look, however, is pretty much the same as all my other expressions, so it didn't seem to have any impact.

Des took a brief look inside the notebook. "At one point I was pretty overwhelmed with all kinds of absurd feelings of guilt, so I had the idea of keeping this sort of *Last Testament* to record the absolute truth of every little bad and terrible thing I did, which I've kept up to this day—"

"So, you *still are* doing bad and terrible things?" I challenged him, practically quaking; the anger must have shown in my voice and body language.

"No, not so much," he replied, utterly calmly. "With Alice, I've really changed . . ."

He sat down again and started leafing through the note-book. "What I really lack is—focus."

For a moment he got immersed reading a passage, then broke off. "It's pretty scabrous," he observed matter-of-factly, as if entirely without any sense of shame or regret.

The intercom buzzer had sounded while he was reading, so now he got up to answer it.

"Of course," he added, walking toward the intercom, "if it later turns into a literary work of some kind . . ."

Under a sofa cushion next to me I noticed a light blue wool fabric which, when I uncovered it, turned out to be a woman's sweater which I believed to be Alice's. My heart sank; suspecting is one thing, knowing another—or thinking one knows, especially after all Des had said.

"Who is it?" he enunciated into the intercom.

"Messen*jah* blah blah," came back the staticky response.

"Okay," he said, and pressed the door buzzer before turning back to me: "Oh, your client friends are finally returning the Oz costumes."

I didn't know what his "oh" was supposed to mean, and at this juncture frankly was not going to ponder it.

"*Whose is this?!*" I asked, somewhat accusatorily in tone, holding up the light blue sweater I was, in fact, almost certain was Alice's.

"Alice was upset about the situation with her Tibet book and just came over here to work on it," Des replied blandly.

As if this were a satisfactory explanation, he stepped out and clomped down the stairs, to intercept the messenger on his way up.

I stood up again, and although I had never in fact taken off my raincoat, now I sort of fluffed it out as if I were putting it on. Then I stepped over toward Des's desk and from amid the clutter grasped the notebook with his scurrilous *Last Testament* inside, smoothly slipping it under my coat.

"Uh—I think I'll be going now," I called down the stairwell a little theatrically.

I started down the stairs, leaving the apartment door slightly ajar. Partway down, I crossed with Des coming up.

"See you tonight," he said.

"Okay."

Des continued trudging upstairs carrying a cardboard costume box and a large white shopping bag with the rubberized Tin Man costume looking up from it.

Tablecloth, candlesticks, a bottle of wine—all the preparations for a romantic dinner had been set. Charlotte liked to entertain and was very good at it. Probably never had the girls' kitchen looked and smelled so well. A casserole was in the oven. Had any Campbell's Cream of Mushroom or other soup been used in its preparation, any trace had since been disposed of. Now Charlotte was toiling at the kitchen counter, preparing a platter of smoked salmon with capers and lemon wedges, taking care not to get any fishy smell on her lovely hands. In those days smoked salmon did not provoke the rather blasé, ho-hum response it tends to today.

"Isn't it a little . . . morbid?" Charlotte asked Alice, hesitating somewhat as if reluctant to pry. Alice, though technically in the bathroom, was in fact just a few feet from Charlotte in the kitchen of the compactly designed flat.

"*Morbid?*" Alice asked. She was in front of the washstand mirror, fully dressed, preparing to go out.

"Why take on all that baggage?" Charlotte asked, carrying the cutting board over to the dining table. "Isn't he a bit of a sicko? From the start you know he's defective—usually you don't find that out until much later . . ."

Charlotte sat at the table to prepare the little pieces of dark bread with capers and horseradish mustard while further developing her thought. "Have you ever thought what he might do in a manic episode, or when depressive? What if you have kids? It *can* be hereditary."

Then she added rather sweetly, "One thing about Jimmy, I know he'll make a good father."

Alice came out of the bathroom. "There's always some problem, some baggage," she said.

"Omigod, you're serious!"

"Not necessarily," Alice said.

The buzzer rang. Alice went to the intercom. "Coming," she said.

She went back for her raincoat, a cool white linen number her Aunt Janet had used in the sixties.

"Tonight I'm going to tell Jimmy," Charlotte said. "Wish me luck."

Alice said nothing.

Charlotte must have heard the jingling of my keys as I approached the door.

"You know," she told Alice sympathetically as she went to open it, "I think my father could have been an undiagnosed manic-depressive."

Charlotte pulled the door open just as I was about to put the key in the lock. She looked fabulous again that evening.

"Hi."

"Hi." To Alice, I asked, "Did you know Josh is waiting downstairs?"

"Yeah," she said. "Thanks."

Alice hurried out, still putting on her raincoat.

" 'Bye," she said.

" 'Bye."

As the door closed, Charlotte looked in the direction Alice had gone. "Alice is so great," she said. "I've got to be a better friend to her."

With this she put her arms around me, leaned me against the wall, and gave me a warm and lovely kiss. The sensation of physical pleasure it provided was intense, but just then, in fact, I was really thinking of Alice.

23

Forgive Our Foolish Ways

At this point the whole thing about Alice liking Josh so much was really getting on my nerves. Had *Alice and I* been free to go out, I'm certain we would have gotten along really well, too. Alice was not the kind of person it was particularly hard to get along with.

One of Josh's strangenesses was being able in later years to remember the exact details of all his early "dates" with Alice. Another was to buy and wear all his clothes several sizes too big, so that although actually quite tall, he tended to have the slightly juvenile look of a youngster whose mother has bought his clothes with too much "room to grow into."

The precise date of that evening was, according to Josh, May 17. In later years he still remembered clearly absolutely every little thing that happened. The evening was quite warm. In May the weather can go either way in New York. It can actually go either way any month, but particularly May. Alice and Josh had already had dinner and were walking side by side along the building side of Central Park South—in my opinion, the coolest midtown street—near where the restaurant San Domenico later became the lunch-hour haunt of many of the country's top graphic designers.

"Before leaving the D.A.'s office," Josh said, "I'd like at least once to use the expression"—acting it out, in a booming voice—'*Book this clown!*' "

Alice laughed. "I thought only police said that."

"No," Josh said, "I think an A.D.A. could too—in certain circumstances, perhaps not very typical."

"Are you aware," Alice asked tactfully "that all your clothes seem . . . slightly . . . big?"

"That's right," Josh said.

"What do you mean?"

"I'm still waiting for my growth spurt. My father and brother are both over six feet. You can still grow in your twenties—there're cases on record . . . Tall people tend to have great personalities—this kind, compassionate comprehension of the rest of the world . . . My father and brother are that way."

"But you're not?"

Josh shook his head. "I'd like to be, someday."

At a break in the traffic, they dashed across Central Park South to the leafy plaza along the rim of Columbus Circle at its juncture with Central Park. They walked toward the tall, very strange monument formed in the shape of the prow of a Teddy Roosevelt–era warship with the figure of a young boy standing on it, his arms outstretched. Several sad or stern sculptural figures gathered round the monument's base: a Madonna with child, a hooded mourner, Poseidon, a warrior from ancient times at rest; then, atop the monument's central column was an extravagant, gilt, horse-drawn chariot symbolizing victory.

Alice immediately sensed the change in Josh's mood as
they approached the memorial. I always felt that part of Alice's
incredible charm was her sensitivity to people's moods and
her ability to change and adapt to them.

"What's wrong?" she asked. Josh had grown silent and
looked a little preoccupied. "I was just remembering something . . ."

"What?"

"It's kind of maudlin," he said. "It was here that my
depression first descended."

"Oh," Alice said compassionately.

Josh looked up at the monument and started to read the
inscription:

> To the Valiant Seamen
> Who Perished in the
> MAINE
> By Fate Unwarned
> In Death Unafraid

"Isn't this the strangest, most forlorn monument?"

Alice nodded.

"Everything about it is so incongruous, forgotten—these
figures must be symbolic, but of what?"

"Yeah," Alice said, looking up also. "It's very sad . . ."

She looked to Josh. "What happened with your depression?"

"Nothing at first," he said. "I just went back to Cambridge, very depressed. Then there was the incident at the
Hayes-Bickford, after which I was taken to Mass. Mental for
'observation.' While there, I cut my hand trying to open a

stuck window, and they put me on a suicide watch—though I don't think I was ever really suicidal, at least no more than a lot of people that age."

They started walking again, heading up the park side of Central Park West, which was exceptionally verdant and gorgeous that night. Except for the distant roar of traffic and the cabs whizzing by on their way uptown, it seemed like a bucolic tree-covered lane. In the old days, when people could walk tranquilly inside the park at night, this corner of the city was said to have been extraordinarily romantic, really breathtaking and magical. You occasionally get a glimpse of how it might have been in old movies, though usually "as recreated" by some studio art director.

"But . . . you're okay now?" Alice asked, picking up the thread of the earlier conversation.

Josh replied with an intentionally drawn-out, self-deprecating "Uh, yeea-ahhh." Josh felt most reassured by not reassuring himself.

"Actually," he said, "a lot of people spend considerable sums of money to get the high I get absolutely naturally. Now, with lithium—which is actually a naturally occurring salt—I can stay on a perfectly even keel . . . perhaps too even."

"Did they prescribe . . . uh . . . lithium right away?"

Josh shook his head.

"Lithium wasn't so standard then," he said. "There was a lot of muddling through . . . Because my right hand was bandaged, I used my left to write friends cards, which was a mistake. My handwriting looked weird and really scared people. I don't think I was ever that, that badly off . . . but others might disagree."

He looked toward her to see what effect all this was having, but at that moment Alice was looking down, her expression essentially unreadable. Then she looked toward him, but he still couldn't tell.

"Do you know the words to the hymn 'Dear Lord and Father of Mankind'? While I was in the hospital, it became a sort of mantra."

Alice shook her head.

" 'Dear Lord and Father of mankind, forgive our foolish ways,' " Josh started in a quiet but poetical recitation of the hymn, using its underlying music, but not exactly singing. The effect was eerie but strangely moving, or at least it might have been for anyone with some emotional distance and the tranquillity to see it that way, which at that precise moment did not include Alice.

"Reclothe us in our rightful mind. In purer lives Thy service find. In deeper reverence, praise," the first verse went.

"Drop Thy still dews of quietness, till all our strivings cease; take from our souls the strain and stress, and let our ordered lives confess the beauty of Thy peace.

"Breathe through the heat of our desire Thy coolness and Thy balm; let sense be dumb, let flesh retire; speak through the earthquake, wind, and fire, O still, small voice of calm!"

When Josh finished, he immediately looked to Alice again.

She said nothing, just continued walking head down, looking up only once.

"What's wrong?" he asked. "You think I'm a . . . wacko?"

Alice at first slowly shook her head no—but then nodded yes.

*****

Alice and Josh arrived back on East Eighty-ninth Street just as the Emergency Medical Services vehicle was pulling up in front of the building. Seeing the ambulance, they covered the last yards at a run.

"What's happened?!" Alice asked.

"I don't know," I said, still kind of freaking out, very worried and not knowing how serious it might be. "Charlotte's in terrible pain—it's her back."

Upstairs, standing in the doorway while the EMS workers prepared to move Charlotte onto a stretcher from the thick carpet where she had lain seeking relief from her back pain (by now already dozing from some very strong painkiller she had taken), Alice quizzed me about what had actually happened.

"No. Nothing happened . . . We were just talking."

"About what?"

"Charlotte said she had something important she wanted to talk to me about, but before we got to that, her period started. Afterward, I mentioned that maybe it was a good time to start thinking about, you know, breaking up . . ."

I turned as the paramedics lifted Charlotte's stretcher. Alice and I followed, joining Josh downstairs as they carried the stretcher to the vehicle. He asked me about it, too.

"I've actually seen this before," I said. "Really bad back spasms."

Several days had passed. Alice in a moody, rather poetic state, looking out Charlotte's hospital window at the boat traffic in the East River. She was still in that bittersweet period when things have started going badly but you still haven't quite realized or accepted how badly, which is when the sweetness tends to disappear and you are just left with the bitter part.

"Josh hasn't called since that night," she said.

"Of course he hasn't."

Alice turned around. "What do you mean?"

"You were *awful* to him," Charlotte said.

Alice looked taken aback.

"Come on," Charlotte said. "You told me. He sang a hymn or something. You were totally weirded-out."

"Well, it was pretty weird—singing hymns on the street."

"I can't believe how intolerant you are," Charlotte said, giving Alice a frank look softened with a smile. "I guess I've always been more . . . open to the spiritual side of things than you . . . Some of those old hymns are beautiful—I've sung them myself—I didn't realize it was so *controversial*."

She looked toward Alice, who had sat in the chair at the foot of her bed and now picked at a loose thread in her skirt.

" 'Amazing Grace'?" Charlotte said, mentioning one of the most beautiful traditional hymns, commercial recordings of which (one, as mentioned, by Carole King) reached the pop charts' Top 10 twice in the seventies—which is not to say Charlotte's interest in spiritual songs was frivolous or superficial (nor that it wasn't).

" 'Amazing grace! How sweet the sound that saved a wretch like me!' " she started to sing, tentatively, in a beautiful tremolo, slowly gaining in confidence and volume, " 'I once was lost, but now am found, was blind, but now I see.' "

Alice's appointment at the Women's Health Clinic came that week. Initially her experience of the "H" infection Tom had mentioned had been asymptomatic, but more recently it had become *not* asymptomatic.

Sometimes, when we're feeling low, small problems start to loom large and get confused with big problems, while impasses that might normally be ignored start to seem enormous. Meanwhile, problems that really *are* big don't get smaller—in fact, the reverse.

When Alice went to a pharmacy to get the vitamins the doctor recommended to assuage the symptoms, she bypassed the one she habitually used in her neighborhood for a more anonymous one midtown. There the pharmacist, a kindly, elderly foreign man, apparently guessing her ailment almost immediately, blurted out "Sorry" as he handed them to her, which, however well intended, depressed her inordinately nonetheless.

One forgets that one of the problems great people have is that they aren't available to themselves for consultation and advice. We get to talk with them, but they don't have that advantage. Oh, perhaps they can mumble to themselves and engage in interior monologues, but it's not really the same as having access to a deeply sympathetic intelligence distinct from oneself. The first person any of us would have consulted had we had a problem of that kind would have been precisely Alice. But for Alice herself there was no one. None of us were as terrific listening as she was, and for that kind of thing in particular, most of us were the wrong sex. She couldn't very well confide in Charlotte, and her own real friends were scattered all over the globe that year with traveling fellowships and the like.

That Saturday afternoon Holly visited the old apartment, which was then, with Charlotte still in the hospital, Alice's alone. Alice made some China black tea for the two of them, which they had in the living room, where the amber hues of the late-day sun now slanted in from the west. Alice did end up mentioning something to Holly, she hoped obliquely, about the situation she was facing. Despite what might seem to have been implied earlier, Holly was not, in fact, "dumb." She was in that category often described as being "not exactly a rocket scientist" but evidently understood immediately what Alice was talking about.

"There *are* a couple of alternatives that aren't that, that bad," Holly said. "First, some guy who's already been around a lot and almost certainly has it anyway, so it'd be no problem and in fact would give you something in common. The other would be some guy so idealistic and in love with you"—she was moved, and there was a catch in her throat—"that he'd want to commit himself to you anyway, *prior* to that step, since his dream would be to be with you forever exclusively always anyway . . . I think Skip's a bit that way."

I visited Charlotte at the hospital every day, doing the whole "devoted jerk" routine, which—if I did not know how painful backs can be—I would say she enjoyed almost more than any other period of our relationship. It was a very strange period for me. Both Des and Josh had chosen me to talk to almost obsessively about Alice while, because of my ambiguous situation, I couldn't say anything. In Charlotte's absence I felt I could not really stay at the girls' apartment, so I also lost the casual, relaxed, everyday contact with Alice I had enjoyed for almost a year. Now we saw each other only in the context of visits to Charlotte in the hospital, which had an entirely different feeling, at times pretty awkward. I actually preferred just being alone with Charlotte there. We ended up doing a lot of reading, and the authors I discovered in this period—the Anthonys Trollope and Powell, and Angela Thirkell—have been those I most often fall back on and perhaps have most influenced my own work.

24

The Woman in Red;
In Fact, Two Women in Red

Rumor had it that the investigation of the Club began after a well-connected lawyer from downtown had problems getting in several weekends running. This lawyer fancied himself a nightlife star; he had gotten into Studio and Xenon in the past, but was embarrassed outside the Club on dates with two different women on successive weekends and was extremely sensitive about such humiliations because of his hair problem, among other things. Rather than coping with rejection the usual way—just walking away, going somewhere else, despising the Club and maybe Disco itself—he nursed a grudge and started to obsess about the opportunities for financial improprieties in a cash business of such obviously high volume as Berrie's.

Though not directly affiliated with any prosecutorial branch or government agency, he was in constant touch with colleagues who were—and was not the only one of them to have been humiliated outside the Club in front of a date.

The first physical manifestation of the investigation, though no one knew it at the time, was the appearance of a woman in a red dress in the crowd outside the Club for several nights running. An odd thing about this woman's behavior, if anyone had chosen to notice, was that she never really tried to get in. Van did notice *her*, but not her holding back; Van was actually a very observant, quite sensitive guy; there was probably no one who showed up outside the Club more than once whom Van did not in a sense "know" and, I would even say, care about—to a degree. But about what the mysterious woman in red might have been doing those nights in front of the Club, he at the time drew no conclusions.

What her role had been, court records later revealed, was to count precisely how many people entered the Club each night. She would stand in the crowd outside the Club from opening to closing over several nights with a counter hidden in the palm of her hand, clicking off each person who entered.

Computing the cover charge and likely drink consumption, a number was arrived at—extrapolated from her count—that became the authorities' estimate of what Berrie and his partners were making every night. This was compared with the ridiculously lower numbers he reported on his sales and corporate tax forms (nearly all filed late).

The Club was so high-profile, and had generated so much ill will, that it became an ideal candidate to be "made an example of" by all the various prosecutors and tax authorities. So started the investigatory process which led to this night many months later with Josh, in a prosecutorial-style tan trench coat, hurrying past an unmarked blue van with police inside near the alley to the Club's back entrance. Next he passed

a pair of plainclothesmen with police radio wires curling up
to earplugs which they held to their ears. One of them seemed
to recognize Josh and nodded to him as he passed. Farther
on, in the shadows of the back court, a red fire marshals'
sedan pulled up, with several white-hatted fire marshals starting to get out. Whatever was happening was about to start.

Josh knocked on the Club's back door. Shad's head
popped out.

"I need to see Des," Josh said. "It's urgent."

"He's busy," Shad said, very truthfully as it later turned
out.

"He'll want to know this," Josh said, and just stepped past
Shad, who, in fact, put up no resistance whatsoever.

"He really is occupied," Shad called whiningly.

"I assure you he'll want to know about this," Josh insisted,
walking at a quick pace down the long back hallway, flashing
his departmental credentials back at Shad, who just followed,
rather lamely.

"Des!" Josh called twice as he approached his office. He
reached the door and started knocking on it. "Des, open
up . . . !"

"I didn't let him in, Des," Shad called plaintively. "He got
by me!"

"Des, it's important!" Josh said. "Open up!" He tried the
door handle again, but it was stuck. Once before, he had seen
Des kick in the door when the latch was stuck, so he stepped
back and tried the same maneuver. It was all too successful,
the door flying open with crashing violence.

Francesca had been wearing a red dress that evening, but
now she wasn't. The red dress—a still beautiful pre-owned
Balmain—was draped over one of Des's office chairs, while

Francesca was on the sofa more or less draped over Des. Both were as God created them—though many years later.

"Christ! Are-you-out-of-your-mind?!" Des screamed, jumping up wrapping the sofa blanket around himself.

"It's about to start," Josh replied in a level tone. "Get rid of all your 'gifts' and anything else you wouldn't want to be found with." Then he turned and left.

Des rushed around looking for all the little plastic coke bags he had accumulated to flush them down his office toilet, mumbling curses as he did so. Francesca—or the Tiger Lady, as the dehumanizers might call her—handled herself with considerable aplomb, regaining her self-possession, crossing her legs and lighting a cigarette, which she proceeded to smoke, making no effort to cover her spectacular body, which looked like the potential subject of a *Playboy* "over fifty" pictorial, as it later would be.

Shad just stood in the doorway gawking, until Des slammed the door shut on him. In any case, by this time the fire marshals had entered the back of the Club.

At the moment the task force struck, I was actually standing near the front entrance with Van. Des later said that he felt that my friendship with Van was something akin to the "Stockholm syndrome," according to which hostages end up identifying with their captors, but I saw its basis as more straightforward: Van was a much better guy than we all had thought, and once I stopped abusing my situation to get agency clients in, there was no reason we should not get along.

The combined task force, including agents of the IRS,

FBI, DEA, EPA, and the New York police and fire departments, entered through each of the Club's main egresses.
Leading them at the front entrance was Hap, the "client" I
had gotten in at such cost the night of my ejection from the
Club, his goofy-yuppie act of the earlier evening replaced by
a cool professional demeanor. Hap's selection for the assignment, I later found out, was similar to Josh's at the D.A.'s
office: he was considered the member of the IRS's regional
investigative unit most likely to be able to get into a "hot"
nightclub, incredible as that might seem.

Hap edged through the crowd at the head of a mixed
group of uniformed and plainclothes agents.

"We're on the list!" he announced, holding up the search
warrant as he and his associates swept past Rick and the rest
of Van's guys, who stood passive and a bit dumbstruck by the
red velvet ropes.

"Hey, Jimmy!" Hap called out happily when he spotted
me. With him I recognized Harry and the red-haired Jack
from Oz night and quite a few other "clients" I had gotten in
on the agency's behalf. Several of them gave friendly nods or
"hi's" as they passed, but I could sense that the stress level was
very high.

Josh, who sat in an unoccupied banquette, still wearing his
raincoat, waiting for the raid to reach the interior, could have
looked like a bit of a nut to anyone not aware of what was
going on. But on the dance floor and elsewhere inside the
Club, everything continued obliviously.

Des, when he finally located Josh, was still buttoning his
shirt, his shirttails hanging loose over his jeans. "Jesus Christ,"

he said, quite agitated, "you're not going to use that against me with Alice, are you? Francesca was just feeling . . . terribly needy tonight. It has nothing to do with how I feel about Alice."

The task force entered the Club from two directions initially, Hap's group closer to where they were.

Des looked over briefly, then continued pleading with Josh. "You're not going to take unfair advantage of that, are you?"

"Okay," Josh said, getting up, not at all thrilled about what he had done that night.

"Coming, Josh?" Hap called.

Josh rejoined the rest of the task force.

"Okay, let's *go!*" Hap said. As the posse of agents, police, and state finance department inspectors entered the crowd, the Club confetti launcher shot off a lovely downpour of shimmering metal flakes on raiders and dancers alike. "Dolce Vita," the late Eurodisco hit, played and on the floor many continued dancing, while others stood around gawking as the assembled throng of tax investigators and law enforcement types crossed the dance floor, some unwittingly moving to the song's rhythm line.

"Downstairs first," Hap signaled. "Harry, Jack!" he called to two of the agents I knew.

I tagged along as they went down to the basement, where, amazingly, Berrie had continued to leave canvas sacks of undeclared cash prior to their shipment.

When the raid began, Berrie had been on the third floor in his suite of offices, which included the cash-counting room, but by now he had left, taking with him the Club's real books and cash records (including statements from the foreign accounts).

He was coming down the side stairs carrying them when he heard Josh's group about to start up, bursts of staticky voices from the police radios of the accompanying cops betraying their approach.

At the landing he dodged down and stuffed all the papers and ledgers behind an ottoman, checking to make sure they were invisible from the staircase, but Hap had caught a glimpse of his looking that way and proceeded to signal an older court officer, still wheezing from the stairs, to have a look.

"You can't touch those!" Berrie shouted, now in outraged constitutional-lawyer mode. "Those are my *personal papers.* I was just carrying them." Sam, the older court officer, stopped and looked to Hap and Josh for guidance.

"Not any longer," Hap informed Berrie, holding up the warrant. "Now they're 'part of the premises' and, as such, the warrant applies."

"Sam," Hap said, signaling him. Sam came forward with a large filing box for documents and evidence. As he removed the ledgers from behind the ottoman, five small plastic packets of familiar white powder fell to the floor not far from Josh.

Josh kneeled down for a closer look and then stood again, finally having the opportunity to utter the words he had longed his whole (short) legal career to use: "*Book . . . this . . . clown . . . !*"

The uniformed cops moved to take Berrie into custody. At this point the older and more experienced professionals of law enforcement, who, more prudent and less agile, had hung back and let Hap and Josh take the point position in the raid, took control, ordering that Berrie be put in cuffs and subjected to most other forms of perfectly constitutional humiliation they had at their disposal. Several of them might have looked familiar to Van from earlier months as among those left to wait outside the Club while more frivolous types were whisked inside.

But within hours Berrie was out, and in two days the Club itself reopened. Des was right. It would not be a meteorite; the Club would not be smashed to smithereens. But Josh and I had opened the door to a process by which the greatest dance club the world had ever seen—in our opinion—could be subject to an unraveling just as terminal in nature. It was "ironic" I suppose that the two of us most in thrall to the Club, who most loved it and what it represented in terms of the culture of the night, should be those who played the most visible role in its undoing. I don't know who is credited with the thought—someone claimed it was Oscar Wilde at a bad moment—but they say, "You always kill the thing you love." I am not sure that is entirely true—in fact, I do not think it is true. Perhaps it could be rephrased, "You almost never kill the thing you love." Only by the sheerest, unlikeliest, and most unfortunate accident do you kill the thing you love. In any case, I hate facile-cynical "ironic" sayings of that kind, which are *always* being cited by "knowing" idiots—from which group I don't exclude myself.

In any case, it is the eternal smoke screen of wrongdoers and totalitarians to make the motives and tactics of those who find them out the focus of all controversy. According to all that is just and true, blame for everything bad that happened at the Club that night and subsequently should be ascribed to the illegalities of Berrie Rafferty, *scumbag extraordinaire*, and to nothing else.

25

Brutus Vindicated

It was already quite dark the next afternoon when I returned to the girls' apartment to collect my things. I came in through the living-room entrance. All was dark inside, so I assumed no one was at home—Charlotte was still in the hospital.

Just as I was heading into Alice's room (having to pass through it to get to the one that Charlotte and I shared), I heard a rustling on her bed as she sat up.

"What are you doing here in the dark?" I asked, passing through.

"I was just resting . . ."

Alice flicked on the light near her. I got to Charlotte's room and put on the lights there.

"Have you seen Josh at all?" she asked.

"Yeah."

"Is he okay?"

"Sure," I said, coming back into her room. "Why wouldn't he be okay?"

"I don't know. He hasn't called in a while."

"Josh's the kind of guy who *will* take no for an answer . . ."

On Alice's bureau I noticed the picture of Alice, Tom, and me together at that party in Sag Harbor Labor Day weekend.

"Did you know I was sort of infatuated with you then?" she asked.

I shook my head. "I assumed you preferred Tom," I said. Alice made a face.

"Also, you seemed a little . . . irritating."

"How was I irritating?"

"Well, you weren't . . ."

There was something I wanted to talk with her about but was absolutely petrified in those days of making a fool of myself in front of women I cared about—an inhibition I later lost.

Finally, I asked, "There's no chance of your getting infatuated with me again, is there?"

Alice said nothing. She just looked to the side, which was enough.

"I just had to confirm that," I said, and took off back to the other room. Alice was disconcerted by my sudden disappearance, but in a moment I was back again.

"Des wanted me to give you this," I said, handing her his leather-trimmed notebook. "It's his *Last Testament*—sort of a personal journal he's keeping. You see, Tolstoy, before he married, gave his wife his diaries to read—the idea being total frankness and candor."

Alice looked at the notebook.

"It's . . . pretty scabrous," I said.

"Des wants me to read this?"

"He feels it'll show you how he's *really changed*."

I went away to pack, pulling my beat-up suitcase down from over Charlotte's closet.

Alice seemed resistant to looking inside Des's book. "You know," she said from the other room, "reading scabrous manuscripts is what I have to do every day at work."

"Well—do what you think best," I said, already beginning to have doubts about what I had done. This has been something of a problem of mine in the agency business, too frequently doubting my own actions when feigning total confidence to the point of cocksureness is usually more effective. It just seems to me that, over the long run, when one's actions *are* doubtful, it is better to indicate you know that. I now wondered if exposing Des's loutishness in the exceedingly graphic terms of his *Last Testament* was really such a wise and heroic act if Alice was lying around in the dark pining for Josh anyway.

"You don't *have* to read it. In fact, maybe it would be best you didn't."

"But you said that Des wants me to."

"Well, maybe that wasn't true."

˟˟*˟*˟*

Outside Des's building in Manhattan's (overrated) Chelsea district, I waited in the street by the cab, semi-pacing, as its meter climbed at the "waiting rate," which was not insignificant. Finally Des pushed out of the doors, carrying a big suitcase and a smaller carry-on bag. Josh followed him out.

"Let me keep your passport for you," Josh said.

"No."

"Come on, Des, help me out."

Des gave Josh an incredulous look, then started putting his bags in the trunk.

"Should people just be allowed to steal from each other and the government," Josh persisted, "and—out of selfishness or indifference or a kind of fashionable cynicism—the rest of us do nothing?" He paused for breath, adding, "You know, I thought much better of you than that."

"You did?" Des asked, closing the trunk. "Well—wrong again, Josh."

It was getting really late; somehow trips to the airport always seemed this way—packed with anxiety about traffic tie-ups and making the flight, etc.

" 'Bye, Josh," I said, and got into the cab.

Before getting in, Des turned back to him. "Listen, you've got all their books and all their documents, you've got *them*—why do you need me, who knew practically nothing?"

Des pointed to his chest. "This is the only body I've got," he said, and turned to climb into the cab.

I leaned forward. "Kennedy Airport," I told the driver. As the cab pulled out, we shouted " 'byes" to Josh.

" 'Bye," he replied in an enigmatically subdued tone, which I could not have figured out then even if I had particularly noticed it—which I hadn't.

In that period, cabs—other than the classic rounded Checkers—had a long, boxy, rectangular shape. They were fairly comfortable, with good suspensions. All were yellow— thank God—and so easy to identify. We were sitting in the back of just such a cab, each looking out of our respective window.

Crossing the East River at the Fifty-ninth Street Bridge—also known as the "Queensboro Bridge" and immortalized in the hit Simon & Garfunkel song "Feelin' Groovy (the 59th Street Bridge Song)"—I could see the hospital where Charlotte was and the actual windows of her room.

As if reading my thoughts, Des pleasantly inquired, "Aren't you a bit of a *cad*, leaving town with your girlfriend in the hospital?"

"It might look that way."

"Yeah, it does. But—it isn't?"

"No," I said. "Not at all. I've been through this before," I reminded him. "You didn't really know Laurie—you'd already dropped out by then—but she was very realistic. We'd agreed that we were going to break up at graduation. The same day, though, she had terrible back spasms, having, in fact, to be hospitalized for them. I felt terribly guilty and ended up hanging around Boston, visiting the hospital, etc., all summer—and almost bankrupting her parents in the process. As soon as I left town, she recovered."

"You're sort of the 'Bluebeard' of backs," Des said.

I nodded. That was how I occasionally felt.

"You don't do anyone much of a favor with the 'devoted jerk' routine," I said. "By going away and putting an ocean between us—i.e., making a definitive break—Charlotte's likely to recover much faster."

Des pondered this. It always pleased me when I could throw him something he could not immediately reply to, and briefly I had that pleasure.

"Why," he asked after a moment, "do you think having an ocean between you and Charlotte necessarily means a definitive break?"

"*That's* a depressing thought."

For a while we both just looked out our windows. The famous Pepsi sign on the other side of the East River, visible from the bridge, grew larger as we approached it.

Finally, Des broke the silence. "I'm going to turn over a new leaf in Spain," he said determinedly. "I'm going to turn over several new leaves."

A poignant aspect of the ride to the airport for flights to Europe—at least if you were not so late as to be obsessed with just getting there on time—was that because almost all were scheduled for the evening, there was often a beautiful crepuscular aspect to the ride, with the sun about to or having just set. Like a rephrasing of the catch phrase from the old travel films, "As the sun sets on the Long Island Expressway Access Road, we say 'farewell' to the continent of North America . . ."

Perhaps that is what put Des in such a thoughtful mood—honest and self-critical—that afternoon.

"Do you know the Shakespearean admonition 'To thine own self be true'?" he asked.

I nodded, of course.

"It's premised," he said, "on the idea that 'thine own self' is something pretty good, 'being true' to which is 'commendable.' What if 'thine own self' is not so good? What if it's 'pretty bad'? Wouldn't it be better *not* to be true to thine own self in that case? You see, that's my situation."

"The one I like is '*Et tu, Brute?*' " I said. "There're different ways of being loyal. Some might seem, on the surface, disloyal—but they're not. There's a higher loyalty. The way I look at it, Brutus was a good friend to Caesar."

"By stabbing him in the back, Brutus was a good friend to Caesar?"

I nodded.

"How?"

But before I formulated a reply Des changed the subject, obviously preoccupied.

"You know, Josh was right," he said. "I probably *should've* stayed and testified. Berrie's a bad guy—probably worse than they know."

"That's what Van thinks," I said. "Van's cooperating."

"Staying and cooperating would be the right thing to do. But instead, I'm running like a rat, because—'To thine own self be true.' "

It was after we had gotten to the airport and Des's passport was confiscated—he was pretty upset, feeling betrayed— that I realized why Josh had been so subdued when we had left him on the street that way. From the way the airline personnel acted, I don't think detentions like that happened too often in the TWA lounge. I had already passed ticket control and was not allowed back to the waiting area, or so I then understood; I was also already on the late side for reporting to my new job and had been strongly advised that any further delay would risk losing it. Still, I'll never forget the look on Des's face that evening.

"I'll wait for you over there!" I called to him. But, in fact, he never came.

The next day Charlotte was up and walking the hospital corridor in her bathrobe, though still quite stiff-backed, with Alice alongside her.

"They say I can probably go home tomorrow," Charlotte said.

"Great."

"There's something I've been meaning to ask you . . ."

Alice's face betrayed trepidation—anyone who knew Charlotte well knew the feeling. The two entered her room, categorized by the hospital as semi-private but with the patient she shared it with off at physical therapy.

"Do you think Jimmy's going away could have had anything to do with him . . . you know . . . having some sort of bizarre, pathetic crush on you?"

"I don't know," Alice said.

"Did he ever say anything?"

Alice delayed replying.

"Yes," she finally said.

"What?"

"Well . . ."

" 'Why don't you love me instead of jerks like Des and Josh?' That kind of thing?"

Alice hesitantly nodded yes.

"I knew it! I thought so!" Charlotte said, quivering with anger. "You *bitch*! I knew it was something like that!"

She climbed back into bed, careful to protect her back while lowering herself onto the slightly tilted mattress.

"*I don't think I want to room with you anymore,*" she said, turning her face away from Alice, controlling the intensity of her resentment with difficulty. "*Being around you hasn't been good for me—or my back . . . I'd like you to move out; I don't know how I'll afford it, but my sanity and my integrity are more important to me than money. I've got to start looking out for myself now.*"

Approaching footsteps could be heard from the hallway and shortly Dan entered in a bit of a "hyper" state.

"Have you heard the news?" he asked, dumping his book-bag on the other bed.

"No," Alice said. "What?"

"They're selling the company."

"What?"

"We're merging with Simon & Schuster . . . There'll be the usual 'consolidation' and 'economies of scale.' A lot of us are going to lose our jobs."

"God, that's sad," Alice said. "I love the company. Everyone's been great to us there."

"Well, I don't know," Dan said, considering this. "We were exploited—but they were nice about it."

Charlotte added bitterly: "Maybe it would be good if they got rid of some of the *deadwood* in that company—particularly if it meant paying the rest of us *decently enough* to live in this city with at least a *modicum of privacy*."

Later, when Alice returned to check on her after having had a bite with Dan in the downstairs cafeteria, she was again calm and apologized for her outburst. They chatted quietly but when Alice was leaving that evening, Charlotte said, "I knew this would happen. I knew you'd end up with all the guys."

Part the Last

26

The Unemployment for Lunch Bunch

All morning Alice had been looking forward to lunch with her Aunt Janet. The time had been set for half past noon, to get in before the quarter-to-one mob scene and allow ample time for conversation. Again it would be at the old Brasserie—the traditional place for them—and Alice would order the delicious hot chicken crepe while gaining sustenance not just from it (and the good French bread) but from her aunt's wonderful true-life narratives and insights. Sometimes she would just sit back and listen, occasionally asking a little clarifying question, or perhaps bringing in some other information from her acquaintanceships and reading. Book publishing was a phenomenal perch for observing and entering into the lives of some fairly interesting people (if at times full of themselves) and acquiring large quantities of information about a diverse array of subjects—Alice would never have learned about the mysteries surrounding the disappearance of ships and planes in the region of the Atlantic Ocean known as the "Bermuda Triangle," nor of the fascinating geometric patterns created on the heights of the Andes by pre-historic astronauts if it had not been for her assistant's work in book publishing. These were not subjects that precisely inter-ested her aunt, but others that she now had an "insider's knowledge" of did, and over the past year, it had been nice to finally be able to bring more to her side of the luncheon table.

The intensest part of the conversation for Alice was always when she got to recount for her aunt—and get her aunt's own invaluable response to—everything, or almost every-thing (she did hold back on a few things), going on in her work and life, which just at that time did seem so dramatic and potentially portentous. She had a lot to tell her, and the prospect of getting away from the office that day seemed par-ticularly appealing. It was nervous-breakdown time at Riley Publishers as the new overlords from Simon & Schuster started showing up. They were not an especially pleasant bunch, their manner certainly not improving a situation anxiety-making in the best of circumstances. Alice was dis-covering that companies in the same business can have very different personalities, which was certainly the case between Riley Publishers and Simon & Schuster. Word had come back even before the merger, after one of the top editors had been lured to S & S with an enormous increase in salary but quickly found the atmosphere toxic and started looking for somewhere else to land—places like Lippincott were still around then. S & S was run as if someone had taken another untrue saying—baseball manager Leo (the Lip) Durocher's terrible "Nice guys finish last," the anthem of obnoxious people the world over—and enshrined it as company policy. While there were some good people at S & S, too, they tried to keep pretty quiet about it. This was about the era when books with titles such as *Winning through Intimidation, Power!*, and *Looking Out for No. 1* were topping bestseller lists, and it seemed that vulgarian ideology was going to dominate everything for all time, with phalanxes of Denbys and B. E. Ellis precursors out to do its assassination work on the Culture Front.

Alice's Aunt Janet had worked at S & S in an earlier, pre-Durocherian era, when nice-guy philosopher Dale Carnegie, its then-bestselling author, set the tone, and the meetings between him and Mr. Schuster were legendary for their exquisite bonhomie and courtesies. But times—and company chiefs—had changed. Heads were going to roll at Riley Publishers, and the bet was it would not be done in the kindest way possible.

Alice arrived a few minutes early and, after checking to see if her aunt might already have been seated, waited at the small open foyer atop the restaurant's interior staircase just off East Fifty-third Street, where a reading room–style wooden rack of the day's newspapers had been placed for the convenience of those obliged to wait. Alice glanced at the *Times*, a little preoccupied—from the headlines it looked like people were getting laid off all over; there was some, not very logical, comfort in numbers.

When her aunt came through the Brasserie's revolving glass door, Alice was shocked at her appearance—drawn and tired as if she had neither been eating nor sleeping properly, her eyes sunken and reddish as if from past crying, looking strangely younger because of her thinness and older otherwise. Nothing of this distraught state had been indicated in her aunt's earlier call; perhaps years of experience in the travel business had trained her how to entirely mask her feelings in her phone voice.

They were seated quickly; her aunt requested a table in the comparatively cramped back section that they normally didn't like especially, but which was less visible and so more private. It suddenly occurred to Alice that the Sloan-Kettering Memorial Cancer Center was very close by—her aunt had once been there for tests—and this thought really worried her. Instantly her eyes watered. Already, in her early twenties, the world had started seeming far more mortal to Alice. Suddenly the generation of her beloved grandparents seemed in peril—become very, very frail—and just the previous month at work a kindly woman, older but not especially so—the "first reader" for her department—had slumped over in her office, dead of a heart attack. Recently she'd heard that someone she had known of in college had also died.

Immediately after they were seated, in response to Alice's concerned questioning, her Aunt Janet clarified that the problem was not medical. She started to explain—it related to Uncle Jack—then stopped. For the next twenty minutes or so she barely said a word. She did not break down in tears; she sat very still, with one hand to her face, while at intervals tears slipped out. Finally, she apologized to Alice for dragging her from her office to subject her to such a spectacle. Not at all, Alice said, and urged her aunt to have something to eat or drink, though at that point only their iced teas and the bread and butter had come to the table. Alice asked a passing waitress if they could both have glasses of water, no ice; water had to be specifically requested in most New York restaurants in this period, since the practice of serving it automatically had been suspended as a conservation measure during a long New York State drought the previous decade.

When the water did come, Alice encouraged her aunt to take a long draught of it. This can, in fact, have an immediately reviving effect, and the distraction also helped her aunt extract herself from the utterly despairing state she had fallen into. The properties of water, drunk at room temperature or slightly below, are practically miraculous.

Slowly, in pieces, the story came out. Her aunt, it seemed, had walked in upon her Uncle Jack, to find him, in the most frank and graphic way possible, in the midst of an adulterous liaison with the young woman who was her aunt's favored protégé in her travel business. For her aunt, who until that moment had thought of herself as one half of a notably romantic, almost model couple, the discovery had been utterly devastating. And also shaming: though ten days had already passed, Alice was the first relative she had even told.

After such revelations do all marriages and romantic relationships invariably end? Would it make a difference if the knowledge of betrayal were just intellectual and not visual? Every time I've heard such a tale narrated in the States—the teller invariably the injured party—the assumption is *always* that *ipso facto* the relationship, or marriage or whatever, is immediately ended. The injured party is immediately *gone*, and whatever efforts the adulterer or adulteress might have made to excuse themselves and patch things up become the subject only of merciless sarcasm. Not a moment's doubt is expressed about the rejectionist course. I've never heard one of these horror stories told and then the teller adding, "Oh well, it was just a fling and ultimately we patched things up." But does that never happen, or are those who go on with such relationships just a lot more discreet about revealing the problems and cataclysms? By the time a victim recounts such a betrayal to a group over drinks, the bitter hurt of the original experience must be essentially gone, while some *rush* of self-righteous gratification remains available for extraction. Perhaps it is only then, when shrunken to a terrible anecdote from a past life that such things can be discussed, or, as was the case with Alice's aunt, when the pain is so immediate and overwhelming that she felt she had to talk with *someone* or go insane.

After the incident itself, Uncle Jack had not behaved in the worst way possible. Under the circumstances, he tried to say and do all the right things, and seemed to mean them. He had the advantage of not having a particularly high moral self-regard in the first place, so he was not subject to the usual irresistible compulsion to justify himself by inventing bitter, retrospective reproaches against Aunt Janet or, alternately, convincing himself that the dalliance with her protégé—pleasant though it had begun—was in fact a *true love*, transforming and redeeming, something out of *Abélard & Héloïse*, which required only her becoming the second Mrs. Jack for all to be correct or at least somewhat congruent. Perhaps they as a couple would not be childless, perhaps they would then even invent some better, romantic version to tell the kids. But never having much prided himself on his "face" anyway, Uncle Jack did not feel honor-bound to begin the matrimonial demolition and reconstruction work of the usual "face-saving maneuver." Instead, he turned to Aunt Janet with a face that was warm, loving, contrite, abject, sincere, and even poetical.

But she couldn't buy it. The moment she had come upon them, she had started down a sort of tunnel of depression and despair that, as if it were some biological process, would not permit the absorption of any ameliorating fact or information. A whole lifetime of Christian education—regarding

forgiveness, redemption, Christ's loving treatment of Mary
Magdalene, casting the first stone, or rather the imperative
not to cast it—either meant nothing or just seemed beside
the point. She could not enter into it intellectually or emotionally. There was a theory of her life that she had lived and
believed in, built on the nearly lifelong romance between
herself and Uncle Jack but connected to everything else, that
was now annihilated, and she could not imagine coming up
with anything to take its place. We are now so oriented
toward the biochemistry of depression—and conditions like
Josh's that come from within—perhaps we discount the seriousness of those depressions that are based on events in one's
life that are truly depressing coming from without. Like a
manic-depressive in a downswing, Aunt Janet could not
imagine going on, and at various moments, had there been a
ledge a little too convenient, she felt she might have thrown
herself off.

I had met Alice's aunt and uncle and had liked them both.
I think Alice was right that her aunt resembled Jane Wyatt—
I would also mention Margaret Sullavan—more than Carole
Lombard. Though her uncle correctly accepted the blame
for everything that happened, I could not see blaming either
of them, either implicitly or explicitly, for the events leading
to the unraveling of their once apparently beautiful love
story. It was just how things always seemed to end up when
"opposites attract."

About two months later, swinging out of the downtown
unemployment office, Des asked the others, "Why don't we
do something?"

"Like what?" Charlotte asked. Josh and Dan came up from behind, making it basically four abreast. All carried with them their unemployment starter kits or, in Des's case, documentation of his job search.

It was one of those rare beautiful New York summer days and particularly glorious on Centre Street, where cooling breezes blew in from the harbor across Manhattan's narrow southern tip. Out-of-towners are often unaware that Manhattan Island's climate varies greatly from one section to another, with the downtown part much better ventilated than midtown in summer due to its geographical position jutting out into a body of water that is essentially the Atlantic Ocean—hence the occasional coast of Maine feeling.

"Well," Des pointed out, "at this time of day, employed people often have lunch."

"I can't," Josh said. "I've got to go uptown."

"Why?"

"Alice and I are having lunch."

"You're having lunch with Alice?" Des asked.

Josh nodded.

"Great—let's all go."

"It's, uh, at Lutèce," Josh said.

"You're on unemployment and taking Alice to Lutèce?" Des sounded concerned. "Uh, doesn't 'irrational extravagance' signal the start of a, uh . . . 'manic' phase?"

"If it were my invitation, you'd be right—but it's not."

"Alice's taking *you* to Lutèce?"

Josh grinned.

"Why? Why would she take you?"

"She's celebrating her promotion."

"When Alice wants to celebrate something, she calls you?"

Charlotte asked, "Alice made Editor?"

"Associate Editor," Josh said.

"What happened with her book?" Des asked. "I thought it was some kind of fiasco."

Here Dan jumped in: "What Alice did, rather cleverly, was shift the category from 'non-fiction' to 'self-actualization.' The book jackets hadn't been printed yet. Reincarnation . . . life after death . . . mumbo-jumbo of all kinds has been highly commercial throughout the history of book publishing. The first printed book was a Bible."

"Actually," Charlotte said, "I'm not upset I was laid off. This will motivate me to find a better job in television, which is where my interests really lie. I've watched television all my life."

Charlotte had completely recovered from her meltdown in the hospital room, which was, in my opinion, uncharacteristic behavior for her, a "bad moment" such as we all have, though Charlotte did have them a lot more than most people. Writing about her, it was hard not to skew the portrayal in an unfairly negative direction, zeroing in on her bad moments—which if you were not the direct target tended to be pretty entertaining—rather than all the times she was really sweet and ingratiating, of which there were also many. Even when Charlotte's behavior *was* a little mean or egotistical, she usually pulled it off in a cheerful manner that took out a lot of the sting.

Charlotte's television comment piqued Des's interest. "If you're interested in television, you should come over and watch *Wild Kingdom* sometime."

"Sure," Charlotte said, flashing him one of her electric smiles. Both she and Des, it turned out, were big television watchers. They would have that in common.

"You're taking the E train?" Dan asked Josh.

"Yeah."

Near them, a taxi pulled up to the curb. "Two dollars, please," the passenger asked the driver, evidently requesting the change from a ten. The voice was familiar.

"Hey, Van!" Des called.

Van was unfolding his long form from the cab.

"What happened?" Charlotte asked.

"The new owners couldn't make it work," Van said, striding over to where they were but in the direction of the unemployment office. This was another phenomenon of the period: everyone from the same company or milieu coinciding at unemployment at the same time. "They finally had to hire people to stand outside and pretend they couldn't get in.

"Anyway, Disco's over," he said quite definitively. "It's dead."

"What do you mean?!" Josh asked.

"People just aren't going out like they used to," Van said. "They're tired. Some are sick or strung out. It's not just the prosecutions and all the owners Berrie squealed on."

"Could it be related to the herpes epidemic?" Charlotte asked. Des looked toward her, and for a moment their eyes met.

"Maybe," Van said. "I've a friend at Casablanca Records & Tapes, and she says that, like, two months ago, the bottom dropped out of disco record sales. Suddenly it's dead . . . Over."

All stood still and subdued.

"God, that's sad," Josh said.

"We're getting older," Des said. "We've lived through a period that's—ended. That's like dying a little bit." Suddenly he looked up toward the sky. Something eerie and beautiful had occurred—from above a lovely, hopeful melody began to sound. Just as they were pondering the death of Disco and, in a sense, of their own young adulthood, music came from the heavens. This actually happened—it turned out to be the carillon of the temple-like church around the corner, but seemed entirely magical and mysterious at first.

Josh took Van's news very, very hard. "I can't believe it," he said, looking around at the rest of us.

"Disco will . . . never be over," he finally continued as if trying to convince himself, too. "Disco will always live in our minds and hearts. Something like this, that was this big and this important and this great, will never die." As Josh spoke, his passion and his conviction seemed to grow in tandem. "Oh, for a few years, maybe for many years, it will be considered passé and ridiculous. It will be misrepresented and caricatured and sneered at—or, worse, completely ignored. People will laugh about John Travolta, Olivia Newton-John, white polyester suits and platform shoes, and going like this—" he imitated the John Travolta dance pose from *Saturday Night Fever*—"though we had nothing to do with those things and still loved disco! Those who didn't understand will never understand! Disco was much more and much better than all that!"

Josh paused and looked around. "Disco was . . . *too great* and *too much fun* to be gone forever! It's *got* to come back someday. I just hope that will be in our own lifetimes."

The others looked shocked by Josh's frenzied tone. His delivery was quite manic, and the over-the-topness of it all perhaps made them fear that the "manic episode" Des had long predicted had finally arrived.

"Sorry," Josh said, suddenly calm. "I've got a job interview this afternoon and was just trying to get revved up. But most of what I said I . . . uh . . . believe."

For a moment they all just stood in subdued silence, including Van.

Des was first to break the silence, approaching Josh. "I was pretty furious when you had my passport lifted, 'confiscated,' at the airport, but . . . you were right. I'm glad I stayed—at least you saved me from being stuck in some foreign city with the likes of Jimmy Steinway—" Hearing this the first time, I had to wince. "But there's one thing I don't get: you did a good job in the prosecution, getting Berrie to squeal that way—why'd they lay you off?"

"Well, there was a conflict involving giving preferential treatment to a friend which they felt I . . . handled badly."

"Oh," Des said, thinking a moment. "Well—congratulate Alice for us."

"Yes," Charlotte put in.

Goodbyes, surprisingly friendly in nature, were exchanged before Dan and Josh ducked down the stairs to the subway station.

Des rejoined Charlotte.

"I don't really envy her, though," Charlotte said, speaking of Alice, "stuck in book publishing."

"Oof. No," Des agreed.

Van started to go. "I've got to get to the unemployment to sign up—going to the Bahamas this afternoon." He raised his arm in a wave. "So long!"

" 'Bye!" they called.

Des and Charlotte watched him go for a moment before turning and starting to walk uptown at a relaxed and enjoyable summer pace.

"One of the things that makes me happy in life is realizing I don't really envy anyone," Des said, mirroring something Charlotte had said earlier. "I don't want to be anyone else and I don't want to do anything but what I'm doing—which, right now, is nothing—but I've got good projects for the future. Can I speak to you honestly?"

"Yes," she said.

"You and I are similar. We've got 'big' personalities. That's good; the world—frankly—needs more 'big' personalities. But maybe ours burn *too* brightly, are *too* big for some people with more normal, healthy-size personalities, like Alice; or *abnormal*, normal-size personalities, like Josh; or itsy-bitsy, teeny-weeny, polka-dot bikini–size personalities, like Jimmy Steinway . . ."

(I should have been prepared for adverse references of this kind, but no matter how thoroughly one might be able to rationalize them—Des's understandable bitterness after discovering my alleged "betrayal," etc.—initially they hit pretty hard. Down through the centuries, a lot of very bad things were said about Brutus, too.)

Charlotte wholeheartedly agreed with Des's egomaniacal—almost crazy—"big" personalities discourse. "That's why I'm confident I'll ultimately be successful in television," she said.

"Absolutely," Des agreed. "One of the problems of 'finding the right person' and 'settling down' is that it takes all the fun and interest out of going to nightclubs. I mean, if you're already living with someone, why bother going out? Getting seriously involved with someone really just means ruining your nightlife . . ."

"I think I agree with you," Charlotte said.

The two continued walking uptown—where to, I don't know but probably in the general direction of lunch and, perhaps, Mutual of Omaha's *Wild Kingdom*. In the following weeks Des did re-create some of the atmosphere of the Club, assembling a growing group of the summertime unemployed around the afternoon *Wild Kingdom* reruns—few had sets of their own and none as large as Des's. One can't really look for work all day long; by three in the afternoon you are generally fairly burnt out. Mint juleps were served—even in Chelsea, mint could grow well, and before long a plantation sprouted along Des's humid back windowsills—and when the lousy afternoon talk shows came on, the set was switched off and music put on, with the first record always *Harold Melvyn & the Blue Notes* (only Teddy Pendergrass seemed able to express what everyone was feeling that summer). Soon it was after office hours, and acquaintances getting off work—including some of the attractive banking jargon–sprouting young women I couldn't get started with at The Raveled Sleeve—began coming by, and the guys interested in them, too, the employed crowd tending to arrive and stay late. Before long the landlord started eviction proceedings (the neighbors had been co-opted by inclusion) and Des had to look for a more legitimate space, which is how his first lounge, the St. Louis Zoo, got started.

27

Cocktails at Petrossian

We saw the rough cut of the movie at a very comfortable screening room below the brassy Planet Hollywood restaurant on West Fifty-seventh Street. Not living in the city, I had never been there and was surprised to find a long line waiting outside in orderly fashion against a red velvet rope on the sidewalk. Someone said they were "tourists," but that term is thrown around pretty loosely these days and they could easily have come from the city or its immediate environs as well. The whole situation was much better handled than in our day. A bunch of jockish bouncers with surprisingly good personalities greeted everyone, keeping those waiting on line for the restaurant in good spirits while ushering in those arriving for the screening with a maximum of Hollywood friendliness.

After accepting the "novelization" commission, I took a leave from Ogilvy et Mather in Paris that winter and spring of 1998 to relocate temporarily in the city so as to have closer access to the underlying research materials available only at the film production company's offices at Lafayette and Spring Streets, not far geographically from where the terrible San Gennaro Festival takes place, but at least far from it on the calendar.

Part of the motivational engine for undertaking this project was to air and, I hoped, exorcise the demons of the past and finally, definitively, "get over" them. "Get over it" was one of the catchphrases of the period. People could be pretty frank with each other in those days without that being taken amiss. Or maybe it was taken amiss but they didn't care. The motto of my favorite boss at McCallum before she got sacked was: "Stop complaining and start working." Recently I copied that out and attached it to a visible spot on my laptop.

In the course of watching many different cuts of the film, I grew pretty friendly with the editing staff and others working on it, coming to identify with their problems, hopes and joys, etc. The Planet Hollywood screening was the first to which the story's other protagonists had been invited. Some I had not seen in years, even if there had been phone or other contact; a few had gained weight and this tended to show in their faces; others had not gained weight and this also showed, making them look a little drawn or "peaked." Overall the effect was as if someone had adjusted downward the color knob on one of the old-fashioned color TVs (who ever thought the futuristic Sony Trinitrons of that period would soon be just "old-fashioned color TVs"?)—though generally everyone looked pretty good, especially Alice.

An appealing aspect of the Planet Hollywood screening room was that cocktails and other refreshments could freely be brought in from the bar area, re-creating somewhat the nightclub environment of the movie. This led to a bit of theater later. A young woman recent college graduate had brought a vodka-tonic into the screening from the bar upstairs and was pretty upset after the film, having felt implicated in it as a "total cliché." She had no idea, she said, that vodka-tonics were considered "unoriginal" in the early eighties and wondered if that was still true in the late nineties. Those she was with said they thought it was. I actually knew some of them and made a mental note to try to find out who she was. There is something about pretty, earnest, insecure, and entirely humorless young women that can be, at least initially, very appealing. Or maybe not but at that point I was just happy to have any evidence someone could distract me from Alice's presence in the room, even for a moment.

What sort of poisoned the screening for me was the way Des acted. Stiff-necked, he held himself aloof from any group I talked with and even pretended not to hear me when I said hello. That anyone could hold a grudge for so long seemed incredible, but this one he had obviously carefully and consciously nursed. I suppose you could say that *whom* we decide to hold grudges against is an important part of our "identity formation." Defining ourselves negatively, whom we choose not to like. In Des's case, that was me. Along these lines, after I found a seat toward the back of the room near Alice, Dan, and the others, Des plunked himself down in the front row.

Coming out of the screening, some of us from the old group tagged along with the film's co-producers and editors for drinks and discussion. They had been heading in default mode to the cheapo Greek restaurant across the street when Des, who knew about such things, strongly suggested either Journeys Bar in the Essex House (for privacy) or Petrossian on the corner of Fifty-eighth Street (for ambiance), and as the production was paying, we decided on the latter.

I was not with them at that point, and I doubt if Des would have been going if he knew from the start that I would be, too. On the walk over to Petrossian (the building is the one with the extraordinarily ornate stonework), Des chatted up a storm with Alice and Dan, but whenever circumstances threw him in my vicinity (at the coat check, for instance), he reverted to tense, stiff-necked, silent mode.

The cocktail debriefing session at Petrossian was intense but, overall, very positive. Alice was in a happy and laughing mood. Dan and I were in pretty good form, too, and the three of us—here I include Des—sort of basked in her presence. Alice had a lot of funny things to say about the movie. She seemed in nearly every regard as charming and delightful as remembered—a little fatigued, perhaps, but that just made it all more poignant. At a certain level the constancy of the attraction was reassuring—that at least I had not been entirely imagining things in the long years of pining for that "lost chance." I assume Des and Dan felt the same way.

While we talked, the film people went through the questionnaires, or "cards," that had been passed out at the screening. Then they quizzed us about our impressions of different parts of the film and were relieved we didn't seem overly critical of their version of events. Halfway through, Josh showed up and stayed for a drink, taking Alice away with him. He seemed fine and was pretty funny. "Manic," Des said after he left.

From other sources I knew that, despite her present cheerfulness, Alice's life with Josh had not been exactly a bowl of cherries. At a certain point the lithium he had long taken threatened to cause kidney damage. While his doctor was trying him on substitute medications, he was all over the place emotionally, with some ominous "depressive" periods that were particularly discouraging for them, as they both thought all that had been firmly consigned to the past. This coincided with the period when many of the old-line New York law partnerships were coming apart in the brave new world of stark competition. Many of the good-student types who had done the work and made partner suddenly had to scramble in the new environment of shifting firms and demands to "bring in business," which Josh finally survived in slightly manic style also.

Next to leave were the film's editors, who said they had to be getting "back downtown." This was something new since my days in the city. Now lots of people would say they "lived and worked downtown." Des and I had ordered fresh drinks, which arrived just as everyone else was leaving. Neither of us was the sort of person to abandon a fresh drink unconsumed, so we ended up stranded there together, alone at a large table full of empty glasses.

"I can't believe you did that," Des finally said after everyone had gone.

He looked into his cocktail glass and shook his head in incredulity.

"What were you *thinking?*" he said, more as an exclamation.

"What?"

"You know."

"No."

Des did one of his trademark "exhales"—a sort of "exhale in anger" or "exhale in disgust."

"You mean, giving . . . Alice . . . your book?" I ventured.

"How could you do that? I thought we were friends."

"Well, I told you on the way to the airport."

"No you didn't."

"I did." Des thought back on the taxi ride, obviously not remembering anything I had said.

"I told you . . . you know, how much I admired Brutus."

Des had not a clue. He put on a quizzical expression. "Who's that—another of Van's guys?" he said, as if forgetting or pretending to have forgotten the scene we had just watched. "I can't believe how you sucked up to them."

"No, not that Brutus. The original one. From *Julius Caesar*. When, out of friendship, to stop Caesar from doing something really terrible—in that case, subverting the Roman republic—Brutus felt obliged to, you know, stab him."

"*That* was telling me?"

I nodded. Des exhaled again. He looked around Petrossian angrily. " '*Woe to the hand that shed this costly blood!*' " he blurted out theatrically and a little ominously. An older romantic couple, sipping martinis in the corner, cast a worried look in Des's direction.

"That's how you feel?"

"Yah."

"It's been a long time, Des. I thought that, by now, you might better understand . . . and have excused me for that. It was for Alice's sa—"

"*Alice's sake?* Give me a break. It wasn't for her. It was some pathetic 'assertiveness training' exercise for yourself." Then he continued, thinking aloud. "Uhh . . . in the play, how does Brutus end up? Not so good, if I recall."

"I don't know. My impression's he did not end up so well. I think Octavian kills him or something. In any case, I never said I ended up well."

"Nor did you start out so well. Why'd you do it? Did your shrink say you had to be 'more assertive' or something?"

"No. I didn't have a shrink—in that period."

"I really *had* changed, you know," he said. "That was no joke."

Des looked toward me and apparently read my disbelief. "Oh, I know. You're so smug. Francesca. You're thinking about her. That was an anecdote. It meant *nothing*. You've now lived some. Haven't you seen how the past doesn't always want to stay that way? No matter how hunky-dory your intentions are, it usually has a few more whacks to give. But that does not mean that it's *not* the past. That it's not essentially *over*, even if not entirely done with. Perhaps someday, when you are older, you'll come to see that."

Des signaled the barman. "Could I have another?" he asked.

As the effect of the booze kicked in, a maudlin quality started to infect the constant of Des's anger and skepticism vis-à-vis me. At the table he started to sag a bit, as if fatigued.

Then he continued: "You ruined my life. I despise you."

"*Ruined your life?*"

"Yes. Whenever I get serious with someone, or even quite far, the thought always comes along—'She's not Alice'—which ruins everything. You and your pathetic 'I thought it would be best, Des' wrecked everything . . . And for what? You never had a chance with her. She never liked you."

"That's not true," I said.

He just stared back.

"In any case, nothing I said or did changed anything with Alice."

"That's crap."

"When I got to their apartment, to pack for Madrid, she was lying around in the dark *pining* for Josh."

"So. People pine. That's hardly definitive . . . How could you know that, anyway?"

"She told me."

"She *told* you?"

"All she did was ask about Josh, wonder about Josh, talk about Josh. She didn't mention you—at all. When I tried to give her your *Last Testament*, mentioning how scabrous it was, she didn't seem especially interested. She said she had to read enough scabrous stuff at work. I don't want to hurt your feelings, Des—"

"Oh, no."

"—but I don't think she was very serious about you. She was toying with your affections."

"*Toying with my affections?*"

"Yeah," I affirmed. "My giving her the *Last Testament* didn't change anything. She was already completely preoccupied with Josh. I knew that before giving it to her. Okay, call it 'assertiveness training' or whatever, if you must. I wanted to act correctly and selflessly about at least one thing, and not just be a tool or lackey of yours."

"Oh, great. You're such a dolt. I really had changed."

Des's eyes watered. "You ruined my life."

Des was like a former high-school football hero still living in his past glories of a near-championship season and moping about the muffed pass that lost the final game.

Maybe it was the "Smirnis" I had consumed, but suddenly I felt I was observing both him and myself as if from very far away and above, two small and rather pathetic figures at a table in Petrossian still fretting over a romantic Waterloo, or maybe Trafalgar (or, in my case, a battle never engaged but still lost), of nearly twenty years before, blaming this defeat for all the emotional-romantic deficiencies of our lives since then, including both our short-lived marriages and our current situations still very much involved in nightlife of the searching kind.

"You lord it over me for being older," I said, "but I've just had the heretical thought that maybe we're both similarly immature for letting our lives be marked by a vain might-have-been. For whatever reason, Alice didn't want us. No matter how wonderful and charming she might seem or be, that sort of cancels out her emotional usefulness to us."

"I don't get it," he said. "Things were going so well."

From the day we met I liked Des, despite the many good reasons not to. Maybe we don't really like or dislike people based on "reasons." I think we had had a pretty good friendship when we *were* friends—perhaps, in ways, the most important I've had, even with the seventeen-year gap. But if I had everything to do over again, I still would have done what I did—anything to keep his disgusting mitts off Alice Kinnon. The very idea of them together made me want to vomit. I could not even think about it.

Leaving the restaurant, Des asked me how long I was staying in the city and offered to put me on the list for the cocktail bar he had recently opened on Mercer Street. Since earlier in the decade, nightlife culture had reconstituted itself in the form of cool cocktail lounges rather than big dance venues. I said I would just go downtown with him, if that was okay. In the taxi, Des said the film had given him the idea of doing a vodka-tonic promotion for recent college graduates.

Another idea of his, building on the tradition of tonic cocktails being a warm-weather drink (related somehow to the
anti-malarial properties of quinine), was to have a gin-and-
tonic festival in late April to mark the official return of Gin &
Tonic season.

Life Among the Moon Worshippers

Obviously I was not so entirely altruistic and other-centered that my "opposites attract" obsession was exclusively about some old-fashioned notion of "protecting" Alice from scum (even if friend-scum) like Des—though, of course, that did play a role. Unfortunately, as is so often the case, there was also some direct, first-person, autobiographical experience involved.

Arriving in Madrid following the drama of Des being intercepted at the airport, I remember passing some of the grimmest days of my life. I had landed at the start of a four-day holiday weekend or *puente*, which was followed by a whole series of them. Alone in a country where you know no one and cannot yet really speak the language, the isolation can get pretty desperate. The image that remains in my mind is of sand held in a wire cage all draining out, leaving one entirely hollow and vacant. Perhaps the abrupt decompression attendant upon leaving the intensely social milieu of the

Club was also a factor. Or maybe I had counted too much on Des's coming with me and not done the usual advance prep you do when leaving for a new city. I remember getting so lonely I could hardly think; I couldn't even have spoken had I known anyone to speak to. The way it just tears you up inside and you go slightly crazy. I think it was in this period that I realized I was basically gregarious in nature.

The Madrid job I originally went over for turned into a somewhat better one in Paris. As anyone finds out who takes an ad job out of New York, once you're away, it's almost impossible to come back. You either bang around the domestic circuit—Minneapolis, Dallas, Atlanta, Richmond, etc.—or, as I did, a foreign one (Europe except for a great São Paolo stint). When McCallum became "McCallum Worldwide" we had not, to be honest, taken it very seriously. Later, particularly after the mergers, the international side became all too serious. One friend, looking for a safe haven when the blood was flowing in the corridors in New York, took the job at McCallum's Djakarta affiliate—and has not been heard from since.

Living on a continent different from one's own, the opportunities for opposites attracting become virtually *limitless*. I've always had a weakness for women who don't speak English properly and soon found myself oppositely attracted into—and out of—two marriages—one facto, the other de facto—as well as some fairly drawn-out relationships. Ariane, my first wife, was named after the European space rocket, or vice versa. Sonja from São Paulo and I never actually married. By the time her divorce came through, things were already pretty rocky: I think we both knew it was over *before* she and the tennis pro at the Casablanca Club Med met. There was also a Brigitte and, finally, Sophie. Then that ended, too.

Recited this way it might all seem pretty unemotional, which was, frankly, the intention. That a certain amount of heartache and wanting to blow one's brains out would also be involved in opposites-repelling-after-previously-attracting might, I think, go without further elaboration. It would be tempting to add, "Well, at least it wasn't boring"—except that, in fact, often it was, excruciatingly so. Mistreatment is not intrinsically interesting.

What kind of opposites were these? Was it *Lady and the Tramp* all over again, but with me in the role of the bubble-headed cocker spaniel? Or was the "oppositing" involved just a matter of accent or nationality? No, the latter I would see as something along the lines of *vive la différence,* in which cultural differences accentuate and even further improve the already very desirable differentiation between the sexes. That *vive la différence* is something actually very good, while *opposites attract* remains purely tragic in its implications.

In any case, once the real emotional bond is finally severed, equanimity is usually restored. As there was no intrinsic likability problem, I stayed fairly friendly with them all, and when the Internet came in, several had me over to their places to set up their E-mail accounts, or at least became E-mail correspondents. What struck me was that each chose as her password, or her E-mail "handle," some variant on the words "luna" or "moon." It was uncanny. Then I remembered that all had been gravely affected or seemingly so by the arrival of every period of a full moon. This absolutely routine lunar phenomenon would drive them to transports of emotion, and it was not just gazing at the moon itself but the

pale, feeble, "magical" light that it gave off or, rather, gave
back, affecting everything the nighttime eye could see.

What follows is going to sound pretty nutty, but if you've
gotten this far, you will probably not be greatly shocked. I
started detecting a pattern behind the lunar stuff. There was a
whole array of preferences and prejudices that went with it.
These were not particularly bad in themselves, or at all, but
the final result was, I believe, to leave me in an essentially
"opposites" situation which had frankly not been detectable
in advance, so it was not just that I had been a dope like Lady.

The Moon Cult tenets I could identify included a passionate devotion to the tepid, lightly lapping, fairly dirty waters of
the Mediterranean; constant discussion of films and other cultural products of the sort "everyone's talking about"; a preoccupation with travel to warm, exotic spots (never Helsinki);
an unwillingness to "close the door" on former relationships, of
which my involvement in their E-mail setups was a perhaps
benign example; and finally that mantra about the need for a
"radical change" in, and control of, one's life, which again
usually ended up meaning going to live somewhere else,
preferably farther south (unless in the Southern Hemisphere,
in which case farther north), such as Rome. Where those
already living in Rome might go, I don't know—though at
one time Ethiopia was a popular Roman destination. I had
time to think about these things because I had been living
among the Moon Worshippers for nearly two decades without ever having taken communion.

What I'm outlining is not the rigorous sociology of an
E. Digby Baltzell, but something a lot more impressionistic
and perhaps dubious. In defining the "opposites" involved in
the dynamic of opposites-attracting-then-repelling, the risk

of sounding like a total nut has to be taken. I saw a distinction and a deep conflict between the sensualist-voyagers of the Moon Cult and the moralist-burrowers of the New Chevalier movement, who sought to delve deeply into the culture of one's own place and past and perhaps open the door onto the spiritual, with which I identified. These were not just differences about where to go on vacation but pretty much everything, leading to the choice of different paths and preferences at every stage of life, with the upshot that quite a few of us were left childless and single at a time of life we hardly expected to be so. While being captivated romantically by a series of Moon Worshippers, that never included being profoundly engaged or challenged intellectually, spiritually, or otherwise. To put not too fine a point on it, the whole Moon Cult tendency seemed pretty moronic at times.

One school of thought sees theology or its remnants behind everything and, coincidental or not, the Moon Worshippers I knew were all from lapsed European Catholic (including of the Brazilo variety) backgrounds. Perhaps this was just the consequence of living in Catholic Europe, where pretty much everyone is going to lapse from it or from nothing at all. Whether Moon Worship had in fact crossed the traditional Reformation "divide"—making just as heavy inroads among no-longer Protestants as no-longer Catholics—I couldn't say; it probably had. Though there were rumors of Protestantism in France—you occasionally came upon the sad little chapels with the "temple" or "Culte Protestant" warnings on the outside—in my experience it pretty much stopped there. Maybe there were a lot of cute Huguenot girls, I just hadn't met them. Or maybe they had turned into Moon Cultists, too; I don't know. I sort of hoped they hadn't, that there were some divides the cult hadn't yet crossed, but maybe that was no longer true.

Of course, a lot of this—all of this—is probably just nonsense, nothing so much as a crystalline illustration of the limits my psychological state had reached and perhaps crossed over.

It's a rather extensive preamble for what I am about to recount. After the film came out in the United States and my temporary leave ended, I returned to Ogilvy et Mather Paris with my writing time limited to the standard hodgepodge of snatched moments before and after work, on weekends, holidays, or the flying component of the short business trips we often took. It was on one of these short-hop intra-European flights, which tend to be so pleasant, that I was working on Chapter 16 dealing with my life in Yorkville when I was living at the girls' apartment but sometimes had to go out and kill time in the neighborhood when one of Charlotte's "ex's" came through town and wanted to see her. Like many writers, I like having the security blanket of "research," even if it is rarely used, and so had brought with me my old copy of *The Lean Years: Hungarian Calvinism in Crisis* in case I might need to dip into it to cite a passage or even just correctly spell the author's name.

For any airplane flight or substantial rail journey likely to involve airtight compartments and claustrophobic conditions, I try to be as freshly showered, shaved, and clothed as I can. It was a little like the preparations for going out on a date. I also found that I actually wrote better when squeaky clean and freshly laundered. I could go back though this manuscript and probably point out the passages written while dirty and unshaven.

On this particular flight the seat next to me had been taken by an attractive—perhaps very attractive, I didn't really look—younger woman. I was following that American frequent-traveler rule of trying not to notice anyone you sit next to on a plane in case they turn out to be one of those nuts who never shut up, or conversely don't want to be disturbed themselves. I also automatically assume that any attractive woman must have already gotten bothered a lot while traveling—it was not something I want to add to. In any case, I felt a little too low in the emotional cycle to make the effort to talk with anyone so impressive.

A natural work break came when the beverage cart arrived and we were offered drinks and those bags of pseudo-nuts the airlines had taken to distributing—roasted corn, I think it was. I was in a fairly virtuous phase and just ordered "Perrier with lemon" (Perrier is a client) when the woman next to me attracted my attention by adventurously ordering—and getting—a Kir Royal. She took several sips rather carefully, as if not sure this was exactly the drink she meant to order, when she apparently noticed my glance in her direction.

"Excuse me," she began, "but I couldn't help notice the book you're reading"—she referred to the title—"*The Lean Years: Hungarian Calvinism in Crisis.*"

Her accent was absolutely lovely, though I couldn't place or unravel all the strands to it.

"Actually, I'm not really reading it—it's sort of a prop."

She looked a little perplexed at this, as if feeling that perhaps her English comprehension was not so perfect, so I explained further: "A prop for a novel, or novelization, that I'm writing."

"You're a writer?"

"Well, not really, but I have a contract to write this, uh, novelization."

I nodded to indicate the laptop open on my meal tray.

She took another sip from her Kir Royal—a pretty cool drink to ask for on an airplane, even if by accident.

"How do you know the book?" I asked.

"It is my godfather who wrote it," she said.

"Hunh."

"He and my uncles were at theological school in Hungary together."

She evidently understood "hunh," which indicated that she must have spent considerable time in America, or at least among Americans. She was tremendously impressed that I was so familiar with the story of postwar Calvinism in Hungary—something her family had, quite painfully, lived. Her name was extraordinarily beautiful—Piroska Szabó—and her accent still bore traces of her native tongue, but as filtered through Paris, Oxbridge, and the Kentucky region where she had been partly educated (others might feel differently, but it has always seemed to me that the music of accents from the Kentucky-Tennessee region could be our country's most appealing).

Her uncles had been in the Reformed ministry in Hungary, but after two were brutally treated by the Communists, the family had fled to the West, where thanks to their scholarly interests and fluency in English they found a home in academia (greatly helped by her godfather, who had gotten out earlier). While the events she narrated were often sad and rather melodramatic, Piroska's tone was not that of one of those glum personalities who revel in life's grim moments and depressing aspects. She was what my brother, citing the old watch ad campaign, used to call a Timex person—"takes a licking but keeps on ticking." She had that combination of beautifully sad eyes but an essentially cheerful and optimistic personality (but not inanely so) that's always so appealing, though in fact I've only really encountered it twice. The rest of the flight seemed to pass in a matter of moments but, landing at Charles de Gaulle, we agreed we would share a cab into town together.

While at the baggage claim area waiting for the conveyor belt to bring out her bag—that she had fallen for the standard airline offer to check her bag made it pretty clear she was not a frequent traveler, with all their hardened habits—it suddenly occurred to me that this mix of European-international background (but with some positive experience of living in the U.S.) with devout and Reformed (but not some nut talking about her pastor all the time) could have been the romantic and personal solution for me, had I met her earlier. Instead, I had built my house—or houses—on the shifting sands of Moon Worship, appealing as they might have been.

Cabs in France tended to be really expensive, so it always seemed appropriate when the one you got at least turned out to be a late-model Mercedes—the price-quality ratio, etc. Sitting in the darkened back of the comfortable cab, night fallen, we drove into town on the A2 and the Périphérique, the conversation continuing in the spirit of fruitful harmony it had begun in courtesy of Air France. We both agreed that the Eiffel Tower was an eyesore and John Calvin incredibly underrated. That he had been at the Sorbonne when he developed his theories struck us both as amazing—so near and yet so far. Piroska said she actually lived near where Calvin had resided in Paris.

When I finally slipped her my standard test question about full moons—to see whether she would maintain her composure or go into transports of emotion—her reply caught me up short.

"Oh, please. Not the moon," she said.

When I explained the context of the question—that I was not trotting it out as some tired pickup line—she was more interested but said that, while she did not have anything particular *against* the moon, or full moons or moonlight, she actually preferred the purer dark of moonless night.

"Or the dark and artificial light of a nightclub with good dance music?" I asked, a little tendentiously.

"Absolutely."

Coming into the city via Bercy, the cab had gotten bogged down in traffic, which I normally hated, but now sitting there, not necessarily saying anything, motionless but higher than a kite, it seemed perfectly fine. Inside the vehicle it was getting warm, so I opened the window partway and Piroska took off her sweater, revealing arms of such exquisite beauty they looked like they might have been made by the Creator on special assignment—not that such things should be given excessive importance. But I couldn't help noticing them.

Suddenly that incredible warm feeling that you have or might have met the most wonderful person who will transform your existence incomparably for the better in ways not entirely imaginable—analagous to the key chemical triggering a formula—descended over me. Not being an agnostic in these matters, I did not think such sensations were necessarily entirely chimerical; sometimes they do happen, sometimes for a while, sometimes for even longer.

I started thinking how romantic life had not necessarily

died with Disco, to which Des, when I later talked to him about some of this, replied, "Of course not; are you kidding?" Des for one had kept the faith; in fact, he asked me if I might want to acquire some token participation in a new club he was opening. He already had the investment, he said, but just liked the idea of sharing the profits—or losses—with a friend from the good old days, and it would give us something to talk about other than the usual lame subjects.

APACK